Love
Blooms

Also by Jamie Pope

HOPE BLOOMS

LOVE BLOOMS

Published by Kensington Books

Love
Blooms

Jamie Pope

Kensington Publishing Corp.
http://www.kensingtonbooks.com

DAFINA BOOKS are published by

Kensington Publishing Corp.
119 West 40th Street
New York, NY 10018

All Kensington Titles, Imprints, and Distributed Lines are available at special quantity discounts for bulk purchases for sales promotions, premiums, fund-raising, and educational or institutional use. Special book excerpts or customized printings can also be created to fit specific needs. For details, write or phone the office of the Kensington special sales manager: Kensington Publishing Corp., 119 West 40th Street, New York, NY 10018, attn: Special Sales Department, Phone: 1-800-221-2647.

Dafina and the Dafina logo Reg. U.S. Pat. & TM Off.

ISBN-13: 978-1-4967-0870-0
ISBN-10: 1-4967-0870-9
First mass market printing: August 2017

eISBN-13: 978-1-4967-0871-7
eISBN-10: 1-4967-0871-7
Kensington Electronic Edition: August 2017

10 9 8 7 6 5 4 3 2 1

Printed in the United States of America

*To everyone who has been knocked down
more than once and keeps getting up.*

Chapter 1

Nova Reed held her breath as she stood outside the door of the shitty one-bedroom apartment that she and her mother had been calling home for the last month. She had been there at least five minutes trying to decide if she wanted to get out of the cold more than she wanted to run away.

This place was the fourth place they had called home that year.

Home.

The word had very little meaning for her now.

They had lived in a hundred different places in her seventeen years. Never staying in one area long enough for Nova to feel comfortable, or for her to find friends, or be normal. She used to wish that they would find that one magical place where they could stay and put down roots. That place they would never again have to sneak out from in the middle of the night, dodging some pissed-off landlord looking for back rent.

But Nova gave up that hope long ago.

When your mama is a raging drunk, you learn from an early age to stop hoping. It was easier than being disappointed all the time.

Nova shivered, still rooted to the spot in front of the door. The cold had seeped through her sweatshirt and hit her bones, and even as her fingers went numb she wondered if the momentary warmth she would feel would be worth the rest of it. Worth what she would inevitably go through with her mother as soon as she stepped inside. But what other choice did she have?

She had stayed out as long as she could, working a four-hour shift at the diner after school today and a two-hour shift before. She wanted to work more but they wouldn't let her. She was still a minor, and it was a school night. So she had gone to the library after work, staying until it closed at nine. And then when there was no place else to go, no other excuses to make, she walked home. In the dark. As slowly as possible.

Mama had been chaos lately. Sick, sad chaos. It was either alcohol-fueled rages, or booze-soaked stupors. No in-between. No peace.

That's all she wanted. To sleep. Just one night of quiet, uninterrupted rest. She had a big test tomorrow. Her guidance counselor told her that if she kept up her grades he could help her get a scholarship to college. She wasn't naturally smart. School didn't come easy for her, but she was a hard worker. She put in the time.

College was her only way out of the shit hole that was her life. It was the only way her mother would let her go. In one of her rare clear moments Mama had been excited about the idea. She wanted Nova to have a fancy job. Something professional, like a lawyer or an engineer. They talked about her living in a dorm with girls her own age. Maybe she would meet a nice boy who was majoring in something like finance or prelaw and they would get married and buy one of the big old fancy white houses. They could put their kids in private school, and go to soccer games and go on boating trips. Mama had encouraged her to get there. Nova tried not to feel guilty for wanting to leave her mother so badly. But getting out was the only way she could help her. Maybe get her into one of those costly treatment programs.

She unlocked the door and walked into the dimly lit space. The smell of cigarettes and alcohol-scented sweat nearly knocked her backward. And if the smell didn't make her fall, the pile of gin bottles littering the floor would have.

But there were beer cans there tonight as well, and the hair on the back of Nova's neck stood on end.

Mama didn't drink beer.

Gin. Vodka. Moonshine when she was desperate. She must have had company today. Mama usually entertained male company when money was running low. When she didn't have enough money to get her next fix. There was no money for her to take this time because Nova kept everything important she owned on her body. Her savings account passbook. Her weekly tips. The gold necklace her grandmother had given her. It was the one that belonged to her father. She had learned her lesson the first time Mama had rummaged through her room and cleaned out her savings to go on a three-day bender with some guy she just met.

She spotted her mother passed out on the couch. Her face and body were bloated. Her bleached-blond hair plastered to her head. Nova was relieved. No raging tonight. No anger about her squandered future. No noise at all. Just sleep.

Her mother had been beautiful once. A Southern beauty

queen, with waist-length dark hair and a body that women would sell their souls to get. But something happened along the way and her beauty queen mother had transformed into a drunk that could barely stand up most days.

She looked at her mother for a long moment before she pulled the quilt her grandmother had made off the back of the couch and placed it over her mother. The stench of booze coming out of her pores was enough to knock anyone backward, but Nova stayed where she was and brushed the hair out of her mother's face. She wondered what her brother would think if he could see her now. She hadn't spoken to him in a few years. They had moved so much that he had lost track of them.

Wylie had escaped life with their mother. They had different fathers and his was a good man who refused to let a sick woman take his child. Even after he died he made sure Wylie was sent to live in Connecticut with a rich family, in a house that had three floors, with people who only drove cars that cost more than most people made in two years. Wylie had gone to prom. He went on vacations. He even got to go to college. And now he was a marine, off in some foreign land, doing something good with his life. Nova almost hated him for it. She loved her big brother. He was goodness personified, but most days she hated him nearly as much because he had the life she had always dreamed of.

He got to go do things, while she was chained to their mother and her illness.

Nova kissed her mother's cheek, heavy guilt creeping up into her throat and choking her. She started to pick up the alcohol bottles and cigarette butts that littered the rooms even though she knew it wouldn't make a damn bit of difference. The apartment would be a wreck again tomorrow.

She should have just gone straight to bed. Her mother was sleeping. She could have her peaceful evening, but she didn't just want to walk away. This was the only time she could spend with her mother. She was drunk constantly now. Not just on the weekends. Not just after work. All the time. Every waking moment. Nova couldn't be around her then, but she could be around her when she slept.

"My baby." Nova heard her mother's slurred words and looked over to her. Her skin was a sickly yellow color, her eyes were bloodshot.

"Have you eaten anything today, Mama? You want me to fix you something?"

"My stomach is bothering me." Her words were so thick Nova had a hard time understanding them.

"Would you like some water? Maybe some juice? I can run out and get you something from the gas station."

"No, thank you, baby. You're my good girl." She rolled over and was out again, knocking the quilt that Nova had draped over her to the floor. Nova sighed, pushing down the large bubble of anxiety that swelled in her when she thought about her mother's health. About how many days her mother had left on this earth if she didn't take care of herself.

So she went into the kitchen, to toss the empties into a plastic bag. The activity would keep her mind busy. Even if she went to bed, tonight would be just as hellish as the night before. She heard the knob of the bathroom door turn. She jumped. She hadn't realized that she and her mother weren't alone. A man walked out. She recognized him.

Archie.

He had been hanging around the apartment a lot since they moved to this building. He was the maintenance man *here, but Nova wasn't sure what he did all day because the place was nearly uninhabitable.*

He was wearing just a towel around his bloated body. She hadn't heard the shower on. There were no signs that he had cleaned himself at all. She had been home for at least ten minutes. It was almost as if he was waiting for her.

"Get your clothes and get the hell out." She went back to cleaning, her head down, but one eye on him.

"Oh, baby girl, you've got a mouth on you, don't you? But it sure is a pretty one."

He stepped completely out of the bathroom and toward her. Their apartment was tiny. One more large step and he would be in her space. She tried not to glance back at her bedroom door. She could run. Try to barricade herself in her room, but she knew that wouldn't work. Even if he left her alone tonight. He would be back. Her mother would always let him in if he came bearing booze. Nova needed to stand her ground with him. Let him know that she wouldn't be pushed around. He wasn't the first friend of Mama's who tried something with her. Just one in a long line of many.

The last time it happened, her father had still been alive. He took her away from her mother and sent her to live in Martha's Vineyard with his mother. It was the kindest thing he had ever done for her. But it was almost cruel, because when he died, she had to go back to Mama. When he died, the tiny bit of peaceful life she had ended and made coming back into hell just that much worse.

Archie walked closer to her, the stench of stale beer on his breath. But Nova knew he wasn't drunk. His eyes were too clear, too calculating. "Your sweet little ass has been making me hard ever since you two moved in here," he said into her ear. His hand settled on her behind and she slapped it away, raising her fist to punch him, but he caught it. Her heart began to slam against her chest, but she refused to panic. She refused to be a victim.

"Don't make this harder than it has to be. Your bedroom is right there. We can just go inside and have a little fun."

"Fuck off, Archie. My mama is right there. You can't seriously be trying something with me."

"Your mama is a drunk. And she ain't waking up. She might be out for the next two days with the amount of booze she threw down her throat."

"And you were right here with her while she was doing it."

"I was keeping her company and waiting for you. I've got a lot of pull around here." He yanked her closer so that her body was pressed against his. "You treat me good and you won't have to worry about your rent anymore."

"We can pay our rent just fine."

"I can also throw you out just fine. You don't think word about your mama has not spread? She screwed so many landlords out of rent money, no one will take her around here. They'll take you though. I'm sure everyone wants a tight little piece." He smashed his mouth to hers and Nova shoved him as hard as she could. He stumbled backward into the stove, but that didn't stop him. It only made him angry. He came at her again, grabbing her arm and pinning her body against the counter. The towel had slipped from his hips. His erection was pressed into her.

"No." She was scared out of her skull, but the word came out firm and clear. "You're not going to force me."

"You'll like it, you little bitch." He grabbed her breast and squeezed it so hard, tears came to her eyes. "I'll show you how a real man does it. It won't hurt. With a body like this you can't be a virgin."

His hand moved toward her zipper and she reached behind her, her hand closing around a handle. She didn't give herself time to think. Her hand swung out wildly and she felt the knife in her hand sink into muscle. Archie let out a horrific scream and fell to the floor. There was so much blood and a naked man squirming on the floor.

Run, *something inside her told her.* Get the hell away from here.

She did and she never looked back.

"Look at who showed up. I'm surprised she even bothers to come here."

They were whispering about her again. The other mothers. As soon as she stepped her foot on the soccer fields it started. The hushed words. The critical looks. The rebel in Nova wanted to flip them off, but the mother in her thought twice about it. She wouldn't embarrass her kid any more than she already did.

Those snobby bitches could go to hell. Nova kept her head high as she walked past them to the visitors' side of the field.

Nova knew she wasn't like most of the mothers on her son's soccer team. She wasn't the wife of a rich man, transplanted here to get away from her stressful overscheduled life in Boston or New York City or wherever the people who could afford homes in the most expensive part of the island came from. She was a single mother with a sketchy past. She lived in a tiny two-bedroom apartment over a vacant store. And unlike them, she had to work damn hard to keep a roof over her kid's head. She was a hairstylist and a makeup artist. She liked her lipstick red, her nails long, and her heels high because it made her feel powerful. It made her stand out in a world she often felt was going to swallow her up.

She was also a walking billboard for her services. She couldn't go out looking any old way and she knew that tomorrow she would get at least three of those stuffy broads in her chair asking her to make them look more desirable for their boring husbands.

She didn't care if they talked, as long as they tipped well so that she could keep socking money away for her future.

She focused on her baby boy, pushing thoughts of those unimportant people out of her mind. He was with the rest of his team, listening to his coach, looking so damn adorable in his blue and white uniform and his halo of black fluffy curls. She wanted to rush across the field and kiss the skin off his sweet round cheeks, but she stayed where she was, as far away from him as possible. She wasn't supposed to be there at all. It was man day. A bonding time with his uncle. It was important because Teo didn't have a father. And she knew that he desperately wanted someone to call Daddy. It was her fault he didn't have one. Not because of anything she had done, but because she should have known long before she conceived that her husband would never be able to be a father to anyone.

But her brother, Wylie, wasn't a bad stand-in. He and Teo went to games and practices and out to lunch and then the two would go back to his house to do whatever it was little boys and their uncles did together. Wylie had her son a lot. He took him on trips, gave him some discipline, and showed him how real men are supposed to act. And that's why her son loved him. Teo loved him way more than he did her. The knowledge of it depressed the hell out of her. But how could she blame her son? Wylie was a war hero, a respected man in their community, and he was a nice person.

She, on the other hand, was screwed up as they came. Way too screwed up to be a mother. Sometimes she thought her son would be better off being raised by her brother, but she just couldn't let him go. He was an accident created with the lowlife she had married when she had escaped home at seventeen. Teo probably would have had a better shot if he were raised by someone else, but Nova was too selfish to give him up. She had no idea what love was until she held him in her arms.

"Why are you all the way over here?" Her brother stomped over to her, looking every inch of the marine he was. He was annoyed with her.

But what was new?

"Hush. I don't want him to know I'm here. I'm just watching. I'm not bothering anyone. Go away."

"You're bothering me," Wylie said, his Southern accent still strong even after having moved from Alabama over fifteen years ago.

They looked as unrelated as two siblings could be. Wylie was a large man, built like a tank. He was fair skinned with hair that was golden brown and eyes almost the color of honey. She was the opposite of him in every way. The blood of her father's family ran strong through her veins. Her hair was jet black. Her skin was brown. She was Native American. Even though her mother was white, Nova connected to her Native side more. And she had come back to this island to be with her father's family. They were the only ones who ever protected her. This island was the only place she had felt close to happy.

But that wasn't true anymore. Wylie had moved here when he got out of the service to be near her. She knew without a doubt that her brother would give his life for her. But that didn't mean they got along. She was fairly certain her brother didn't like her at all.

"Go away, jarhead." She turned back to the game, her eyes glued to Teo. "You're going to give me away. Can't you go put a damper on someone else's day?"

"If you didn't want him to see you, you shouldn't have come. You aren't one of those women who blends into the crowd."

"I don't think she knows how," Nova heard a deep voice say and goose bumps broke out all over her flesh. She recognized the voice of her brother's best friend all too well. She didn't want to remove her eyes from the spot on the field that she had fixated on, but she couldn't help but look at the man whose deep, almost commanding, voice did something odd to her insides. Tanner Brennan was no ordinary man. He was a giant. Six foot six. Long body, wide stance, powerful shoulders. His skin was just a shade darker than sun kissed and he was beautiful. If someone wanted to create a race of perfect men, Tanner Brennan would be the man they modeled them after. He was a former Army Ranger, a war hero, and good with his hands.

He annoyed the hell out of Nova.

"Tall, dark, and dummy," she said, passing her eyes over him. He was in a navy blue T-shirt and well-worn jeans. His arms were folded over his chest, his biceps bulging beneath the sleeves. "I've always heard that the freaks come out at night, but here you are in the light of day for all to see."

His eyes narrowed as the shot hit him. She could never describe their color. Hazel didn't seem to encompass it. They were brown with flecks of gold, but sometimes they looked green. Whatever they were Nova always had a hard time looking away from them.

"I was made this way," he said. "Can't help it." His gaze traveled down her body in a slow leisurely way. "Unlike you. Red shoes, red lips, red nails. You say you don't want to be seen but looks like you're shouting to the world that you're here. I think someone didn't get enough attention when they were a kid."

"Isn't there a short person in need of something on a high shelf? Go bother them and disappear from my presence. It's straining my neck to look up at you."

"I wasn't aware that you were a queen and could banish people."

"I wasn't aware that you were the king of the pains in the asses," she snapped back.

"I—"

"Enough," her brother barked in his most authoritative voice. "There's a bunch of five-year-olds here and they are better behaved than the two of you.

Nova, go say hi to your kid. Tanner, stop trying to get my sister charged with assault."

He walked away from them then, heading back to the stands where most of the parents sat. They fought, she and Tanner. Every single time they saw each other. She wasn't sure why. She wanted to say that there was something disrespectful about him. He stared at her. She had been stared at by men her entire life. Men who wanted to get into her pants. Men who would use her and discard her, and she wanted to put Tanner in that category, but she couldn't. He didn't stare at her breasts or ass. He never made a move on her, but he still stared. Into her eyes. Every time he spoke to her, he gave her unwavering eye contact. It was disconcerting. It was like he was trying to strip away something besides her clothes every time they spoke.

Nova turned back to watch the game. Tanner came to stand by her, his body close to hers. That was another thing he did to bug her. He never gave her space, but he never stepped over the line. He never groped or grabbed her. It was a touch of the hand here and there. It was an arm brushing hers. And now it was his side, not exactly touching her but close enough that she could feel his heat radiating to her body on this cool morning. She wanted to stand closer to him. Feel his long hard body pressed against hers. It was a crazy urge considering that the thought of any man touching her in the past five years turned her stomach. But she had very different feelings in her stomach whenever she saw him and that made her really dislike Tanner. It made her dislike herself.

"Why are you here?" she asked him. He didn't even live in town but she ran into Tanner seemingly everywhere. At the grocery store, at the post office, and family functions. He even came to her to get his hair cut once, and now he was here at her son's soccer practice. It wasn't the first time he had come, but it never ceased to surprise her when he did.

"You know why. Teo asked me to be here."

"You could have told him you couldn't make it. You're a single man in your thirties. Surely you must have something better to do."

"My father wasn't around, even when I asked him to be. You think I could deny your son? Besides, I like him. His mother is a loud-mouthed, hostile pain in the ass, but the kid is damn near delightful. Cantankerousness must skip a generation."

And there it was . . . The reason she couldn't really hate him. Only he could manage to be so sweet and so shitty in the same breath.

"You bug the hell out of me," she said truthfully and without heat.

"You're no goddamn picnic yourself. But the real reason I'm here is because I like to see the daggers the other mothers throw at you."

"Judgmental bitches. They don't even try to get to know me. I may not have been born with a silver spoon in my mouth, but I work hard. Harder than they ever have."

"You know it has nothing to do with your work ethic, Nova. Even you can't be that dense. It's how you look that has them wanting to brand you with a scarlet letter."

"Because I'm Native?"

"You may look dumb, but Lord knows you're not." He sighed in frustration. "Don't make me say it."

"This is one of the few times I actually want to hear you talk. Speak, man, speak."

He glared at her. "You're walking sex. You have to know that. Your thousand glances in the mirror a day should confirm that."

"I'm wearing jeans, a T-shirt, and a cardigan!"

"And heels. High red heels and tight jeans that make your ass phenomenal. It's not you personally they hate. It's the way you cause their husbands to look at you." He turned to fully face her.

She had always had this problem, even when she was a teenager. Men looked. They always looked. And sometimes they touched, and it didn't matter what she was wearing. She had tried to cover it all up, tried to hide her body, but it never mattered. She had waist-length black hair. She had brown skin and wide slanted eyes. She would always stand out. She might as well feel good while she was doing it. "I don't ask for it, and if you are suggesting I am in some way inviting these men not to pay attention to their wives and look at me, you can shove it. I shouldn't have to wear a potato sack just to make other people feel comfortable."

He grinned, showing off his perfect teeth, before he leaned over and spoke into her ear. "You have no idea what kind of effect you have on them, do you?

A man sees your pouty red lips and all he can think about is the way they would feel on his body, traveling down his body and wrapping around his . . . ." He trailed off. "And your nails . . . A man sees them and can only think about how they would feel scraping down his naked back. And your body . . . It doesn't matter how much you cover it up. It's the type of body that begs to be undressed."

She was feeling breathless. Excited. These were new sensations for her. Only they weren't so new right now. They were becoming commonplace whenever she was around him. "You want to undress me?" she asked him, knowing she shouldn't, but the question had just popped out. He managed to suck her in to his sensual vortex. Her clothes felt too tight and too hot all of a sudden. Her nipples tightened in her shirt and she could see herself running her nails down his bare back. She could see herself kissing him all the way down his long hard body. She could envision herself wrapping her body around his and letting him explore her every dip and bend. But she shouldn't be having those thoughts about him. She had never considered herself a sexual person despite what the world thought of her. But whenever she was around Tanner, sex popped into her mind at the most inconvenient times.

"Me?" He pointed to himself with a shake of the head. "No. I can see right through your act. Undressing you is the last thing I want to do."

* * *

Tanner looked down at Nova, watching as her eyes widened as she took in his words. He was waiting for the returning shot, one of the barbed comebacks that Nova was so quick with. But it never came. She just turned away to watch her son. He turned back too, feeling her inch closer to him, and then lean against him. Slightly. Just her arm resting against his. It would have been an odd reaction to that exchange from anyone else, but he knew enough about Nova to know that men had been trying to sleep with her since she was a girl. She was that rare kind of woman who could walk around wearing a garbage bag and still make men go crazy with desire.

People assumed she was a bad girl because of that body. The talk around town was that she dated a lot. She told people she dated a lot, but he knew she didn't. No man in the area had boasted that he'd had her. No one had actually ever seen her with anyone. She was all talk.

He hadn't lied to her when he said undressing her was the last thing he wanted to do. Undressing her *was* the last thing he wanted to do before he tumbled her into bed. Somehow she had become the first thing he thought about when he woke up in the morning, which was crazy. He had a million other more pressing things to think about. But there was Nova.

All the time.

Driving him insane even though she was nowhere near him. She was an extraordinarily beautiful woman. Astonishingly so. And he didn't use those words lightly. He had been around socialites and beauty queens, exotic women from all over the world. But they couldn't compare to Nova, a true American beauty.

She had the body of an old-school burlesque dancer and a strut to match. She was glamourous. The type of woman that women emulated.

He wanted her. It was a fact of life. Earth was round. The ocean was wet. And he wanted Nova with every cell in his body. But she was the sister of his overly protective best friend and she was the mother of a sweet kid who didn't need any drama in his life. And Tanner knew that as much as he wanted Nova, he couldn't have her. He had made up his mind that she was strictly off-limits, even though she was leaning slightly against him, making him want to feel even more of her.

He knew he should walk away, go sit with Wylie, wait for Teo to be done with practice, but he didn't move. He simply couldn't move away from her. This was the only contact he would allow himself to have with her and he wasn't about to break it.

"Mommy?" Teo spotted her and ran full speed toward them and through the opening of the gate. It was clear he was excited to see her there, but he didn't leap into her arms as most five-year-olds might do. He stopped before them and approached her slowly, looking up at her with uncertainty in his eyes. Nova looked back at her boy, just as uncertain. Mother and son had an odd relationship; it was distant and yet incredibly close at the same time. Tanner always found it interesting to watch them together. It made him think of his own troubled relationship with his mother. He hadn't seen her in years. Neither one of them bothered to attempt to make contact.

"Hi, love," she said softly.

"Hello, Mr. Tanner," Teo said, sparing him a quick glance, before returning his attention to his mother. "I didn't know you was coming."

"I didn't want you to see me."

"Why?" He scrunched his face in confusion. He looked just like her. Same beautiful brown skin. Same jet black hair.

"Because it's man day. And I'm not a man, little one."

"You can always come see me, Mommy," he said, sounding like a little adult. "Everyone else's mommy is here."

"I'm glad you don't mind." She knelt down beside him. "You look so gorgeous in your uniform. Can I hug and kiss you?"

"Yes," he responded, and before he could get the entire word out Nova had swept him into her arms and was kissing his apple-round cheeks.

"You are a perfect boy, do you know that?"

"You tell me that," he said with his eyes closed. The boy looked damn near blissful, adoring every moment of his mother's affection. Tanner couldn't take his eyes off Nova. There was tenderness in her face, overwhelming love combined with a little bit of sadness.

And that sadness intrigued him. It made him want to know more about it, about her.

"I only tell you that because it's true."

Her tough chick shtick was all an act. He could see right through her. There was a sweet, sensitive lady inside of the woman with the bad girl body, and as much as he knew that he needed to stay away from her, a bigger part of him wanted to know every little piece that made her up.

"I've got to go back to play now, Mommy," he told her when she let him go.

"Okay." She stood up again, looking sad. "Have fun."

"Are you going to stay the whole game?" he asked so hopeful, that Tanner would tie Nova to the bleachers himself if she refused.

"Of course."

"You could come to man day if you want. I have to ask Uncle Wylie, but he'll say yes. Right, Mr. Tanner?"

"I'm sure he will," Tanner agreed.

Nova shot him a look before she looked back to her son. "This is man day. I'll go see Mansi. You have a good time. Go play."

"Okay, Mommy." He turned away, giving her one last look before he walked back to his team.

"Why do you ask your son if you can hug him?" Tanner asked when Teo was out of earshot.

"Because it's important for him to know that no one can touch his body without his permission. If I ever teach my kid one thing, it's that."

The hairs on the back of Tanner's neck stood up. "Did something happen to him?"

"No. Not to him."

But to her. The words were unsaid, but were hanging thickly in the air between them.

He grabbed her hand. It was an impulsive, probably foolish thing to do, but he did it and he didn't want to let it go, promises to himself be damned. "You're coming out with us for man day. We won't take no for an answer."

Chapter 2

Mama had moved them to Texas two years ago, chasing after some boyfriend who was on the rodeo circuit. Max had been a heavy drinker, a world-class bar fighter, and an all-around wreck, but he was one of the few boyfriends that Nova had liked. He had been fatherly to her. He warned his friends away from her, gave her a curfew, took her to get her first job. He had set boundaries for Mama, too. He only let her drink on the weekends. He made sure she went to work every day. He made her be an adult. She bristled at it and ended up sleeping with one of his friends. He had kicked her out that night.

Max told Nova that she could stay, that she would be better off with him, and for one traitorous moment she thought about it. But she had gone with Mama. They had stayed in Texas because there was no home to go to, moving from town to town, only staying long enough to piss off a new landlord, or to cheat some man out of something valuable.

Texas was such a huge place, it was easy to get lost in it. But Nova didn't want to get lost here anymore. She kept seeing Archie's naked bloody body on the kitchen floor, and when she ran out of her apartment that night she knew she had to get the hell out of Texas. She had gone right to the bus station. Her first bus took her to Oklahoma. Then she headed to Missouri before getting on this bus to take her to Florida.

It seemed like a good place to get lost.

She was running like hell again. It seemed as if so much of her life had been lived on the run. Her long black hair was hidden under a hooded sweatshirt. She bought cheap sunglasses to wear over her eyes. She didn't speak to anyone on those long bus rides. She didn't look at anyone. If she could have melted into her seat she would have.

She thought about the scene that she had left behind. Thought about her mama and what she would think about all of it. Wondered how her mother was going to survive without her. But the thing that was in the forefront of her mind was how the hell she was going to survive alone in a new state. She had every dime she had ever made on her. Almost two thousand dollars. She could get a cheap room for a while. Eat cups of soup, packages of mystery meat hot dogs. But then what? She had no ID. She couldn't tell anyone who she was.

She looked out the window. They were heading into the city now. To another bus station, to drop off and pick up another set of people who looked like they were trying to get lost. They were at the station a little longer than usual and an unnatural hush fell across the passengers. Nova looked up this time to see two state troopers walking up the aisle. Her hands started to tremble and she clenched them into tight fists to try to stop it. She looked back out the window, hoping they would pass by her. But they didn't.

"Excuse me, ma'am," one of the officers said.

She slowly turned to look at him, warning herself to stay calm. "Yes, Officer?"

"Would you mind removing your glasses?"

She did, her eyes unaccustomed to the brightness because they had been on her face since she had started this journey ten days ago.

"Take down your hood." She swallowed but did as she was asked. The urge to barrel through them and run overwhelmed her, but she knew that she wouldn't get anywhere. "And your hair, ma'am?"

She unwound her tight bun, her heavy hair cascading around her shoulders. The police officer's eyes widened. "It's not her," his partner mentioned.

"I can see that." He looked troubled, but Nova felt more than relief. She almost sagged into her seat. "You're traveling alone?"

She nodded.

"You shouldn't be."

"I've got no other choice. I'm going to live with my grandmother." It was a lie, but Nova knew she couldn't go to Mansi. She couldn't bring chaos and shame to the peaceful tribe on Martha's Vineyard even though that's where she had longed to go.

"Cover up," he ordered, knowing what could happen to a young girl traveling alone.

"Yes, sir."

"Make sure someone knows where you are during every leg of your trip."

"Yes, sir," she said again as they turned to leave. She couldn't do as he asked because that was the point of running away. She wanted to get as lost as possible.

* * *

"Ouch!" Nova felt a sharp smack to her side as she leaned over her grandmother. "Mansi! Stop hitting me."

"Don't you ouch me. You're the one who's inflicting torture on me!"

"I'm cleaning up your eyebrows."

"Torture!"

"I have to master eyebrow threading if I'm going to be good enough to work in Boston. You want me to be good, don't you?" She removed a few more hairs and attempted to dodge a few more slaps. "Old woman! You're not being very helpful."

"Why is this taking you so long?"

"Because you have caterpillars growing up there. I'm trying to shape them."

"Why do I have to be your porky pig? There are a hundred women on this island you could practice on."

"It's guinea pig, Mansi. And I want you, because you are the most beautiful person I know."

Her grandmother smiled slowly, revealing her gap-toothed smile. "You're full of it."

Her grandmother was in her mid-seventies, and the opposite of petite, standing at nearly six feet tall with a soft round body that looked like it was made to give comfort. Mansi may not be the American standard of beauty but Nova did think she was one of the most gorgeous women she had ever seen. She had waist-length silver hair that she always wore loose, brown skin, high cheekbones, and deep, dark eyes. She had given birth to six children and faced the hardest of times and Nova wanted to be just like her when she grew up.

Mansi had saved her. More than once. She would have been dead or in prison without her.

"I'm only a little full of it. I can't have you walking around town looking like you don't give a damn about how you look. I've got a reputation to uphold. How can I be known as the island's beauty diva if my own family looks like they just rolled out of bed?"

"I rarely leave the house. In fact I'm mighty annoyed that you made me come here today. We could have done this at home."

"No. All my tools are here."

"You could have brought them to the house! You travel all over the island to do weddings."

"But I wanted you to get out of the house. You haven't been out since Wylie and Cassandra's wedding. You can come sit in my salon for a couple of hours. Now sit still for five more minutes and I'll let you go."

"I want to go now," she complained.

"You're worse than Teo."

"Are you going to leave him at my house tonight?"

Mansi had a lovely gingerbread cottage that Wylie had built just for her. Her brother had originally come to this island as a government contractor, building affordable housing for the people who had been on Martha's Vineyard since the beginning of time. Mansi's home had been his special project. There was a kind of warmth there that was impossible to find anywhere else, including her own tiny apartment in the center of town, and that's why she left Teo there often. Nova worked a lot of nights and weekends doing hair and makeup for the weddings of the island's wealthiest. But there were a lot of nights when she wasn't working that she had left him there, thinking that her son would be much better off under her grandmother's stable influence. He was. He was a respectful, intelligent, insightful little boy. But leaving him in another's care all the time had made him think that she didn't want him around. It wasn't true. Everything she was doing, every extra class she took, every job that took her away from him was all for him. To give him a better life, a more stable life than her mother gave her.

But his little five-year-old mind didn't see it that way. He confided to his uncle that he thought that she didn't want him anymore. Hearing that was devastating to her. The worst moment of her life.

She had done so many things that she wasn't proud of, but those things were in the past, those things she couldn't change. She could try to change how she was with her son. She never wanted him to look back on his life and think for one moment that he was unloved.

"I would like to stay over, too. Is that okay?"

"Give up your apartment and come live with me. I have the room. I don't particularly enjoy your company but it would be nice to have a live-in servant."

"You're so funny, old woman." She kissed her cheek and then grabbed the finishing spray off her station and gave her grandmother's hair a liberal dose.

"First you try to yank the skin on my face and now you're trying to suffocate me! If I didn't know any better I would say you are trying to kill me to get your inheritance."

Nova slanted a brow at her. "What inheritance?"

"My entire collection of tiny spoons goes to you, my child. I've got well over a hundred now. You could get good money for them."

"Ah." Nova grinned at her grandmother. "Well, in that case you had better watch your back. I want those spoons so bad I can taste it." She turned away to get her phone out of her bag. "Now look gorgeous. I want to take a picture of you for my Instagram account."

"What?"

"I put pictures up on my social media account so people can see my work."

"You're going to put my picture on the Internet?"

"Yes, Mansi. I am."

"Turn me toward the mirror. If you're going to put my pictures up, I want to see myself."

Nova paused and put her hand on her hip. "Are you going to let me take the picture after you see yourself?"

"Maybe. I might kick your butt if I don't like the way you cut my hair."

"Fair enough." She spun her grandmother around to face the mirror and held her breath. She was nervous. She had done thousands of good haircuts at this point, but her grandmother's approval meant more to her than any stranger's.

She watched as Mansi scrunched her face and studied herself. She was silent for so long that Nova was starting to get scared. Her grandmother usually told her like it was, so silence was far scarier than any words she could say.

"I want you to contour my face."

"Say what?"

"And give me red lips, too. I want to look like one of those girls on the TV with the big bottoms."

"A Kardashian?"

"Yes. One of those. Do it." She spun her own chair around. "If I'm going on the Internet, I want to go all out."

"You got it. There's a new technique I've been dying to try out."

Nova pulled out her makeup kit and went to work. She had never thought she would ever go into beauty for a living. She had dreams of college, of a professional job where she wore a suit to an office every day, but life didn't work out that way for her. She never even got to finish high school because she had to run away. She spent too long in a bad marriage before a brutal beating brought her back here where she got a job answering phones and sweeping up hair. If it weren't for her boss suggesting that she attend cosmetology school, she would still be in the same place she was, going nowhere fast, not sure how she was going to make a better life for her baby.

She was good at beauty—for the first time in her life, really good at something—and her skills were going to take her places.

"There." She studied her work with satisfaction. "You want to see?" she asked, spinning her grandmother back around. "What do you think?"

"I look like a hooker. I love it!" Mansi flipped her gray hair that was freshly cut and softly curled.

Nova laughed hard, feeling it deep in her belly. She didn't remember smiling before she came back to this island and her grandmother. This was the only place in the world she had ever felt safe, ever felt calm, and now she was planning to leave it.

"Let's take a selfie," her grandmother said, surprising her.

Nova frowned at her. "What do you know about selfies?"

"I know a lot of things. I keep up. I'm much smarter than you, girly."

"I can't argue with that. Stand up. We have to find our right angle."

"Maybe I can help with that," she heard a familiar male voice say. She didn't have to look up to know that it was Tanner. And it was him, wearing work boots and a button-down shirt.

"Stretch!" Mansi grinned widely. "Come take a picture of us. We're going to be on the Internet."

What was he doing here?

The last time she had seen him was at Teo's practice. He had made her join them for man day, buying them all giant hamburgers and ice cream floats. Teo had been overjoyed to have the attention of so many adults. Nova felt differently. She had been counting down the minutes until she could get away from Tanner. It was hard to think clearly when he was around.

"Give me your phone," Tanner said, looking her directly in the eye, in that way that only he could manage, in the way that made heat creep up her spine.

"It won't be a selfie if you take it, dummy."

"Give me the damn phone, Nova."

She held it out to him and he took it from her hand, and his lengthy fingers brushed hers, lingered just a moment too long, shooting heat up her arm and causing her breath to catch.

"Get my good side, Mr. Giant. I'll smack you if you don't," Nova told him.

"In order for me to get your good side, you'll have to turn around." He delivered the line with a little smirk, and Nova wasn't sure if she wanted to punch him or compliment him on his comeback.

"That was a good one, Stretch," Mansi said, laughing.

"You're supposed to be on my side," Nova complained.

"I will be when you deliver a comeback to match that one."

"Smile for the camera, ladies."

Tanner took a bunch of pictures, showing them to Mansi for approval.

Smart man.

"This one," she finally said after ten minutes of posing. "This one will go up on the Internet and cause all the men to fall in love with me."

"Men are already in love with you, Miss Mansi." Tanner winked at her. "You're very beautiful."

"Give me a kiss, Tall Drink of Water." Mansi grabbed Tanner by the collar and planted one right on his lips.

"Oh, Mansi." He played along, grinning. "I might become addicted to those."

"No more for you, Daddy Long Legs. You'll muss my makeup." She turned to Nova and pulled her into a hug. "You're a good girl. I'll see you later tonight. Right now I'm going to the senior center to see if I can scrounge up some male company."

"Mansi!"

"Don't wait up." She wiggled her brows at them before she walked out.

"That old woman." Nova shook her head and went to clean up her station. "I think she is going to put *me* in an early grave."

"She's hot. I think she's going to give you major competition for the most beautiful woman in town."

He had called her beautiful. She had heard that word bandied about when it came to her, but she mostly brushed it off. There were a lot of things that made a person beautiful. She wasn't sure she possessed many of them, but she liked it when she heard the word from him.

"Why are you here?" She turned around to face him. He was standing a few feet away from her. His arms were crossed over his massive chest. The air was thick with something she couldn't exactly explain. Maybe it was filled with the memory of what happened the last time they were alone in this salon. It was the thing they had never spoken of after it happened, but it was something that crossed her mind from time to time and she hated herself for wondering if it had ever crossed his mind, too.

"Why do you think I'm here, Nova? I'm a stubborn man, but even I have to admit that you are the best. I need a haircut."

"Can't trust the barber in town?" She motioned to her chair.

"You saw my last haircut," he said as he sat.

"He hacked it up." She ran her fingers through his hair as he sat. It was thick. There was a curl to it. She could tell he would have ringlets if he let it grow out. The thought of this six-foot-six man with ringlets made her laugh. "You should have come back to me sooner."

"I think we both know why I didn't."

She didn't respond to that, but of course she knew why he hadn't. "I need to wash your hair with a moisturizing shampoo. You're dry." She led him to the sink. "What are you using to cleanse?"

He looked at her blankly for a moment. "I'm using that combination body wash, shampoo, and conditioner stuff."

"Are you trying to give me chest pains? That stuff is garbage. You're not a teenager. You need to use real products."

"That is real. You know I'm a Ranger. You know that I spent months in places that barely had running water, much less shampoo. I was lucky to have a bar of soap."

"Well, you're home now, soldier. You don't have to worry about it anymore. I'm going to give you some products to take home with you. You better use them or I'm coming after you."

"Does Wylie use them? He's a marine. I imagine he would be even more resistant."

"He uses the entire line of products. He thinks I don't know much, but he trusts my judgment when it comes to hair. Lean back." She turned on the water, making sure it was the right temperature, and looked down at him. His eyes were closed. His face was relaxed. His lips were full and pink.

Pink?

Mansi had kissed him. He still had lipstick on his mouth. "You had better stop kissing my grandmother." She rubbed her thumb over his lips to remove the pigment. "If you walked out of here looking like that, there would be rumors about you."

"Nova." He grabbed her hand.

She had been touching his lips. It didn't register until this very moment. She was just supposed to be washing his hair, not stroking an intimate place.

"I'm sorry."

"You're apologizing for something? What's today's date? I need to mark this down for the record."

Her cheeks grew hot. "I shouldn't have touched you. Or at least I should have asked your permission."

"You don't need to ask permission to touch me. You probably shouldn't touch me, but I will never be upset if you do. But right now I need you to wash my hair."

This was a bad idea. A hellishly bad idea, Tanner thought as Nova washed his hair. Her breasts were dangerously close to his face, brushing his cheek as she vigorously massaged his scalp. It felt heavenly, but it also was torture.

"Relax," she murmured. "Don't fight it. It's supposed to feel good."

It was feeling too good. That was the problem. He was already wildly attracted to her. It was an exaggeration. The way he felt about her verged on primal. She could be a hundred miles away and just the thought of her aroused him. But now that she was here, so close to him, her breasts brushing his skin, her scent affecting his senses, he felt about ready to jump from his skin.

She rinsed his hair, and as soon as he was sure the suds were out, he grabbed her hand, preventing her from touching him further. "What?"

"Stop. I have to go."

"What do you mean you have to go? You're dripping wet."

"I need to get away from you."

Hurt flashed against her face, but hurting her was the last thing he wanted to do to her. He pulled her into his lap, so that she could feel the size of his erection.

"You feel that?" Her eyes went wide as he asked her. "I can't be this near you without this happening. I don't want to feel this way, but I do. So I need to leave right now. For both our sakes."

"No." She slid her hand up his cheek, and kissed his lips very softly. It immediately brought him back to last time he was here with her. They had kissed then. Not hot passionate kisses, but soft deep ones, which were far more dangerous for him. "Don't be a damn coward. You're not leaving here without a haircut."

"Nova," he groaned. "You can't make me stay. I'm much bigger that you. I could flick you off of me like a gnat."

"But you wouldn't. You wouldn't lay a hand on me."

"Because your brother would kill me."

"It has nothing to do with him and we both know it." She kissed the side of his face. "You would never touch me unless I wanted you to." She slid her hand beneath his T-shirt, stroking up his belly, making him harder in the process. "There's something inherently good about you, Tanner Brennan."

The air wheezed from his lungs.

She was telling him that he was good. He had been a bratty kid, a shitty teenager, and a wild young man. He had hurt people and for the past fifteen years or so he had been trying to make up for it, and he wasn't sure that he ever would.But hearing the words from her was like a balm on a raw scrape. It made him feel better.

Her curvy bottom in his lap didn't feel too bad either. He could sit like this with her for hours. It was like she was meant to be there. He buried his fingers in her thick dark hair and pulled her face to his. He just rubbed his lips against hers, giving her every opportunity to pull away, but she didn't. So he kissed her, a real kiss this time. Her mouth was hot. It was the only way he could describe it. He felt heat travel down his neck and throughout the rest of his body. He wished they weren't in this shop. He wanted to be home. In his bed. Without clothes on. Inside her.

She broke the kiss. Her eyes were closed. Her lips swollen.

"Do you want me to touch you, Nova?"

"No." She opened her eyes and then stood up. "Keep your big paws off me. And put that thing away." She glanced at the erection tenting his pants. "Let's get this hair cut."

* * *

An hour later Tanner entered his house. Actually it wasn't his house. It was the home of his grandparents. Naval captain turned senator Bryce Edmonds and his wife, Mariam. The oceanfront estate was actually their vacation home. Their third and rarely used home. They spent most of their time in Washington, D.C. When they weren't there, they lived in a multimillion-dollar condo in Boston. The house had been without a visit from its owners in nearly two years before he came to stay there. He had spent summers there as a kid. They were good summers. Little blissful escapes from his parents and their turbulence. Tanner was born into one of the oldest and wealthiest families in the United States. His grandmother boasted that they could trace their lineage back to *The Mayflower*. Tanner was born with a silver spoon in his mouth and was educated at the most exclusive private schools, had experienced the best money could bring him, but walking into this house, with its five bedrooms and indoor pool, he felt he didn't belong here.

It could have been the six tours of duty he had done in the most dangerous parts of the world. It could have been that he was so used to the simplicity of life on base that all this seemed incredibly extravagant and unnecessary. But he had always felt out of place in this world. In the schools he attended. With the friends he had. Even within his own family. He didn't feel connected to them at all. He didn't feel connected to anything.

It had become even worse after the accident. Not even the army felt like home anymore.

He walked into the kitchen and opened the refrigerator, remembering that he was supposed to go to the store after his haircut. The chore had flown right out of his mind.

Damn, Nova.

He wasn't sure what the hell she was trying to pull in that shop. Touching him like that. Kissing the side of his face. Pressing her hot little body against his like she wanted him.

And then she pushed him away. Made him stay to get his haircut. And it just wasn't a regular haircut like he got in the army. There was no quick buzz to his head. She touched him. Her fingers brushed the sides of his neck. Her hands cupped his cheek as she studied her work. She stayed close to him the entire time and it drove him insane.

It was a great haircut and what made everything worse was that she wouldn't let him pay for it. She even sent him home with shampoo. She was a single mother with a kid. He was a grown man who never spent the money he earned and had an unlimited supply of money he didn't.

Not that Nova knew anything about that. No one knew he was the grandson of a senator. That his father was a giant in real estate. Even his maternal grandmother was from old money.

In his family, money married money. No question about it. He was thirty-four. Married to no one, not even his career, and wealth was the farthest thing from his mind.

He dug through the freezer, finding a pan of something that Wylie's wife had made for him a few weeks ago, and put it in the oven. He smiled as he thought about Cass. She was a sweet, gentle woman, who loved his best friend.

Wylie was like Tanner. Battle scarred and hardened, but Wylie had found Cass again and he came alive.

Tanner never thought he would get married, but if he ever did, he would want his bride to be someone like Cassandra. A sweet, pretty, former schoolteacher, who loved to take care of people and openly showed affection.

But he knew himself too well. A woman like Cassandra would bore him after a while. He wasn't used to sweet. He was used to explosions, and jumping out of planes and being in fear of his life every day, and that's why he was so damn attracted to Nova.

She was all of those things wrapped up in one beautiful creature. He sat down at the kitchen table with his laptop while he waited for his food to heat up. He was still signed in to his video chat and not four minutes into his e-mail check he saw that his grandfather was requesting to chat with him.

He sighed. He didn't want to speak with his grandfather tonight. He never liked to talk to him, but he respected the man and he knew that he was probably the only person in his family who truly cared about him.

He accepted his request. "Hello, Captain."

"Hello, Sergeant Major."

They always addressed each other by rank. His grandfather was a naval officer and Tanner was an army man, but the military was the thing they had in common. A love of serving. He never thought they would have this. His grandfather was the one who blackmailed him into service nearly fifteen years ago. At the time he thought he could never forgive him for that.

Maybe he still hadn't forgiven him for that, but his grandfather had been right. Joining the army had saved his life. He wouldn't have made it to twenty-one without it.

"You've gotten a haircut." His grandfather nodded in approval. He sat behind his giant cherry oak desk. He had been retired from the navy for many years, but he still carried himself as an active officer, his bearing straight, his presence large even through a computer screen.

"Just a few minutes ago. Wylie's sister cut it for me." He wasn't sure why he felt the need to give that last detail. Maybe because Nova still hadn't left his thoughts or maybe it was because conversation with his grandfather was always so damn strained.

"Ah, yes." He nodded. "She did the hair and makeup for our friend's daughter's wedding."

"You keep up with the stylists of Martha's Vineyard, Captain?"

"Don't be ridiculous, son. Your grandmother told me. Apparently she is quite talented. You've met Johnson's daughter. She's a lovely girl, but she wasn't blessed the way some other women are. Apparently Nova transformed her, or so your grandmother says."

"You're being quite politically correct, Senator. I

believe I once heard you say that the girl has a face as pretty as a sack of old shoes."

His grandfather revealed a rare grin. "I don't say such things . . . anymore."

Tanner grinned back, but then a silence fell between them again. Things should be easier between them. But there was always some kind of thick but invisible wall up between them. He couldn't figure out why that was. It's not like his grandfather ever tried to keep him at a distance. If anything, he tried too hard to be in his life when he was a kid. But there was something there. With his grandmother, too. Something they were holding back.

"Was there something you wanted to speak to me about, sir?"

"I just wanted to know if you had heard from your mother. From either of your parents."

"I think you already know the answer to that question."

His nostrils flared a bit, a sure sign that he was annoyed, but Tanner knew that his grandfather's annoyance wasn't directed toward him. "I find your mother exasperating to say the least. This news should come from her."

"What's wrong?" Uneasiness spread through him. He wasn't close to his parents. Most of the time he was fairly certain that neither one of them cared if he lived or died, but he didn't like the thought of something being wrong with either of them. He didn't want them to be sick, and it was for selfish reasons. Because then he would be forced to make some kind of push in their relationship. To make amends or just resolve some of the shit that was left floating between them.

"I feel like it will only make the news seem worse if it comes from me."

"You can't tell me there is something wrong and then refuse to tell me what it is. If my parents didn't call me, then it must be something they don't want me to know."

"Everyone will know eventually. It will be a matter of public record."

"What will?"

"They are getting divorced."

Tanner threw back his head and laughed loudly.

"Is that funny, Sergeant Major?"

"Of course it is, sir. They have been married nearly forty years and have one of the worst marriages in the history of marriages. Divorce was created for people like them."

"Your mother wants to remarry. He's a sculptor. She met him in Italy."

"She's a walking cliché. Let me guess. He's younger and has exotic good looks."

"Your mother has always had a taste for good-looking ethnic men. I would say men like that are exclusively her preference."

"Maybe she should have just married one of those men in the first place. I think she would have been much happier."

His grandfather opened his mouth to speak, but no words came out. He was stopping himself again.

"What is it, sir?"

"Nothing. It's just that I agree with you. I think

she would have been much happier, if she had followed her heart thirty-five years ago. I've got to go, son. Speak to you soon."

His grandfather disconnected, leaving Tanner confused. His parents were married for forty years. What that hell was his grandfather talking about?

Chapter 3

Nova wiped down the counters of the diner as she glanced at the group of guys sitting in the booth in the corner. It had been a slow night. Her manager told her that she could go home but she decided to stay. She was renting a room in a rundown motel with dingy décor and shitty, paper-thin walls. She'd much rather stay at work in the gleaming fifties-style diner. She had lied about her age when she applied, assuring the manager that she could work as many hours as he could possibly give her.

Her twelve-hour days there gave her the opportunity to observe a lot of people. Families on vacations. College kids down for a weekend of fun. It made her sad seeing those people. It made her think about the life she could have had. It made her think about the life she had run from three months ago. She was careful to watch her back, to listen for any signs that the cops were looking for her. But there were none. She had gone to the library and searched on the Internet for news in her former town. No murder had been reported. No assault charges had been filed yet. It made her want to call her mother and ask her what had happened after she had left. But she could never bring herself to dial *the number. More than she was afraid of being found, she was afraid of finding out what became of her mother.*

With nobody left there to protect her, to take care of her, how long could she possibly survive?

"Hey, gorgeous," a guy, maybe a few years older than her, said as he walked up to the counter. He was with the group who had been sitting in the booth for the past couple of hours. She had seen him a few times before and always took note of him. He was unlike anyone she had ever seen before, except on Martha's Vineyard in her father's tribe. "Can I get a chocolate milkshake?"

"You sure can." She felt shy around him. He was beautiful with long black hair and a slender, but hard body. "My manager is going to start kicking you all out if you don't keep ordering."

"They wanted to go hours ago, but I'm making them stay."

"Really?" She knew he had been the leader of the group as soon as they walked in. He wasn't the biggest one, but he had the most presence and a bad-boy gleam in his eye that she knew was trouble. "Why can't they go?"

"Because I wanted to stay and talk to you." She had been hit on before there; in fact, not a day went by when she wasn't, but this time she was flattered. She had been lonely these past few months. She had her coworkers, but she needed a friend.

"Why would you want to talk to me?"

"Because you are the sexiest thing I have ever seen in that uniform," he said as his eyes passed over her slowly. "You're Native, right?"

"Yes," she admitted. She had never spoken to another Native person outside of her family and even then she had spent so little time with them.

"Where are your people?"

"Up north."

"You're here alone?" He took a little more interest in that than she had expected.

"There are more jobs here."

"And yet you're working in a shitty diner. You don't have to, you know. There are plenty of ways for a pretty girl like you to make ends meet around here."

She had been approached before by men. They offered her a few extra dollars to come home with them. They always seemed to know a great club where she could become a star. "I'm not a whore or a stripper, so you can fuck off."

She turned away from him, but he grabbed her wrist, which caused a visceral reaction in her. She still remembered the way it felt when Archie had grabbed her, how violated she had felt.

The guy dropped her hand as soon as she raised her fist. "I'm sorry, sweetheart. I didn't mean anything by it. I was suggesting that you need a man to do right by you, to take care of you."

It was foolish, but it sounded nice. She'd never had that. She had lived her entire life knowing that she would never have anyone to depend on but herself. "Who exactly is going to take care of me?"

He stood up straight and smiled. It was one of those too-charming smiles, the type that men who were up to no good excelled at. "I'm here for that job. My name is Elijah. I'm at your service." He extended his hand.

She shook it, knowing that she shouldn't engage, but her lonely heart wouldn't stop her. "I'm Nova."

"Nova." He nodded. "What's a man got to do to get you on a date?"

* * *

A week later Nova crept into Teo's bedroom at Mansi's house. She had just come home from doing the biggest styling job of her life. For the past year, her profile as a stylist on the island had been growing steadily.

It had all started with one wedding. Something she had taken on for extra money when the original stylist from New York had canceled. She had no idea that that wedding was for a congressman's daughter, but the family had liked her work so much that they recommended her to their friend, who asked if she would do the hair and makeup for their wedding, too. And then word of mouth spread and she was *the* stylist to come to if you were getting married on Martha's Vineyard.

She felt kind of funny being around all those fancy ultrarich people. They were kind to her. They tipped her well, but she felt incredibly out of place when she was with them. Even though she knew she was the hired help, she still felt like a fraud. She had to make sure she spoke properly, that she kept her voice quiet. She wore her hair up in a tight bun. She wore lighter lipstick and looser fitting clothes, trying not to draw any attention to herself, trying not to give them any clue that she was as uneducated as they came, the child of a drunk, the ex-wife of a degenerate. They were all so educated. She overheard them talking about their days at Emerson, and Yale. The yachts they traveled on. The only boat she had ever been on was the ferry that shuttled them off and on the island. They wore fifty-thousand-dollar wedding gowns. Ate world-class chef-prepared lobster entrées. Her wedding gown had been a T-shirt and a pair of ratty jeans. She had been married at the courthouse and had fast-food hamburgers for dinner.

Her son, however, was going to have it better than she had. She had been stockpiling money for his education. She wanted him to have the best. She wanted him to have every opportunity there was, and the only way she could do that was to agree to these gigs. Her goal was to get off the island. Get to Boston and into a high-end salon there. She could still do events on nights and weekends so she could afford to get Teo into one of those nice private schools. That's where the connections were made. He was a smart kid. He could adapt. He made friends easily. He could go far. He could be the lawyer or doctor that she had once dreamed of being. He could go to college and live in a dorm like she had always wanted to.

He would never have to wait tables in a shitty diner, or sweep up someone's hair, or put up with some asshole's abuse just to keep a roof over his head. She was going to give him what her mother couldn't give her.

A chance.

She knelt on the bed lightly, trying not to wake him up, but as soon as her knees touched the bed he turned to face her. "Mommy, you came back."

She nodded and lightly set her hand on his hair. She set her other hand on her stomach as a funny feeling churned inside of it. It was guilt. She had left him with Mansi so often. While she went to beauty school, when she was working, at nights when she was too caught up in her dark side and didn't trust herself to be alone with him. He was waiting for the day that she wasn't coming back for him. Her mother had done that to her once. She had been gone for three days, but Nova was thirteen then. And she still had been terrified. No five-year-old should have to fear the same thing.

"I'm not going to leave you, Teo," she said softly as she lay down next to him.

"Uncle Wylie told Aunt Cass that you wanted to go live in Boston."

"I want to work there, but I would take you with me. I can't leave you behind. I would be too sad."

"But what about Mansi?" he asked seriously. It was a very good question. Her grandmother was elderly, but by no means frail. She still drove. She did all her own shopping. She still was sharp as hell. But what would life be like without her in it every day? Wylie was still there. Their village would always make sure that she was okay, but how would Teo be without her? How would Nova be without her?

"I don't think Mansi wants to leave her home. This place is very special. Uncle Wylie built it for her."

"But what about Uncle Wylie? He's going to be a daddy soon. I want to be here when the baby comes. If we go to Boston we can't have man day anymore."

"Not all the time. But Boston isn't so far away from here. You'll see him a lot if we go."

"And Aunt Cass is your best friend. She said you're going to be the godmother to her baby. You can't leave her before that."

"We will be here for the baby. I promise you that. Boston was just something I was thinking about. I want to send you to a good school, and all the best ones are there."

He didn't look convinced. "Mr. Tanner told me he went to school in Boston. He told me he had to wear a uniform. He hated it."

"Did he?" She found herself grinning at the thought of Tanner. "For a man who doesn't like uniforms, he spent his entire army career in one."

"He said they made him wear a tie. He don't like wearing ties, Mommy."

"No. I guess not. When did he tell you all this?"

"At man day. I like Mr. Tanner, Mommy. He's really tall."

"He is, baby."

"I want to be tall, too. Was my daddy tall?"

Nova hesitated before she answered him. He had been asking more and more questions about his father lately. It made sense, especially since he had entered school. He saw all the other fathers coming to pick their kids up. They went on field trips and came to concerts. Teo had Wylie, who was frankly a better father than ninety-nine percent of the world, but her son wanted to know where he came from. What he would look like when he was older.

"Yes, your father w-was tall." She stumbled over the word *was*. Elijah was dead to Teo. Dead to her. But the state of Mississippi had a different record of that.

"I look like him?"

"A little, but I think you really got all your good looks from your mama." She pushed her fingers into his curls and stared down at him, her heart feeling so heavy. She thought back to that time just before she had him. Things had been bad between her and Elijah. He had been furious when his parents cut him off and cut ties after he stole from them to fuel his growing substance abuse. Nova had felt so damn stupid then. She had escaped one life with one substance abuser only to start a new one with another.

But she had been determined to save him, to fix him like she had failed to do with her mother. She should have known better. You can't fix someone who doesn't recognize that they are broken.

She didn't want to expose a baby to that, but she just couldn't bear the thought of being without her son.

He was her blessing. She knew she wasn't a great mother, but she had tried her hardest to give him a better life than she had.

"I'm going to give you a bunch of kisses and then I want you to go back to sleep. I didn't mean to wake you. I just wanted to say good night."

"Why do you always tell me before you kiss me? Aunt Cass never asks. Mansi tells me I have to give her kisses."

She didn't know how to explain it to him without scaring him. Without making him distrustful of everyone he encountered. She didn't want him to be like her. "I just want you to know that you are in charge of your body and you shouldn't put up with anything that makes you uncomfortable. From anyone. You have to tell me if someone is touching your body. You have to tell me no matter what and

I'll make it stop." She would kill for him. Without a doubt in her mind she would murder anyone who harmed her boy. It was another thing she would do for him that her mother couldn't do for her.

"Mommy, are you going to cry?"

"No. I'm sorry. I'm being silly. I think I'm just tired."

"It's late." He nodded. "You should go to bed."

"Okay, Mr. Reed. I'll go to bed." She kissed his cheeks half a dozen times. She had to put up a front. She was the Teflon tough girl. Nothing bothered her. Everything bounced off of her, and she could maintain that face in front of nearly everyone. Except Teo. Tears always lurked beneath the surface and he could make them rise with just one look, or question, or smile. She didn't want him to see that side of her. To know that she was a basket case. She didn't want him to see the real her.

But if she took him to Boston, if it was just him and her, he would know. He would see the real her. She wouldn't be able to hide it. "Good night, little one."

"Good night, Mommy."

She left the room and went to the other spare room that Mansi kept just for her. She felt dangerously close to sobbing. Not quiet crying. Not silent tears running down her face, but full chest-heaving sobs. It had been a good long while since she cried like that. And for some reason in that very moment, Tanner popped into her head. The night she cut his hair still hadn't left her. The memory of his kiss stayed on her lips. His big hard body beneath hers. Supporting hers.

Somehow, some way she had come to trust him. Trust that he wouldn't take advantage. Trust that he wouldn't use her up and discard her. She had never felt like she was in control of him, but she did feel like she was in control when she was with him.

They had been dancing around this attraction for so long. She was woman enough to admit that her body wanted to be with his. That there was something insider of her that craved his touch. But she couldn't allow herself to go there. She just couldn't. And yet her phone was in her hand and she had already dialed his number.

He picked up immediately. "Nova, what's wrong?" She could hear the alarm in his voice. "Where are you? I'll come get you."

"I'm fine, cowboy," she told him, feeling a little warmth spread through her at the thought that he would drop everything if she needed him. "You don't need to come charging to my rescue. I would call Wylie first anyway."

"You're sure? It's one A.M."

"I just got in from working a wedding. I guess I didn't realize it was so late. I'm sorry. Go back to bed."

"What's wrong? The only late-night calls means something went wrong or something salacious is about to happen."

"Are you suggesting that I am giving you a booty call?"

"I know you too well to suggest that," he said chuckling. It was a low deep sound. It soothed her raw nerves. "Tell me what's wrong, princess."

"Can you just say something mean to me? I need to hear it tonight."

"Okay," he agreed easily. "I think about you far more than is healthy or necessary. I go to bed thinking about what it would be if you were curled up beside me. I think about kissing you all the time. I think about you, Nova, and I cannot seem to stop."

She didn't realize that she had been holding her breath until she felt dizzy. His words were mean, almost brutal. He knew how to get to her, how to knock the breath out of her. "You went too far," she managed to say after a long silent moment. "You're supposed to say that I look like a tramp, or that I don't have the brains God gave a fish. You weren't supposed to say that."

"I don't think you're a tramp. I think you're smart. I think you're one of the smartest, most talented people I know."

She had felt something then, something real and intense that only one other person in the world could bring out in her. And that person was her son. But there was Tanner with his silly little words, making her heart squeeze. Quite painfully. "I want you to stop this right now, Tanner. This is not funny."

"Okay, Nova. You're a tramp and you're dumb. Are you happy?"

"What's with you?"

"What's with you? You call me at one A.M. and expect me to be on my best game?"

"I'm sorry I called."

"Why? I'm not sorry you called."

"There you go again. Quit it."

"Are we ever going to talk about what seems to happen to us whenever you cut my hair?"

"It doesn't just happen when I cut your hair. It's just that we're alone then and everything is heightened."

"I don't want you to stop cutting my hair. I look damn good. Maybe I should just come during the day when there are other people in the shop."

"No." She was going to say that maybe he shouldn't come at all, but she couldn't muster the words. "Come after the shop closes."

"Why?"

"You know why." She disconnected from him then, not wanting to say anymore. They had just admitted, aloud, for the first time, that there was something between them, and Nova realized that more than anything she was scared.

Tanner looked up from the wiring work he was doing to see a heavily pregnant woman standing in the doorway.

"Cass." He grinned at Wylie's wife. "What the hell are you doing here? Your husband is going to pass out if he sees that you're on your feet. I heard you were supposed to be in bed."

"I don't want to be in bed anymore." She waddled over to him and kissed his cheek. "He's been treating me like I'm sick. I'm not sick. I'm pregnant. And I wanted to see how things were going here. It looks like you guys are nearly done."

"Yeah." He looked around the house that some grateful family would be moving into soon. He

and Wylie were government contractors here on
Martha's Vineyard to build affordable housing for
middle-class people and to start a work training
program for individuals who needed a fresh start
and kids who were at risk. "We've already lined up
another community on the Chilmark/West Tisbury
line. We'll have work there for at least the next two
years."

"I'm happy for you. You all do such good work. It
makes sense that people would want you to stay here
on the island."

Cassandra's statement made him pause.

Stay here on the island.

He only took the job because after he left the military he didn't know what the hell he was going to
do with himself. He had been in active war zones.
He had been shot before. Hit by shrapnel, but it was
a training exercise gone wrong and the death of a
twenty-two-year-old kid that made him want to hang
it all up. To take a break from the constant motion
for a while. He thought he would die from the lack
of action, from the complete stillness at first. Even
now, after a full year and a half out, sometimes the
nights were so quiet he thought he would go insane.
Because that's when all the thoughts flooded him.
Thoughts of his childhood, his way too wild teen-
aged years, his time at war. But his brain didn't
explode. Those thoughts hadn't killed him.

He never planned to stay here for even this long,
but if he stayed till the completion of this next
community, he was committing to staying for a long
span of his life. He didn't have a home.

Could he see himself making one here?

"Should I take you around the community for a tour?" He extended his arm to her.

"I would love that." She smiled. Cassandra was pretty, but pregnancy had transformed her into something truly amazing. He had met her as a frail, devastated woman, reeling over the loss of her first husband and unborn child in a shooting. But in the past year he had seen her bloom into a happy and beautiful woman.

He took her around the community, showing her the playground and the little pond they had put in. Most of the people who lived in the community were Native. They had been on the island since the beginning of time and had watched their land being sold away from them for millions of dollars, making it impossible for regular people to buy property there.

Wylie had been passionate about the project. He was from Alabama, born as white as white could be but his sister was Native through her father's side. His adopted family was Native. And with their help he was making this island a place they never had to leave.

"It's so wonderful here," Cass said with a sigh. "I'm sorry we have to move so slowly. I'm as big as one of these houses you've built."

"It's not every day I get to take a walk with a beautiful woman."

"I'm sure it could be every day, if you wanted it to be. I've seen the way the women around here look at you. You could have them eating out of your hand."

"It's not fun when they eat out of your hand. It's

the chase that excites me. Didn't your husband have to chase you a little?"

"I think we had to chase each other. I wouldn't take back marrying my first husband. I don't think I would be the person I am today without having been married to him, but lately I find myself wishing that I could have started this life sooner. That I could have been married to Wylie longer. It's a beautiful thing to wake up every morning and know the person you are meant to be with is right there beside you in bed." She rubbed her belly. "And I get to make a family with him."

"I've never seen him so happy, Cass. I didn't think he could smile before you came here. Now he smiles all the time. You did that."

"You know Wylie didn't really have his own family growing up. He lived with my first husband's family after his father died. He didn't have contact with his mother for years. He never had a place to call his own, a family that he truly felt he belonged in. But now he does. He had Nova and Teo and Mansi. And now he has me and this baby and the other babies we are going to make."

"You're sure you want more kids already?"

"Of course. It would make Wylie so happy to have a large family."

"And you?"

"Cass!" Wylie stepped out of one of the houses and came barreling over to her. "What's the matter? Is it time? Why didn't you call me? You know I have my phone on for you."

"I'm fine, honey. I was just getting lonely at the house and wanted to see you."

Wylie looked at his wife with such intense tenderness that Tanner had to turn away. "I would have come home." He took her in his arms.

"I was bored there. You won't even let me do laundry."

"You've got one job and that's to grow our baby. I can do everything else. If you would have called me, I would have kidnapped a circus troop to come entertain you."

"You see, Tanner? This is why I want a big family with this man."

Tanner left work that day feeling restless. He should be tired—building homes was hard, physical work—but he didn't want to go back to that huge empty house. He got in his car and drove in the opposite direction, into town, and ended up at the soccer fields. It was Teo's practice night. If someone would have asked him which night practice was, he wouldn't have been able to tell them, but he must have subconsciously known. Subconsciously he wanted to be here. He spotted Nova immediately, his eyes zeroing on her even though there must have been twenty other people there.

She was alone in the visitor stands, far away from the other parents, as she watched her son.

It was still fairly cold for spring and she wore an oversized sweater that hung off of her shoulders, tight black pants, and black leather boots. Her hair was loose and softly curled. She was gorgeous as usual and he knew in his gut that she really had no idea how perfectly beautiful she was.

"Daddy Long Legs," she said to him as he approached. She tilted her head to the side and studied him, almost as if she wasn't sure she was seeing him correctly. "What are you doing here? It's not even man day."

"I was bored. Peewee soccer practice is the only thing going on in this town."

"You need to get out more."

"Do I?" He sat on the bleachers next to her. He didn't know if it was purposefully or instinctively, but she moved closer to him. Her thigh pressed against his, their warmth combined. The urge to wrap his arm around her became overwhelming very quickly.

"There's fun to be had here if you look for it in the right place."

The look in her eye was seductive, but he knew that she wasn't trying to seduce him. She was naturally sexy. It was why she was sitting on the opposite side of the field, away from the other mothers, a self-imposed exile. She may say that she didn't care what they thought, but she did. She didn't want to rock those women's boring little worlds. "Do you have fun here?"

"I go out. I see people."

"What people?"

"I date."

"You lie."

"How would you know? Everybody on the island knows how much I enjoy the company of men."

"Don't do that, Nova. Not with me. I know you aren't seeing anyone. That you haven't seen anyone since I've been here."

"Then what's your explanation for where I spend my Thursday nights?"

"I don't know." He frowned. "You're going to tell me one day. But I know you aren't with a man. You don't let just anyone touch you."

"Going on a date with a man doesn't mean I'm having or will have sex with him."

"I know that, but you're the most beautiful woman in this town. If you went out with someone here he would brag about it. He would tell the whole damn world."

Something flashed in her eyes, but it had disappeared so quickly that he wasn't sure he had seen it in the first place. "Maybe I'm seeing an older man. A rich, powerful man that needs to keep things discreet. Maybe he's married and has a wife and three kids that he needs to protect."

"And maybe you're full of shit." She was no man's mistress. No man's secret. No man's second place. and more than that, he knew she wouldn't do that to another woman.

"Everyone else is quick to believe that about me, even my brother. Why won't you?"

"Why would you want me to?"

She said nothing, just picked up his hand and stroked his callused palm with her long-nailed fingers. The simple touch sent a wave of intense sensations through his body and he knew that again, she wasn't trying to turn him on. That this touch was absent-minded, purely innocent on her part.

He didn't bring attention to it. He didn't want her to stop. Her touch was something only a very select few got to experience and he wanted to cherish it.

"I spoke to my grandfather last week," he started. "He said my parents are getting divorced." Tanner wasn't sure why he felt the need to tell her, but this was something that had been sitting beneath the surface for him since he learned of it.

"Why was he the one to tell you?"

"I guess you could say that my parents and I aren't very close."

"Not being close is one thing. Completely disregarding you is another."

"I think you just summed up my entire relationship with them." He was an adult. He had lived a full and exciting life without them. He shouldn't be thinking about his childhood, or how lonely it had been. But the news of his parents' divorce coming from his grandfather brought all that shit up again.

Why couldn't one of them just have told him? How much effort would it have taken? He was their only child.

"They sound like assholes to me," Nova said softly. He looked into her eyes and she gave him a sheepish grin. "No offense."

"You're right." He grinned back at her. "They fought. Incessantly. I think I was seven before I realized that all parents didn't scream at each other all day, every day. They need to divorce. They should have gotten one thirty years ago."

"And yet?"

"And yet they couldn't pick up a goddamn phone and tell me. I had to hear it from my grandfather."

"You should call them. Confront them. Tell them how pissed off you are about it. Throw a few cuss words in there."

"Is that how you would handle it?"

"I might. The best part about having a family is being able to tell them how you feel about them. I tell Wylie all the time."

"You tell him that he's an annoying pain in the ass."

"He is. I love him though. He has made me want to be a better person."

"Does he know that?"

"Of course not. And you better not tell him, or I'll knock you out."

He chuckled. "Do you think you need to become a better person?"

"Oh, hell, yes. Don't you?"

"I like you the way you are."

She looked away from him and down at the field. "You only say that because you don't know me," she said in a soft voice.

"I do know you. Better than you want me to, and that's why you hate me." He tucked a piece of hair behind her ear so that he could kiss the side of her face. She looked up at him, eyes wide, mouth slightly opened.

He wanted to kiss her again, pull her into his lap and kiss those sweet pouty lips until his mind went completely blank.

"Mr. Tanner!" He tore his eyes off Nova when he heard Teo's voice. The boy was running toward them as fast as his little legs could carry him. Tanner felt a smile spread across his face. No one had ever been this happy to see him. It made him feel . . . good.

"Hey, little man!" He stood up, caught Teo before he barreled into the bleachers, and swung him into the air. "How are you?"

"I'm fine. My class took a trip off island this week. It was just to a museum. It was kind of boring, but the boat ride was fun. My friend Bluebell says her daddy has a boat and it has a living room and a kitchen and they can sleep in it. I don't know why they got one of those when they have a house. They should just sleep in their house."

Tanner laughed again. "Your friend's name is Bluebell?"

"A bluebell is a flower, Mr. Tanner. Did you know that? It's like being named Rose or Lilly. At least that's what my teacher says. I said it was weird, but Valerie said the name Teo is weird, too."

"Teo is a nickname. Your full name is Theodore," Nova explained. "Theodore is a very good and normal name. You didn't tell me any of the stuff you just told Tanner."

"I didn't know you wanted to know." Teo's tone had changed. That excitement that he first exhibited became subdued now.

"I always want to know, Teo."

"Mansi says I talk too much."

"You do," Nova said with a small smile. "But that doesn't mean I don't want to hear it."

"Danny is having a birthday party at the bouncy

house place. His mommy said that you should come talk to her about it."

Nova nodded and touched Teo's cheek. "I'll go talk to her now." She looked into Tanner's eyes. "He'll be okay here with you?"

"Go. We'll be right here until you get back."

She nodded and walked away. He still held Teo and looked at the boy whom he genuinely liked. He wasn't a kid person, but this one had something special about him. "You know your mother loves you a lot, don't you?"

"Yeah." He sighed. "She's trying."

"What do you mean by that?"

"I don't know." He shrugged. "I hear Aunt Cass say that to Uncle Wylie a lot."

"Well, what do you think she means when she says that?"

"She sees me more. She used to leave me at Mansi's house when she worked late, but now she comes over at night and sleeps there. And she makes me breakfast now."

"She wasn't feeding you before?"

"She would give me cereal, but now I get pancakes, or waffles, or eggs with cheese on them."

"Sounds good."

"Mommy likes to cook. She says we have to eat together every day no matter what. She said the best time she had with her mommy was when they were eating."

"Have you ever met her?"

"No." He shook his head. "She died a long time ago."

"I'm sorry to hear that."

"You should tell Mommy that. She still gets real sad about her mommy sometimes. Mansi said she had a hard life."

Tanner knew that. Nova had never complained about how tough she'd had it, but he knew how bad her past had been. He had heard little bits from Wylie, who had escaped life with his mother. But Nova hadn't. She had lived with someone who had the stability of a tornado and there was some strong need in Tanner to make her life easier.

What right did he have to want that? His own life was still a mess, but there was something inside him that wanted to fix things for her, to take care of her.

He knew if he tried, she would probably crack his skull open, and that made him want to be there even more.

"I didn't know you was coming to see me practice."

"I want to take you and your mother out for dinner."

"I think Mommy would like that. She don't want to cook every day."

Chapter 4

Nova had been a little annoyed when she had returned from speaking to Danny's mother only to learn that Tanner had promised her son that he was going to take them out for dinner. The man was trying to torture her with his presence. How dare he show up at her son's practice? How dare he kiss her cheek like that in public where anyone could see?

How dare he be sweet to her?

She didn't like it, didn't know how to handle it, or him for that matter. She had wanted to tell Tanner no, but she couldn't do so without coming off like a world-class bitch to her kid. How could she tell Teo that they couldn't eat at a restaurant with the best lobster fritters on the island because they were going home to eat box mac and cheese and chicken nuggets because she hadn't been able to get to the grocery store that day?

How could she tell him that he couldn't spend more time with Tanner, who was kind to him and attentive and genuinely seemed to want to hang out with him?

She couldn't.

And she certainly couldn't tell her son that it royally ticked her off that he was so much easier around Tanner than he was with her.

Teo told Tanner stuff about his life that he never once mentioned to her. It was hard not to feel a little hurt by it. He was her kid and yet he felt more comfortable with everyone else.

But that wasn't his fault. It was hers. She hadn't always been the best mother she could be. She was trying to make up for it now, but she was afraid the damage had already been done.

"Mommy? Can Mr. Tanner come in to see what you gave me?" Teo asked her as they were heading back to their apartment in Tanner's car. They lived just a few blocks away from the fields and Nova had taken to walking Teo to practice, just to get a few more quiet moments with him.

The walk was her favorite part of the week. He would slip his little fingers through hers and they would talk. She would tell him things about her mother, about her childhood that were safe for him to hear. Good memories that she had. She told him about Wylie and their visits when they were kids.

He wasn't going to be five forever. His birthday was at the end of summer. She wasn't going to have this kind of time much longer. A big part of her didn't want to share any more of her son than she already had.

She looked over at Tanner whose expression was neutral. He wasn't going to try to influence her decision either way, which she appreciated and which annoyed her at the same moment. He made it so hard for her to dislike him.

"Baby, I think Mr. Tanner might want to go home now."

He gave a subtle shake of his head. He didn't want to go home yet. He would stay as long as she would have him. She was surprised that he had shown up today. They always avoided each other after she gave him a haircut. The energy between them was too charged, too much for her to handle in large doses. She needed space from him after those encounters. She needed time away from him to dull the memory of his kiss. To forget about his touches. But lately those feelings were refusing to go away.

Her heart kind of tumbled in her chest when she saw his long body making his way toward her. She was happy to see him, she realized. It was lonely being a single mother in a town where all the mothers avoided you. But there was no place for him in her life. No place for any man. And yet she wanted him to come inside tonight as much as Teo did.

He gave her knee a slight squeeze. He didn't have to say the words, but he was telling her that he wouldn't make her look bad in front of her kid.

If she sent him away, he would go without an argument.

"Okay. You can show him, but then you have to get ready for bed right after."

"Thank you, Mommy," he said softly. She looked back at him. He was smiling. Happy that he got the extra treat of spending time with Tanner.

She knew he wanted a father. She just hoped that he wasn't starting to think that Tanner could be his. She'd promised herself that she wouldn't let men into her son's life, that she would protect him completely—and that included his fragile little heart.

Tanner pulled up in front of her apartment. They lived in a tiny two-bedroom above a now-abandoned record store. Tanner had never been inside before and she felt herself grow a little nervous as he followed her up the stairs. She didn't do this. She didn't take men to her apartment, to the home she shared with her son. In fact, so few people came here. Wylie. Cassandra on occasion, but that was it, really.

Her walls were painted a neutral taupe, but that was the only thing that was understated about her apartment. She had been so poor growing up. They had moved around from place to place. From motel to motel. Sometimes leaving in the middle of the night with nothing more than the clothes on their backs. She always dreamed of having her own home, but marriage didn't make that dream come true. And it was more of the same. Living like a nomad.

But this was her first place and she wanted everything in it to be comfortable. She had a huge overstuffed couch, piled high with pillows and throw blankets. She had a chaise lounge in the corner draped with a quilt that Mansi had made for her after Teo was born. There was a lot of artwork on the walls. Unique, sometimes bold paintings, stuff she had picked up at flea markets and yard sales over the years.

"You got to take your shoes off in the house, Mr. Tanner. Mommy don't like it when you mess up the floors," Teo said when she let them in.

"Oh, that's okay, Tanner. You don't have to take them off."

"If that's the rule, Mommy, then that's the rule." He grinned at her and then removed his huge heavy work boots.

"I hope your big feet don't stink up the place."

"My feet smell like spring flowers." He lifted one up. "Want to smell them?"

She bit back a smile. "I'd rather eat a live snake."

"Come on, Mr. Tanner. I want to show you what Mommy got for me." Teo grabbed him by his hand and pulled Tanner into his room. Nova followed him, trying to ignore the cute image of her tiny son, leading the enormous grown man.

"What did you get?" Tanner asked. "A remote-controlled truck? A new video game?"

She bought Teo a lot of stuff. He had more clothes than three little boys combined, and shoes to match every color and shade invented. It was too much, she knew, but she'd had two pairs of jeans and three shirts when she was a kid. She only had one jacket for years and she wore until it literally fell apart. Teo would never know what it was like to go without warm clothes, and good shoes. He would never spend his childhood in a sparse motel room.

"No." Teo pointed to the corner in his room. She had bought him a large bookshelf and filled it with books, and she found a little desk and chair for him. And in the corner she placed the biggest bean bag chair she could find to complete her vision.

"Mommy made me my own library. She got me a hundred new books and said we could read a new one every night."

"Wow, Teo," Tanner said quietly. "You have the best room I have ever seen."

Teo beamed. "Thank you."

"Go get ready for bed and if your mom says it's okay, I would like to stay here for one of your stories."

"Is it okay, Mommy?"

"Yes." She walked to his drawer and took out his pajamas. "Go put these on and brush your teeth. Make sure you get all of them, even the back ones."

He nodded and was off, leaving Tanner and her alone again. He said nothing to her at all, just walked around Teo's room, looking at all of his things. She had hung up his team photos, mounted his old soccer jersey, displayed every ribbon, trophy, and certificate in there. She hoped he was happy there, that when he looked back on his childhood that he would remember how hard she had tried.

"I'm finished." He came back in the room with toothpaste dribbled down his pajama top. "Pick a book, Mr. Tanner." He got in his bed, beneath his covers, and waited.

"Oh, that's a big decision. Are you sure you want me to make it? What if you don't like the book I choose?"

"Mommy says that there are some things in life that you aren't going to like and you just have to deal with them. I'll deal with it."

Tanner laughed, his entire face transforming from merely handsome to absolutely gorgeous. It was probably one of the reasons she was so drawn to him. He smiled easily. She knew his life hadn't been easy, but he still found happiness in small things and she admired that about him. "Okay. Sit down, Mommy. Let me read to you both."

Nova found herself being pulled into the story as soon as Tanner started reading. He made funny voices. He read with such expression and she wondered where he got it from, where he pulled this talent from. He was a single man. An Army Ranger, a decorated hero, and veteran of two wars. How the hell did he have time to become an expert kid's book reader?

When he finished the story Teo let out a groan. "One more story?" he asked.

"Go to sleep, little man." He bent to kiss his forehead, as though it was the most natural thing in the world, like Teo was his son and not the nephew of his best friend. Nova felt funny about it and she couldn't exactly pinpoint what it was that made her so damn uneasy.

"Your turn, Mommy." Teo held out his arms, which was not the norm for him. But there was something about Tanner that was infectious.

She hugged her son, wrapping her arms tightly around him and kissing his face as many times as she could before he squealed.

She plugged in his night-light and with Tanner walked out of the room. As soon as they stepped into the living room, he grabbed her by the waist and planted his lips on hers. It was a hot kiss, one that caused warm tingles to snake through her body. Her nipples grew tight, her skin felt too restricted covered in all of her clothing, and Nova had the urge to break free. Not from his kiss, not from his powerful hands curled around her waist, but break free from all the crap that bogged her down, and made her scared to take a leap.

Her feet left the ground and Tanner carried her to the couch where he lay her down and covered her body with his own. The last man to lay on top of her had been her husband. She had been disgusted with him by then; there was no love left. Not even any like left, but she had pledged herself to him. She had made a family with him, but he left her cold. It was very unlike the way she was now. Tanner's body was heavy and warm. He had her pinned down to the couch, but instead of feeling trapped, she felt protected, safe in his hold. He looked right into her eyes, regarded her tenderly, like she was fragile, as he stroked his thumb along her cheek. Then he kissed her again. It was a slower kiss this time. A deep slow kiss, which made her breathless and languid and never want to get up from that spot.

"My kid is in the other room," she whispered, not wanting things to get out of hand. They could, with Tanner, they easily could.

"I know. I just want to kiss you, Nova. I need to kiss you."

"Why?"

"You got him a library and I'm not sure who is sweeter—you for thinking of it, or him for loving it so much."

"He really does like it, doesn't he?"

"Yes, Nova. Did you think he was being polite?"

"Yeah, he's very polite with me."

"You're a good mother. You've given him a good life."

She slid her hands up the back of his shirt, feeling his hard muscled back. "This has to stop. I need this to stop."

"Do you want me to get off of you?" he asked her.

"Yes," she said, and as soon as she said the words, he went to lift his body from hers, but she tightened her arms around him.

"You're not letting me go." He gave her a confused frown. "You're the queen of mixed signals."

"Mentally, I want you to go, but my body wants you to stay right where you are. Besides, I really didn't think you were going to go. I'm not used to men listening when I tell them I don't want to be touched."

His nostrils flared, and she felt his anger immediately. "What the hell happened to you, Nova? Real men listen. Real men understand the word *no*."

"It's none of your damn business what happened to me."

"I'm making it my damn business."

"You're my brother's best friend. It's barely his business so how could it be yours?"

"I'm not just your brother's best friend, damn it. You know that."

"What are you? My friend? You just want to get in my pants."

He sat up, completely disconnecting his body from hers. The loss was quick and brutal, but it was what she wanted to happen, what needed to happen. She wouldn't have been able to send him away. She loved the way his body felt. She would have become addicted to his closeness. She couldn't risk that. She had goals and plans and he wasn't a part of them.

"You know that's not true. I want you. God only knows why, but I want more than what's between your legs. You know that."

"What could you possibly want with me if not my body?"

"I don't know, but it's real and it's powerful and we would both be better off if we just admitted it."

"I was fine sparring with you and keeping my distance. You changed the rules. You started being nice. You started kissing *me*."

"Don't act like it was one sided, Nova. You feel the same things that I feel."

"I was feeling boredom."

"I hope you're feeling full of shit too, because that's what you are." He stood up. "I'm getting the hell out of here."

"Good. Get out."

He grabbed his boots and he left her. Nova had never felt so relieved, and so much like she had just pushed away one of the few good things in her life.

Chapter 5

"Tanner."

He turned around at the sound of Wylie's voice. It was near the end of their workday. It had been a busy one, but Tanner wasn't ready to quit just yet. He thought after his run-in with Nova a few days ago that he'd welcome the solitude of his big empty house. But he didn't. The house felt even emptier now that he'd spent a few hours with Nova and her kid. Maybe it was a size thing. Maybe a man wasn't meant to live alone in an estate home, and an apartment would serve him better. He made a mental note to start looking for places.

"Yeah?" he responded.

"Cass has issued an order for me to invite you over for dinner tonight. She wants to have a bonfire on our beach and told me that if you don't come she's going to cry. If my wife cries, I'll be forced to kick your ass, so just do me a favor and agree."

"Is she really emotional these last few weeks of her pregnancy?"

"She's really happy. She's nesting. I've told her to

stay in bed and let me handle everything, but she's been cooking all day. And every time I come home there is something new in the nursery. One day I caught her trying to put the crib together by herself. She's going to give me a heart attack."

"I'll be there. What should I bring?"

"Nothing, but she told me she wants you to make your special hot chocolate that you made for us at Christmas. She says she wants to drink it by the fire."

"Far be it from me to ignore a pregnant woman's request. I'll go home and shower and be over after that."

Tanner went home and took a quick shower before he dialed his grandmother's number. She answered immediately. "Tanner! I'm so happy to hear from you."

"How are you, Gram?"

Tanner and his grandmother didn't speak often. He couldn't say they were close, but out of everyone in his family, his relationship with her was the least complicated. He liked her. For a woman whose blood was as blue as could be, she was pretty down to earth. "I'm alive, sweetheart, and that means I'm wonderful."

"That's good to hear."

"To what do I owe the pleasure of this call?"

"I was wondering about your hot chocolate recipe. I tried to make it at Christmas, but there was something missing."

"What did you put in it?"

"Milk, chocolate hazelnut spread, sugar, and cocoa powder."

"You forgot to add a pinch of salt. It makes all the difference."

"Is that what it is?"

"That's all. I'm surprised you made it. I didn't think you noticed much of what we did when you were a boy."

"I noticed. I remember a lot of things we did when I was a kid. I remember my time on the island."

"Those were good summers, weren't they?"

"Yes, and then I turned fifteen."

"It was like an adrenaline junkie demon possessed you. I'm glad you've calmed down some."

"Drag racing loses its thrill when you're dodging IEDs."

"I'm so glad you're done with your service. I hated when the phone rang. I always thought it was going to be bad news on the other end."

He had survived. No calls had to be made about him, but he had been the one to notify a family once. It hadn't been his job to, but he had been there. He had watched the kid die and he had felt responsible. He put in his papers three days after that.

"I made it out."

"I'm infinitely grateful for that. Why don't you come to see us? Your grandfather will have spring recess soon. We could meet in Miami or even out of the country. Someplace warm. It has been a dreadfully cold spring in D.C."

"Things are just starting to pick up for us again. We had to slow building down in the winter months.

The goal is to have all thirty families moved in by summer."

"There was a time when your grandfather and I were sure you were going to end up in prison, but you are more dedicated to your work than most people I know."

"I guess I have my grandfather to thank for that."

"You don't have to thank him. He's happy enough, just seeing how you turned out." She paused for a long moment. "Listen, sweetheart, your mother is here. Would you like to speak to her?"

"Does she want to speak to me?"

"I don't see why she wouldn't. Did you find out the truth about . . . ?" She trailed off. "It doesn't matter. I'll get her."

"Wait!" he said but she was already gone. He knew that there was something his family wasn't telling him, something that they had kept hidden from him for years, but he couldn't figure out what the hell it might be. He knew it had to do with him. His grandparents always watched him, looked at him a little too long, studied him a little too closely. But his parents were the opposite. They acted like he didn't exist.

"Hello, baby boy!"

He hadn't heard his mother's voice in nearly two years. He would get a birthday card, an occasional e-mail, but that was it. Now she was on the phone sounding as if they spoke every few weeks.

"Hi, Mom. I heard your news."

"Isn't it wonderful? I can't wait for you to meet Ilario. You'll adore him."

"It's great that you've found someone to make

you happy, but I'm wondering why you couldn't be bothered to tell me that you were getting divorced."

"I was sure your grandfather would have told you. You speak to him much more than you have ever spoken to me."

"And whose fault is that?" he asked, unable to hide the edge in his voice.

She was silent on the phone for a long moment. "Are you trying to imply something, Tanner?"

"No, Mother. I'm not implying anything at all." He thought about Nova in that moment. She told him to tear into his parents, confront them, but something inside of him made him pause. "Is there something you need to tell me? Something you've been keeping from me?"

"Why would you ask that?" she asked in a way that was so defensive, he knew she couldn't be innocent. "Your father and I are getting a divorce. We were unhappy together. That is all."

"I really don't think it is."

"Well, that's all you are getting from me. I have to go, Tanner. I hope to see you at my wedding."

She disconnected and Tanner sat in his chair just staring at the phone still in his hand. There was something gurgling in his chest. It was the anger returning. That sick, hot burning anger he used to feel so much of as a child. When he was a kid he would do something destructive, punch a wall, break something, pick a fight, but he was too old for that now, too disciplined. He was a grown man, but it didn't seem to matter how old he was; his parents still managed to disappoint him and he still was having a hard time letting it go.

* * *

Nova glanced down at the diamond ring Elijah had just given her. It was a large marquise-cut diamond in an old-fashioned setting. It was real. She could tell it was real, and it was expensive and it was on the tip of her tongue to ask him where he had gotten it from. Or, more importantly, how he got it. She wanted to think he just walked into a store and purchased it with the money he had been saving for the past few months. But in her gut she knew that wasn't the case. Her ring had belonged to someone else, and she knew if she asked him who, it would cause him to lie, or worse, get angry.

They had been dating for six months now. Elijah was true to his word. He took care of her. He moved her out of the rundown hotel and into a one-bedroom apartment. The neighborhood wasn't the best, but the apartment was nicer than any she had ever lived in. He had a king-sized bed and a big-screen television. There was a state-of-the-art stereo system, and every video game imaginable. At first she thought his parents had bought these things for him. They were good people. His mother was a college professor. His father was an author and historian of Native culture. They made good money. They had a big beautiful house. They were the kind of people Nova wanted to be, but they had cut Elijah out of their lives.

He had brought her to his parents. Showing her off to them. Making sure they knew that she was Native, too. He thought that that would make them proud, that it would get him back in their good graces. But she could tell they weren't impressed by her. Why would they be? They were two Ph.Ds. She still hadn't finished high school.

Elijah seemed so disappointed when they didn't care that he was in love with her and planning to settle down. Nova wondered if it was because he wanted his parents to love the woman he loved, or if he had wasted his time courting a girl who couldn't get his parents to reconsider letting him back in their good graces. Nova had been worried for a while. Worried that he really hadn't loved her. Worried that it was all a game, but then he gave her this ring and promised her that they would make their own home and have a family of their own.

And the thought of that warmed her, but it didn't prevent that little voice in her head from speaking.

There was a reason his parents cut him out of their lives. There was a reason he had hushed meetings in the living room that she wasn't allowed to be involved with. There was a reason all of their possessions just appeared in the apartment and nothing ever seemed to come from a store.

"Come on, Nova." Elijah came up behind her and grabbed both of her breasts. "I got rid of everyone. Why do you still have all your clothes on? You said you wouldn't do it if my friends were in the house. Now they're gone."

"I know." She swallowed hard. Sometimes she liked the way Elijah's hands felt on her body, but there were some times when he was too rough with her. Tonight was one of those nights and it made her think twice about going through with her promise. There was a heavy scent of alcohol on his breath and his eyes were glassy. The air in the house smelled like whatever it was that they were smoking before she walked in. "Maybe we should wait until after we're married. We've waited all this time. What's another week?"

"Fuck that, Nova! I've never waited more than a week to get with a girl and you have me waiting six months. Do you know how many girls I could have gotten with? I come home to you every night. I proposed to you. You think I've ever done that before? I'm going to be your husband and it's your duty as a wife to have sex with me. If you don't want to be with me tonight, then I don't want to marry you. You can go back to living alone in that shitty motel rather being with a man who protects you. A man who loves you."

Elijah hadn't been perfect. There were things about him she didn't like, but he had been there. Every single day. He made sure she was fed and clothed and had a home. With him she finally had a place to live for more than a few months, and she couldn't risk losing that so soon.

"Okay, Elijah. I'll do it. Be gentle."

He pushed her down on the bed and tore at her jeans. "I don't think I can be. I've waited too damn long for this."

Nova had to give it to Tanner. He was a hell of a good faker. She could tell he was on edge the moment he had walked in that night. His long body was tight. He smiled, but it didn't quite reach his eyes. He joked and laughed with Wylie and Cassandra and ate heartily. He even played endless hands of Go Fish with Teo, but something was up with him. She could feel it and every time she looked at him she wanted to go over to him and make him tell her what it was that was bothering him.

But she stayed where she was. She hadn't seen him since he stomped out of her apartment. At first she thought he might have been on edge because of her, but she knew that couldn't be it. He wasn't the type to hold a grudge over something like that. It was one of the reasons she liked him so damn much.

"He's asleep." Cass came over to her and rested her head on Nova's shoulder.

"Before the bonfire? He was so excited about it. It was all he could talk about when I picked him up from school."

"I was excited for it, too." She rubbed her lower back. "But I'm kind of glad he's asleep. I don't think I could waddle all the way out to the beach."

"You're in pain, aren't you?" Nova had noticed Cass wincing when she moved, and how hard it was for her sister-in-law to move.

"Please don't tell Wylie."

"Is it your hips?"

"Yes. How did you know?"

"I've been pregnant before. Are you sleeping with a pillow between your legs?"

"No."

"Try that and take warm baths and tell your husband to book you an appointment for a prenatal massage. In fact I'll book you an appointment. There's a place in Edgartown with a great therapist."

"You don't have to do that, Nova."

"I want to. Wylie," she called to her brother who was speaking with Tanner near the kitchen door. "I'm stealing your wife tomorrow afternoon."

"Oh, no, you're not. She's eight months pregnant

and you'll have her going off island or flying out of the country."

"She's a grown woman with her own free will, Wylie James. If she wants to fly out of the country, she'll fly out of the country."

"Oh, you two, don't start," Cass chided. "Nova is taking me to get a prenatal massage. She noticed that I was in pain and offered to book me an appointment and take me."

"You're in pain?" Wylie looked horrified and rushed over to his wife. "Why didn't you tell me? Do we need to go to the hospital?"

"No, dummy." Nova rolled her eyes. "Cass's body is preparing her for labor. Hip and back pain are common. She needs to take warm baths and sleep with a pillow between her legs. Not rush to the doctor. You are making her anxious with all your anxiety, so quit it. You've been to war, you'd think a little childbirth wouldn't scare the crap out of you." She looked back at Cass. "There are some stretches you can do, too. I'll show you tomorrow."

"How do you know so much about this?" Wylie asked her suspiciously.

"Hello! My kid is in the next room. How do you think he got here? I assure you it wasn't magic. The twelve hours of labor I experienced wasn't a dream."

"Sometimes I forget you actually had a baby. I didn't even know you had been pregnant until Teo was almost three," Wylie said to her, guilt in his eyes. "I would have tried harder to find you."

"You came when I needed you," she said, suddenly uncomfortable with her brother's softness to her.

"I didn't. If I had known what he was doing to you—"

"Quit being such a girl! I'm fine." She squeezed his arm before she walked away from him and toward Tanner. She had never told Wylie about her life before she came to the island. He'd learned bits and pieces over the years. But she could never tell him everything. It wasn't good for him to know. He would feel guilty for not being there and she would resent him more for escaping that life.

Tanner gave her a long look as she approached him. The edge was still there. "My kid is sleeping," she told him. "I don't think we are going to have a fire tonight."

"He was so excited about it." Tanner looked a little disappointed himself.

"There will be other nights."

"I made all this damn hot chocolate."

"We can still drink it inside." Cass came over to them, Wylie behind her, his hand on the small of her back. "I can open all the windows so it gets cold in here."

"You don't have to do that." Tanner grinned at her.

Nova studied the mugs. They really were quite beautiful with toasted marshmallows, whipped cream, and a chocolate drizzle on top. She hadn't expected such a presentation from him.

"You know, Tanner, I really can't believe you made these. I didn't think soldiers had any imagination. I thought you all were trained to point, shoot, and blow things up. But these mugs are damn near beautiful. Where did you learn how to do this? Home ec?"

"My grandmother used to make these for Christmas."

It was sentimental and sweet and maybe a normal person would have left it at that, but she wasn't a normal person. There was something up with him. "What else did you learn from your grandmother? Can you knit? Maybe do some watercolors. Mansi loves to play mahjong. Maybe you two can get together and have a tournament. You seem to be up on what all the little old ladies are doing."

More than annoyance flashed through his eyes. "I'm not in the mood, Nova," he warned.

"Really? That's not something I hear men say to me a lot. What's the matter? You have an accident at work today? Did your nail gun go off in a sensitive place? That's enough to make any man grouchy. Maybe you need to call your grandmother so she can kiss it and make it better."

"Damn it, Nova. Enough!" he barked at her in a way that caused her to jump. But she got what she wanted. The act was dropped and she saw the man who had really been here all night, the pissed-off guy who would rather be anywhere other than here pretending he was having a good time. She also saw a little glimpse of the commanding officer he had been in his previous life. A giant. Imposing. Not a man to be messed with.

Maybe that was the reason he got under her skin so much now. He was always quick to smile, to joke, to tease. She knew his life had been tough. She knew there was darkness there. It didn't seem right that he could go around so seemingly happy, so unaffected by it all.

So she pushed his buttons, because getting a rise out of him somehow made her feel better about herself.

"I'm sorry," he apologized immediately to Cass. "I shouldn't have raised my voice in your home. I think I need some air."

He walked out quickly and the three of them stood there for a moment in silence.

"Why do you have to be such a pain in the ass, Nova?" her brother asked her.

"Something has been bothering him all night," she said looking at the door he'd escaped through. "I wanted to get it out of him. I'm going to go talk to him."

She left them, grabbing a couple of throw blankets off the couch as she went outside. Somehow she knew he would be on the small private beach that was just a few hundred steps from Wylie and Cassandra's house.

She took off her heels, even though the sand was freezing in the early spring, and walked over to him. She said nothing, just spread out one of the blankets on the sand beside him and sat down.

"I know you're always a giant pain in the ass," he said after a while. "I shouldn't have snapped at you like that. I'm sorry."

"Don't be. I wanted you to snap at me. I was

wondering how long it was going to take. I was afraid I was going to have to start making some low blows."

He looked down at her. "You want to run that by me again?"

"Something is bothering you. I want to know what it is."

"What if I don't want to tell you? What if it's none of your goddamn business?"

She held out her hand to him. "I brought two blankets. We can wrap the other one around us."

He shook his head as if his choice went against his better judgment, but he sat down beside her and she went up on her knees to wrap the blanket around him and while she was there she kissed the side of his face. Once. Then twice. Then half a dozen times.

He exhaled heavily. "Don't kiss me."

"You need to be kissed and hugged and babied. But if you don't want me to touch you, I'll stop."

"I don't want you to stop. I'm going to want more than just a kiss from you. Don't tease me. Just walk away."

"I'm not teasing you." She set her lips on his and swept her tongue into his mouth. She could taste his surprise and his arousal. "I want to feel your hands on my skin."

It was all she had thought about this past week. His big hands, his heavy body, his warm breath. She took his hand and placed it beneath her shirt on her back.

"What are you doing?" Even in the darkness she could see the bewildered look in his eyes.

"There's something up there I need you to remove

for me. You've got long arms. You're the only man I can think of to reach it."

He trailed his fingers up her back, his eyes never leaving her face, as if he were waiting for her to change her mind.

"Tanner, I don't ever ask a man to unhook my bra, but I'm asking you. You want to snap to it?"

"Please don't play with me tonight," he begged, and she felt a little bad for him.

She went back on her heels and pulled her sweater off over her head and removed her bra.

"Are you insane? You're going to freeze to death."

"Then keep me warm." She wrapped her arms around him.

He tumbled her onto the blanket. She should have been cold. There was gooseflesh all over her exposed skin, but she didn't feel cold, she felt exhilarated.

"You're freaking crazy." He kissed the side of her neck. "I can't stand you. Sometimes I hate you."

"I know. Sometimes I hate you, too." She slid her hands up the back of his shirt. "Touch me. That's all I can think about some days."

He pushed his mouth against hers and gave her a fiery kiss. There was so much pent up inside him at the moment, there was a little bit of wildness there. Part of her liked it. Part of her was scared. He slid his hand up her side and then covered her breast. Her nipples had already been hard due to the chilled air, but now there was a new sensation there.

Pleasure.

He stroked her nipple with his thumb, just across

it at first and then in circles. She hated to compare him to her husband, but when she met Elijah, he hadn't been much more than a boy and she was a virgin. She didn't know what to expect, that he was supposed to care about her pleasure.

But right now she was with a man who seemed to instinctively know what felt good.

"Don't moan like that," he said, his breath coming out labored. "You know we can't finish what we've started here."

"Why not?" She reached for the button of his jeans. "I'll make sure you finish."

"Nova." He grabbed her hand. "Nova, Nova, Nova."

"What, Tanner?"

"Not here. Not here in the cold sand. Not walking distance from your brother's house."

"I just wanted to feel you up a little."

He chuckled and gave her another scorching kiss. "Not here. Not tonight," he panted.

"Okay, then tell me what's wrong."

He sighed and she knew he was contemplating if he was going to tell her.

"Please, Tanner."

"I spoke to my mother today."

"Did you let her have it?"

"No. I did ask her why she didn't tell me she was getting a divorce. Most of my life, I've had the feeling that my family is hiding something from me, but none of them will fess up to it."

In the moonlight she could see pain flash across his face. "Tell me about your family. I don't know much about them."

"I'm the black sheep. The only child of only

children. I was supposed to go to a good school and then go into finance or be a CEO of a large corporation. My parents didn't expect me to stay in the military as an enlisted soldier for fifteen years. They sure as hell didn't expect me to go to war and love being there."

"Did you really love being at war?"

"I loved the thought that I was fighting for my country, fighting for something bigger than myself. And if I died in battle I would know that my death would be for something. That I would have honor."

"Like a warrior."

"Yeah, but it sounds kind of stupid when you put it that way. I was a messed-up teenager. I was wild. I was beyond wild. I was headed toward killing myself."

"What do you mean by that?"

"I drank. I did drugs. I shoplifted and wrecked cars and fought and fought and fought. I didn't care if I got hurt. I didn't care about the consequences. I just needed to feel something. Something that was a clear sign that I was alive."

Nova was alarmed at his confession. He didn't seem like the type. He was too noble. Too upstanding. Too kind. But she of all people should know that appearances didn't matter.

The revelation of the substance abuse made her want to shy away from him. Her mother drank herself to death. Her husband abused. She couldn't be around it. But she had known Tanner for a year now. He wasn't a drinker, or druggie, or maniac. He was good. He felt good to her. "Why did you need to feel like you were alive?"

"Because to them, my parents, I was invisible. I didn't exist."

"How could that be? They made you. They had to have loved you."

"I think my mother did in her own way. She spoiled the hell out of me, protected me from my father's wrath when I was little. I was like her little accessory. She would dress me up and parade me in front of her friends. My father would try to make decisions about me and she fought him at every turn, most of the time for no reason. But then I wasn't so little or cute anymore and she got tired of me. She started taking trips. Long trips to Europe, or across country. My father was always away on business so I was left alone."

"And you wanted them to notice you."

"I didn't realize what I was doing at the time, but yeah. I wanted that one thing that was going to make my mother come home and stay home. That one thing that was going to make my father see that I existed, that I was his son. That I mattered."

"And did it work?"

"No." He gave a humorless laugh. "Well, it got my grandfather to notice. I had gotten in trouble when I was nineteen. My friends and I took a car. We were going to bring it back, but to the police, breaking into someone's garage and driving off in their car was a serious offense."

"How did you get out of that?"

"My grandfather has some pull. He could have made the whole thing go away with a snap of his fingers, but he told me that if I didn't straighten

up my act and enlist that he was going to use his pull
and make sure I went to prison."

"He wouldn't have really done that."

"I told him that he was full of shit, and then
he made me stay in jail for two weeks. By the time he
came back to see me I knew better than to call his
bluff."

"So you joined the army."

"So I joined the army," he said with a small laugh.
"And I loved it. Every goddamn minute of it until
the end. I hated my grandfather for it. For so many
years after that."

"Why?"

"Because he knew what was best for me. And
when you're young and pissed off, you don't want
to hear anyone tell you that they know what's best
for you."

"He ended up saving you from yourself." She
sighed and snuggled closer to him. "You're lucky.
Not everyone is lucky enough to have someone who
wants to save them."

"No." He kissed down the side of her neck, and
then that very sensitive spot where her shoulder
and her neck met. It felt heavenly. To be this close
to him, underneath the stars with the waves crashing against the shore and no one around them. It
was intimate, more intimate than she had been with
anyone else before and that scared her, too. "I can't
believe I have you half naked and beneath me and
I can't even enjoy it."

"Why can't you enjoy it?"

"I can't see you very well. I need to see you. I've

been dreaming about what you look like naked for the past year and I need to see if my imagination conjured up anything nearly as good as the real thing."

"I might disappoint you. I could be a hot mess under my clothes."

"It wouldn't matter if you were. I would still want you."

She was glad it was so dark because he would have seen her blush. No one had ever spoken to her the way he did. She didn't know how to handle it. "Because you had a bad night, I'm going to let you get away with being sweet to me."

"I'm not being sweet to you, I'm being honest."

"What else is stopping you from enjoying this?"

"I keep worrying that you're going to freeze to death."

"I'm fine. There's a giant man on top of me."

"The cold from the sand has to be seeping through this blanket." He rolled off of her and reached for her discarded clothing. "Put this on." He helped her redress and then wrapped the blanket around her. It was another one of those unconscious sweet things he did.

"You're very motherly."

"I'm not. Trust me." He hauled her into his lap. "It's taking everything inside of me not to yank down your jeans and slam myself inside of you." He put his lips on her ear. They were warm and they sent tingles all throughout her body. "I keep imagining how warm and wet and tight you'll be, with your legs wrapped around me and your nails digging into my back. I want to make you come, Nova, and after I'm done, I want to start the process all over again."

Coming from another man, his words might have been crude, offensive, but they weren't. They were erotic and beautiful, and as much as he wanted to feel her around him, she wanted to feel him buried deep inside her.

"You could have had me tonight. I would have let you."

"I couldn't. Not here."

"Why?"

"Nova!" She heard her name being called in the distance.

"That's why." Tanner kissed her cheek. "I would never be able to look your brother in the eye again. A man can't have sex with his best friend's sister on the cold sand a few hundred feet from his house."

"You have a point." She sighed. "We're over here, Wylie," she called back to her brother.

"Are you okay?"

"Tanner hasn't killed me if that's what you're asking."

"We're just talking," Tanner yelled back to him.

"Cass is worried. She thinks you're going to freeze out here."

"We'll be in soon."

Nova rested her head on Tanner's shoulder, kind of upset that whatever it was they had just been engaged in was now over. "Do you really think your family is keeping a secret from you?"

"I know they are."

"What do you think it is?"

"I have no idea."

"Well, there's only one thing you can do in this situation."

"What's that?"

"Keep digging until you find out what it is."

Chapter 6

Tanner and Wylie's work building the community was slowing down. Nearly all the homes were done; there were just little things here and there, but they could wait. It had been a rainy morning and as Cass got further along in her pregnancy, Wylie took off more days to be at home with her. And when Wylie took off, he let everyone take off. But Tanner had enjoyed working. Most of the time he went to the community site anyway and completed small jobs. Sometimes he did paperwork. It was that and Wylie's incredible leadership skills that made them so far ahead of schedule. Tanner was planning to go in today anyway, but he realized that if he completed all of his work early he would have a long stretch of time off later and the thought of that much inactivity was making him twitch. So instead of heading to the work site at seven, he got in his car and headed to town, to Nova's apartment.

It wasn't a plan, or conscious thought. But he wanted to see her. She was waiting outside when he pulled up. Teo was at her side, dressed for school, prepared for the rain in his matching green raincoat and rain boots. Nova wore rain boots, too. Hot pink plaid ones. She had on jeans, an oversized Marine Corps sweatshirt, and over her head she carried a huge umbrella with butterflies printed all over it. Her face was clean of makeup. Her hair was up in a tight bun. She was still absolutely gorgeous.

He stepped out of his SUV and walked over to them. Teo's face lit up with he saw him. There was surprise in Nova's eyes, but she smiled, too. Her smile could make any man feel warm, even on a cold, wet spring day.

"Sasquatch!" she greeted him.

"How are you, Mouth? Good morning, Teo."

"Good morning, Mr. Tanner. I'm waiting for the bus."

"I can see that. You're dressed perfectly for it."

"Mommy bought me these boots," he said, looking down at his feet. "They got frogs on them. She says they're adorable. I didn't used to like to wear them, but three ladies stopped to tell me I was *so* cute the last time I wore them so now I like them."

"It's a good thing that you realize the importance of pleasing women."

"Yeah. Mommy said when I become a teenager she is going to buy a big stick to beat the girls off me. I told her that she shouldn't hit them, because hitting people isn't nice."

"You're right. But sometimes mamas need to protect their babies and your mother doesn't want any other girls kissing you but her."

Teo looked up at her.

"He's right, kid. I'm the jealous type. I don't even

like it when Aunt Cass kisses you. But I deal with it because she is such a nice lady."

"I think your bus is pulling up," Tanner said looking down the street.

"Time for kisses," Teo announced. He lifted his arms and Nova picked him up.

"Have a good day in school and a good time at your friend's house tonight." She kissed his cheeks. "Call me if you need anything, or if you want to come home early."

"I won't want to come home, Mommy. It's restaurant night for the school and before then we have a Scouts meeting and I'm going to be busy."

"You're always busy." She sighed. "I'm going to have to buy you a day planner to keep all your appointments straight," she said with a grin.

"I would like that. We could keep it in my office."

"Go to school, you little old man," she said, squeezing him one last time.

"Good-bye Mr. Tanner." Teo turned to him. "You could hug me too, if you want."

"I want to." He took him from Nova and hugged him before setting him on the ground. "Thank you for offering."

The bus pulled up and Teo got on it, looking back once to wave to them before the doors closed. "He's the cutest freaking kid on the planet," Nova said when the bus pulled away. "I know I must be biased, but who else do you know who has a kid that gorgeous?"

"No one, but then again, not many people look like you."

"His father was incredibly beautiful." She sighed.

"It was the only thing he had going for him. Teo has a lot of his features and none of his personality. Thank the Lord."

"Tell me about him."

"Ugh. Don't make me. The only good thing about him just went away on the bus."

"Wylie said he's also Native."

"Yes. I think that's why I fell so hard for him. He had the most gorgeous hair when we met. Thick and inky black. It was longer than mine. People used to stare at us whenever we went out. He was both insanely jealous and incredibly proud. Toxic combination." She stared off into space with some sadness in her eyes. Wylie had told him that her husband was a deadbeat who Nova divorced shortly before his death. Tanner wanted to ask her a dozen more questions about the man who let her get away, but he refrained. Nova would shut down if he pushed.

"You busy today?"

"Today is my day off. I think you know that." She looked at him, into his eyes, and there was something there. Awareness maybe. They had shared something incredibly intimate the other night. And it wasn't just the fact that she invited him to touch her in a way few other men could. He had talked to her about his life, his childhood. He had barely scratched the surface, but she had gotten more out of him than anyone else had.

He could hold a conversation with anyone. Make small talk about the most inane things. He could talk to Wylie, his best friend, about his time in the service, about his time at war. He could discuss his

PTSD. But that was it. He never could go deeper than that. He could never talk about his other life.

And it was another life, because he didn't feel like he became who he was until he put on that uniform. He had conveniently shut out everything that reminded him of his past, but he could no longer do that, because now he was entering into a new life. And if he didn't merge the two, he would be nowhere.

"Will you come with me somewhere?"

"I hope it involves food."

"I will feed you whatever you want."

"Where are we going?"

"Boston."

"Boston?" She was quiet for a moment. "Will you take me to Newbury Street? There's a salon I want to stop in to. We won't be there more than fifteen minutes."

"Of course."

"Thank you. Come upstairs. If we're going to Boston, I need to look the part."

He liked her cozy apartment; somehow it was everything and nothing he had expected at the same time. She portrayed this image of feisty screw-up to her brother, but she was so far from it and he could tell by the meticulous placement of everything in her apartment.

"Shoes off. I almost forgot," he said when he saw her remove her boots.

"You don't have to. I just make Teo take his off. That kid can't resist a pile of mud."

"No. I want to." He kicked off his shoes and followed her back to her bedroom, even though he knew he should probably stay in the living room while she got ready. But she didn't say anything to him. Sometimes he felt she needed to be near him as much as he needed to be near her.

Her bedroom had the same bohemian feel as the rest of the apartment. None of the furniture matched. It was all refinished and distressed. She had a fluffy cream colored throw rug that looked like it would be perfect to make love on. But her bed was the centerpiece of the room. It was large, large enough for him, and piled high with pillows and a huge down comforter. It looked like the kind of bed you would want to stay in all day.

She opened her closet door to reveal black colored clothing. It was her uniform when she worked.

"Why do stylists wear black anyway? I've always wondered."

"There's a couple of reasons. It's chic. Stylists want to be seen that way. Plus we use a lot of dyes and products that might stain. Black makes it harder to see."

"And that's why you always wear red to break it up. I don't think you like walking around in all that dark clothing. I notice you never wear black when you're away from work."

"Reminds me of a funeral. I think I'll wear a dress today and some black pattern tights and my booties. What do you think?"

"Do you see what I'm wearing?" He motioned to himself. "It took me a good ten minutes to put this together."

"I think you look handsome, for a giant, that is."

He had put on a thin sweater over his plaid

button-down shirt and a pair of dark wash jeans that were free of paint, and holes. "Thanks."

She turned back to her closet and began to take off her jeans. He got hard, immediately. It wasn't a slow process, but quick and painful. She had the most beautiful ass. Round and perfectly formed. She wasn't even wearing sexy underwear. No thong. No lace. But cute ones that had the solar system printed on them.

"I like your panties."

She grinned at him. "They glow in the dark."

"I would pay good money to see that."

"One day," she said, and sounded like a promise he prayed she would keep. She pulled off her sweatshirt and top and walked over to her dresser. It was the first time he got a glimpse of her unclothed body. She was just as beautiful as he expected she would be. Lush. Curvy. Her body covered in rich-looking brown skin. She could be a pinup model. If he had gone to war in the forties, it would be her picture he would have hanging in his locker.

He watched her pull out a different set of underwear from the drawer. It was basic black and boring.

"What's wrong with the ones you have on?" he asked seriously.

"I need more structure," she said to him as if he knew what the hell she was talking about.

She removed her bra, like it was nothing, like she didn't have a fully aroused man sitting on her bed, staring at her. "You realize that I'm here, right? I'm not a figment of your imagination."

"Is this bothering you? I figured since you have already seen me naked it wouldn't be a big deal."

"I have not already seen you naked. It was dark. I remember expressing how terrible it was that I couldn't see you."

"Well, here I am." She stood still for a moment, swallowing hard as if she were nervous to be appraised by him.

Her breasts were as beautiful as the rest of her. Teardrop shaped and high with small brown nipples that were hard little peaks.

"Come here."

She obeyed his request and stood in front of him. He touched her. She had to know this was coming, that he couldn't be in a room with her alone without doing so. He ran his hand down her belly. She was soft; he remembered the intense pleasure he got lying on top of her body.

"See? I'm far from perfect. I've got a little pooch. There's stretch marks on my hips. You should have seen me when I was eighteen. I was the hottest thing on two legs."

"You're beautiful." He kissed her belly. She had given birth. Lived a hard life. This was the body she should have. He wouldn't want her any other way.

"Don't start kissing me," she moaned. "I can't think when you do."

"So don't think." He pulled one of her nipples into his mouth and gently sucked on it.

"You're making me . . ." She trailed off.

"What were you going to say?" He blew on her nipple. "Wet?"

She nodded, biting her lip. Big-mouthed Nova was a bit of a shy girl. "The last time we were together . . . That night after I left you, I couldn't sleep. I throbbed for you. I can't go through that again all day."

He pulled down her underwear. She was wet. So ready for him. His manhood was pressing against his zipper so hard he was afraid his pants were going to burst. "I won't let you go through the day like that. Why didn't you just touch yourself?" He opened her lower lips and stroked her with his middle finger, sliding his finger inside her. Hot, tight, wet. Just like he thought, like he'd dreamed about.

"I don't do that."

He paused and looked up at her. "Why not? It's natural."

"I turned off that part of me. I'm not sure if it was ever on. Ever worked properly. But then you came around and you make me feel sexual. You made me want something that I thought it was impossible to want again."

It was right then he knew he had to have her. Not just her body, but all of her. She needed someone to take care of her, to show her how a man was supposed to treat a woman, and he could do that for her. He could make her happy if she would let him.

"I'm glad to see I'm good for something." He rolled her on to the bed so he would have easy access to her mouth. She had a set of lips that were hard not to kiss. His hand migrated back between her legs and he stroked her in slow firm movements. He was proud of a lot of things he had done in his life, but being here with the gorgeous Nova Reed, making her moan, feeling her body shake with pleasure was probably one of his best moments.

"Tanner. It's too much. I'm . . ." She let out a deep earthy moan that nearly sent him over the deep edge. She came hard. She wasn't quiet about it and he loved every second of it. He held her for a long time, not wanting to let go of her beautiful warm nude body. But he knew he had to step away from her, if only for a few minutes.

He kissed her, as deeply as he could, and then left the bed. "Get dressed. Call me when your clothes are on." He walked out of the room.

"Tanner?" Nova called thirty minutes later. "Come in here." She was seated at her vanity when he walked through the door.

He looked relieved to see her dressed. She smiled at him. He probably hadn't realized how much of a gift he had given her. In those few minutes he made her feel alive, more in tune with her body than she had ever been. And he didn't even ask for anything in return.

"For a glamour girl, you work fast. I thought it would take you at least an hour to get made up."

"Did you think I was very high maintenance?"

"I don't know if I would use the words *high maintenance.*"

Her eyes met his in the mirror as she placed the last few curls in her hair. "Are you one of those men who think women who don't wear any makeup are somehow more real and down to earth? That they are better than those who like a little cosmetic enhancement?"

"Hell, no. I like those red lips. I like your long

nails. I like your beautiful hair. If you cut your hair short and no longer wore makeup, I would still want you, because you are you. But the idea of walking down the street with an insanely sexy woman on my arm does something powerful to my ego."

Nova unplugged her curling iron and faced Tanner with a smile. She didn't know exactly what was going on with him and didn't know how to describe what she was feeling, but she was glad he had stopped by today. He would have been on her mind all day anyway. She didn't want him to be, but they had crossed a line the other night and there was no going back.

"I'm ready to go."

He skimmed his hand down her side and kissed her exposed collarbone. "You look damn good."

"Thank you. How did you occupy yourself after you left me?"

His lips touched her ear. "I had to go into the bathroom and take care of something."

The words excited her. She felt breathless and flushed. "I would have taken care of that for you."

"If you had touched me, we wouldn't be able to go to Boston today. We wouldn't have been able to leave this room." He kissed that sensitive spot beneath her ear. "Let's go before you start me up again."

"I'm not doing anything."

"You're existing." He grabbed her hand, slid his fingers through hers, and pulled her out of her apartment.

She didn't like where this was going, how she was feeling. She preferred the bickering. The barbed shots. The walls that were there between them. He had already knocked down a few of them. She needed to stop him, or at least slow him down before he crashed through all of them.

She thought they were going to take his car on the ferry and then drive to Boston, but he drove them to the airport instead. She had never been on a plane before. She hadn't said anything as they were boarding because she was a little overwhelmed. The short forty-minute flight was nothing to him. Of course it was nothing. He had been overseas. He was a Ranger, a paratrooper. He was highly decorated. He had lived a hundred lives. She had been dragged around the country, but those weren't memories she cherished. They were tainted by having to follow around a drunk mother.

There was a rental car waiting for them when they landed. A black Range Rover. She wanted to ask how he afforded it all. She knew for a fact that the SUV he purchased when his truck died was used and that he wore his clothes until they fell apart.

But she remembered Teo saying something about him living in a big house on the water. She had thought he was confused, because the man she had come to know, come to like, couldn't be one of them. One of those people who inhabited those enormous homes in Chilmark that mere mortals couldn't dream of affording.

"We're on Newbury," he said pulling up. "You let me know where it is you want to stop."

She looked at the numbers of the shops on the busy street. It was so different from the Vineyard with its old brick buildings and high-end boutiques. She was dressed just as well as anyone who frequented these places, but in her heart she was a small-town girl who never got the hang of city life.

"It's up here. Just on the left," she told him, feeling a little distracted. "There's a space right there."

He pulled in and she sat there for a moment, not at all sure about what she wanted to do. "Why did you want to come here?" Tanner asked softly.

"I just wanted to see what I would have to do to be able to work here. This is the dream for me, to be good enough to work in a place like this."

"Are you thinking about leaving the island?"

"I think about it all the time. It doesn't mean I'll be good enough to ever work here. I haven't been licensed that long."

"You've given me the best damn haircut of my life. I think you can handle a few stuffy rich broads."

"That's not saying much. You have shitty taste."

"I've got a thing for you. My taste . . ." He trailed off. "You're right. I don't know what the hell I'm talking about." He gave her a devilish grin before he placed his hand on her knee and gave it a comforting squeeze. "There's nothing to be nervous about. You're talented. Where's the loudmouthed confidence that I've grown to equally hate and love?"

He made her smile. She relaxed a little. "Come inside with me?"

He nodded and got out of the car.

She could go in alone. Maybe she should have gone in alone, but he was here and her entire life she had to be forced to do things by herself. Sometimes she wanted someone beside her.

The inside of the salon was ultramodern. The equipment was state of the art and all the stylists looked so glamorous. It was a far cry from her little salon on the island, which hadn't been updated since the nineties. Even the receptionist looked like she walked off the pages of a fashion magazine.

"Hello. Welcome to Salon Cara Bella. How can I help you?"

"Um." She hesitated, hating that she sounded so unsure of herself. "I was just wondering how a stylist would go about applying to this salon."

"You would have to speak to one of our senior stylists. Magda does all the hiring." A woman with bright red hair came around the corner. "There she is."

Nova recognized the woman, who was the best known in the area. She was so successful that she had opened sister salons in New York and Miami, but Boston was her home.

"Magda, this stylist would like to talk to you."

"You're Nova Hair MV."

Nova blinked at the use of her Instagram handle. "You know me?"

"I follow you. You have a very large social media following for working where you do. Your bridal hair is some of the best in the business, but your makeup skills are out of this world. Where did you train?"

"Mr. Roy's School of Beauty," she said sheepishly. "But I keep a close eye on trends and try to stay ahead of them."

"I know." She glanced over to Tanner. "I saw you on her Instagram page. You're even better looking in person."

"It's the haircut. I look somewhat like a sheepdog normally."

She grinned at Tanner, her eyes changing slightly. There was interest there, and for one brief second Nova wanted to smack the woman. "You do good men's cuts too, Nova Hair MV. Can I ask why you're here?"

"I was just wondering what it would take to work here."

"You want a chair in my shop?" She pulled a card out of her pocket. "Call me. We'll find space for you. Just let me know when you want to start."

Nova walked out of the salon a few minutes later. She was quiet, her mind too busy spinning. Nothing in her life had gone that easily. She had to fight for everything she had. Prove that she was good enough. But all she did was walk through the door and the job had been placed in her lap.

She felt Tanner's hand slip into hers. "Of course they offered you a job, Mouth. You can thank me for it, too. If I wouldn't have walked in with you and dazzled them with my good looks and fine haircut they would have booted you out of there."

She looked up at him, a rush of feeling coming over her. Boston has just been some far-off dream. Something she didn't think she could achieve so soon. She thought she would really have time to think about how she would get there. Now it seemed the time for thinking was over.

All she had to do was act.

Why wasn't she more excited?

"What errand did you need to run here today?"

"I'm here to see my father. I haven't seen him in six years."

"Oh. I just love a good family reunion."

Chapter 7

Tanner wasn't sure how he would be received in his father's office. There was no falling-out, no one thing his father should be angry with him over. But they hadn't spoken in so long. They were strangers. They always had been. They probably always would be.

Work was his father's life. He was a real estate tycoon and as they entered the shiny new high-rise building they saw evidence of that wealth. The name Brennan was everywhere in New England, including big bold letters on the front of the building. He wondered what Nova thought about it. She said nothing to him when they got on the plane, but he could see her eyes go wide and the gears in her head turning. He was career military. He shouldn't be able to afford it, but she had no idea that he was sitting on an untouched trust fund. She had no idea that he stood to inherit hundreds of millions. No one knew. Not even Wylie.

When he went into the army he had been treated like everyone else for the first time in his life. He wasn't an outsider. He was part of a group working for something bigger than himself and he had never wanted to set himself apart from it, so he kept his background quiet. He never told his new friends how he grew up or who his people were. The only time anyone found out was when he became decorated and his grandfather came to the ceremonies.

He had lived off of what he made. He put money away. He bought used cars and lived in base housing when he wasn't deployed and even now he made good money. He could have blown through his trust fund. Spent it all on various stupid shit like other spoiled rich kids do, but he wanted to prove to his father, and to himself, that he didn't need him for anything. But Tanner wasn't sure his father had noticed what kind of man he had turned in to. He was probably glad just to be left alone.

Well, that ended today.

He walked up to the receptionist in the main lobby, Nova at his side. "I need to see August Brennan."

The receptionist looked up at him, her surprise clear. It wasn't every day that people walked off the street and asked to meet with the CEO of a billion-dollar corporation. "Mr. Brennan is very busy. You should contact his assistant about seeing if you can make an appointment."

"I'm his son. Tanner Brennan. I'm pretty sure if you check on the Brennan Corp.'s Web site, you'll see a picture of my father and me together. I'm the one in the dress blues."

The receptionist looked at him for a moment and then checked her computer. She then picked up her phone and called upstairs. It was less than a minute before she said, "He'll see you."

"Thank you, ma'am."

They walked to the elevators. He could feel his body grow more rigid with every step. He hadn't been here since the building had opened right before his last deployment, but he knew the way to his father's office. His father had spent most of Tanner's life in his office. It was one of the fights his parents had over and over.

If you didn't leave me alone so much, it wouldn't have happened!

I feel like I'm in this marriage alone.

If this marriage is broken, it's because you destroyed it when you broke my trust.

The elevator doors opened to the executive offices and there was a hush in the room when he and Nova walked onto the floor. They all stared, as if they knew he and his father hadn't spoken in years. Maybe they did know. Maybe August Brennan acted as if he didn't have a son at all.

His father's assistant stood up as soon as they approached. "Tanner," she breathed. Helga had been with her father for over twenty years. She knew him when he was just a punk kid, doing crazy shit in the hopes of getting his father to notice him. "Look at you. You're so handsome."

"How are you, Helga?" He leaned in to hug her.

"I'm fine. I heard you left the army. I was surprised you entered in the first place, but you're a hero and from what I hear one of the bravest men around."

He was embarrassed by her description. He was a

lot of things. Hero wasn't one of them. "I don't think I'm brave. Just too stupid to be scared. Remember that time you had to come bail me out of jail when I got caught base jumping?"

"Who on earth jumps off buildings for fun?"

"It made paratrooper school a breeze." He took Nova's hand and brought her forward. "This in Nova. Nova, this is my father's long-suffering assistant, Helga."

"Hello," Nova said quietly, seeming much shier than he knew her to be. But this quiet, gentler person was probably more Nova's inner personality compared to the brash woman he often sparred with. The closer he got to her, the more he saw the side of her she hid so thoroughly. "It's nice to meet you."

"It's wonderful to meet you. I was surprised when Tanner showed up out of the blue, but now that I see what a beautiful girl he has brought with him, I know why. He's never brought a woman home for his father to meet."

Tanner didn't say anything to correct Helga's notion. It was true that he had never brought a woman home. He had never even thought about bringing a woman to meet his parents. He had never been serious enough with anyone, but he had brought Nova here with him. They weren't even a couple, but he wanted her by his side today. "Can I go in?"

"Of course. I think he's happy you're here."

Tanner nodded, but he wasn't so sure about that. He walked into his father's office. Not much had changed since he was a teenager. The décor had been reflected to mirror the times, but the layout was the same. A large wall of windows overlooking the busy downtown street greeted him. Various awards and degrees hung on the wall. The smell of musky oak scented the room. If felt like the office of one of the country's richest men. His father was seated behind his enormous desk. He looked all-powerful sitting there. Tanner would rather have his toenails yanked out than admit that he was intimidated by his father when he saw him here as a kid. But today his feelings were different. His father looked older. He *was* older of course, but he looked more than his sixty-three years. And Tanner wondered if nearly forty years spent in a bad marriage did that to a man.

"Tanner." He stood up. He was average height. Maybe seven inches or so shorter than Tanner. He was missing the large build. The skin that was just a shade lighter than brown.

"Hello, sir." He couldn't bring himself to call him Dad this time. "I want to know, who's my biological father?"

"What?" The question literally knocked August backward. He placed his hands on his desk to steady himself; the look of bewilderment that crossed his face was all the answer Tanner needed.

He hadn't meant to ask that question. He didn't wake up this morning with the plan to come here to ask it. But seeing August Brennan again after all these years, up close, it was like all the puzzle pieces finally snapped into place and he couldn't believe it wasn't abundantly clear to him early.

Maybe he had been in denial. Or maybe fifteen years spent in the most dangerous parts of the world pushed those inconvenient family matters out of his head. He had been too focused on his survival and getting his men out alive to think twice about his parentage.

"I know you're not my father."

"I am your father! Everything I have is yours."

"I've been lied to my entire life, by my entire family. You could barely look at me growing up. You owe me this. You owe it to me to tell me who I really am."

"Sit down. Please." He motioned to the large leather sofa in his office, instead of the chair in front of his desk. He looked at Nova.

"She stays," Tanner barked out.

"I wasn't suggesting she leave," he barked back. "I thought you were here to tell me you were finally getting married. I think I'm allowed to be curious when my son shows up in my office after not speaking to me for five years."

"I didn't speak to you? You were the one who has remained silent for all these years."

"That's crap and you know it! You barely spoke to me when I came to your Bronze Star ceremony. You wouldn't even look me in the eye. It was clear that day you wanted no part of me, and even after that I still tried for a year to connect with you."

"Turnabout is fair play. You wanted no part of me since I was born. You only showed up to my Bronze

Star ceremony because it looked good for your company's image."

"I showed up because I was proud of you. I showed up because it was the only time I could see you. You haven't been back home since the day you enlisted." August let out a frustrated breath. "And I wanted to tell you, but I promised your mother that I would never say anything to you. This was her secret."

"The secret is dead now. How stupid do you all think I am?"

August was quiet for a long moment, weighing his words. "She had an affair. I don't know with whom. We were married young. Our fathers were friends. The whole damn world thought we were perfect for each other. Two wealthy families brought together to make a perfect union. I loved your mother. I still do, damn it. She has one of those personalities that sucks you in, but she was in love with someone else. I was blindsided when she told me that she was pregnant with another man's child. I was angry as hell about it. What man wouldn't be? It was very hard for me to look at you and her because it was a reminder that everything I thought was real and true was a lie."

"Why didn't you just leave? You would have been happier. We would have all been happier."

"And admit I was a failure? That I couldn't keep my new wife happy? You may not know me very well, Tanner, but I have never failed at anything in my life and I wasn't going to start with my marriage. Plus the scandal in our community would have been huge. I did love you, even though it hurt like hell to look at you and know you came from another man. You may not believe it, but I did. You had one of those personalities. I knew you could do great things if you just applied yourself. Why the hell do you think I was so hard on you?"

"Thank you for telling me." He was overwhelmed by the truth even though he knew it was coming. But he also felt numb. Not happy about it. Not angry anymore. He just didn't really feel a damn thing. There were too many thoughts in his head to sort it out. "This is Nova, by the way." He took her hand. "Come on, baby. I promised you lunch."

He turned and walked out of his father's office, ignoring his call to come back and talk.

They didn't need to talk. There was nothing more to say. He finally got the answer he had been searching for his entire life.

Tanner was stonily silent as they left the office. When she set out to Boston with him this morning, she hadn't been expecting this, to be there at the revelation of a dark family secret. And as uncomfortable as it was to be a witness to it, she was glad she had been there. And now she didn't think it would be good for Tanner to be alone right now. No one should be alone when they learned that everything they thought was true is a lie.

His father wasn't his father. He didn't know who the man was. He had no idea where the other half of him came from. She didn't have much, but she knew who her parents were. Both of them. She knew what her father looked like, and smelled like. She knew where she got her skin from and her wicked sense of humor. She knew him and, even though he was a very limited part of her life, she could always say that she had known him, that she had loved him.

They walked outside and back toward the car, his fingers tightly locked with hers.

"What kind of food are you in the mood for? There's good seafood, or I could take you for steak. Hell, I could eat pizza right now if you want to."

She stopped and looked up at him. His expression was neutral, but he was hurting. She could feel it, radiating off of him. "I'm sorry," she said to him.

He frowned at her. "For what?"

"I'm sorry your parents are shitheads. I'm sorry they lied to you. I'm sorry you have to go through this. I'm sorry." She cupped his cheeks and pulled his face down to hers. She kissed his lips. Once. Twice. Half a dozen times, not caring that they were in the middle of a busy street.

"You have to stop it, Nova." He shut his eyes and rested his forehead against hers. "I can't take it anymore."

She looked into his eyes. "Then take me somewhere."

"Where?"

"Someplace where I can make you feel better."

He looked at her for a long moment and then nodded. They got back into the car and a few minutes later pulled up in front of a very swanky-looking hotel. She was coming to the realization that Tanner wasn't just some regular soldier. He was one of those Brennans. The ones with their names all over downtown Boston.

He must have grown up with everything, but he seemed far from one of those über wealthy people, the New England elite that she encountered working at weddings.

He was hardworking and got his hands dirty and treated her like she was his equal.

It was a hell of a thing.

He got a room for them and led her upstairs to a suite that overlooked the harbor. It was by far the most beautiful place she had stayed and she wanted to press her face against the window and soak it all in, but she resisted. She knew Tanner was used to roughing it, but he must be used to this kind of luxury, too. He must have grown up with it. This was probably commonplace for him. While she felt so out of place here, she was afraid someone was going to burst through the door and order her to leave.

But no one was going to force her out of there. There was a man who wanted her very much.

She turned to face him. He stood in the center of the room looking taller than his six feet six inches. She swallowed hard as her heart went into overdrive. She realized that she was shaking, ever so slightly. It had been years since she'd had sex. And even then she hadn't wanted to. She did it because she was married to a man who expected it. Who would mope and rage and pout if she withheld herself from him. But this time was different. She was willingly giving herself to this man. For the first time in her life she wanted to be intimate with someone.

The knowledge of that was nearly overwhelming.

"Are you sure you want to do this here, today? We don't have to. I can wait for you. I will wait for you."

Tanner knew how she was feeling, how huge of a deal this was for her, and it made her want him even more. "I'm sure."

She closed the distance between them and kissed him, softly at first, but she could taste the need in him, the hunger he had for her, so she deepened their kiss. The heat built slowly, starting in her toes and snaking up her body until it was all the way up to her cheeks.

"I'm serious," he said after he broke the kiss. "We can get room service and rent a movie. We don't have to do this. I don't want you to do this just because my family is shitty."

She thought back to her first time. Elijah making her feel guilty for wanting to wait, him pawing at her breasts. His breath tasting of alcohol. His scent of smoke.

Tanner's hands grazed her waist. His breath tasted of mint. His scent of aftershave.

She pulled his shirt from his pants and then removed the sweater that was over it. She began to unbutton his shirt, growing a little more aroused with each piece of skin that was revealed. "Next time we do this, you'd better come to me with less clothes."

"Is there going to be a next time?"

"That depends on how well this time goes."

He flashed one of his devastating smiles at her and her insides completely went to mush. He was the only person who had ever made her feel this way. She really had been in love with her husband at the very beginning, but he never once made her feel like this. What the hell did that mean for her and Tanner?

She finished unbuttoning and pushed the shirt off his shoulders. He was covered in muscle. His body long, but not lanky. A nice, thick, hard body that seemed almost too perfect for words.

He had scars. A semi-circle on his stomach, a dozen or so smaller ones on his left arm and shoulder. He didn't have to tell her what they were. She knew he had been hit with shrapnel. She kissed him there, glad he was alive. Glad she had met him.

She focused on his pants, her eyes zeroing in on his zipper, which was bulging. She had felt him pressed against her, his hardness never failing to arouse her, but now she was going to finally get to see him and touch him. It felt like a gift she had waited all year for.

She unbuttoned his jeans, unzipped his fly, and slipped her hand inside. He was large, smooth, hot, and impossibly hard, and with one yank she had his pants down to his knees. "Chair," she ordered, looking behind him to the big armchair in the corner of the room. He grabbed her hips and kissed her as he walked backward towards it. She felt like she was being swept away.

He tripped and landed in the chair, pulling her on top of him, but she scurried off and went to his feet, removing his shoes, socks, and pants quickly so that she could see him completely naked.

He looked like a king sitting in that chair, or maybe some kind of marble Greek statue. His skin was bronzed, every muscle was flexed and tight, and his erection stood proudly waiting for her to soothe it.

She settled herself between his legs and took him in her hands and just ran her lips up and down his shaft. He smelled clean and felt good against her lips. She kissed him, just slow pecks at first, before she opened her mouth and gave him wetter, hotter kisses. He groaned deeply, which spurred her on. She placed his head into her mouth, her eyes on him, watching his every expression. His eyes were open too and he was watching her with so much emotion she had to look away. She slid her mouth farther down on him, stroking him with her tongue. His breath came out ragged.

"Does that feel good?"

"Too good." He tugged on her hand until she stood up. "I want you naked."

She kicked off her boots just before he grabbed her and pulled down her tights, taking her underwear with them. He cupped her bare bottom in his hands and squeezed. She loved the way it felt, the possession of it all. She had never wanted to feel owned, trapped again, but there was something different about this. She knew she could still keep herself and be with him. She knew if she walked away right now, he would be fine with it, that he wouldn't hurt her.

They were crazy thoughts to be having right before sex, but being with him brought up a lot of things she tried to keep buried.

"Do you have a condom?" she asked him.

"There's one in my wallet. Let me get it."

"No. Don't move." She backed away from him and bent to retrieve the protection from his wallet.

He moaned. "Your ass is outstanding. Have I ever told you that?"

She smiled and walked back to him. "Keep telling me that."

With her teeth she ripped open the packet and straddled his lap, rolling the condom down on him.

"You have too many clothes on."

Before she could respond, her dress was pulled up over her head and she was just in her bra. Tanner ran his knuckles over her cleavage, seemingly caught up in the way her skin felt against his hand.

"There's more, you know." She unclasped her bra, dragging it off of her and tossing it to the side. "I like it when you put your mouth on me."

He took her nipple in his mouth and gently sucked on it. "Like this?"

She moaned her answer. He cupped her other breast while he bathed her breast with his tongue. She was so aroused that she knew that if he kept it up she would come.

"Let me take you to the bed. There are some other places that I have been meaning to taste."

"Later. I want to feel you inside of me now."

"Are you ready for me? I barely got to touch you." He placed his hand between her legs and stroked her.

He made her so wet she was almost embarrassed by it. Almost. She wanted him too bad to think about it too much.

"Do you think we would be here if I weren't ready

for this?" She cupped his face and kissed him, but the kiss only lasted a second before he pulled away.

"I know how lucky I am to be here with you right now. Don't think I'm taking you or this day for granted."

His words did something to her chest again, to her heart. She felt it crack. She hated the feeling, but it wasn't going away, and with every beautiful thing he said to her, the crack grew deeper. "No more talking. We've got some work to do."

She rose slightly and Tanner grabbed her hips, guiding her down on him. She couldn't stop the noise that escaped her lips. He filled her up with his thickness and she had to clench every muscle in her body to stop herself from coming right then. There was only one shot at a first time with someone. This time had to be good for both of them.

"You're going to kill me," he said to her. "You feel too damn good."

She moved on him, slowly at first, finding her rhythm. It had been so long. She wasn't sure if she was any good; she wasn't sure she would be able to please him. But she looked up into his eyes. He was staring at her with such intensity, such passion. No one had ever looked at her like that before.

"I'm not going to be able to last long." His words came out choked, as he placed his hands on her hips. He moved her on him, pumping into her at the same time. She felt each slide of him throughout her entire body.

She couldn't prolong this, even though she wanted to. She wanted the feeling to last for hours but her climax was building so fast and every little pleasured groan that escaped Tanner's lips brought her that much closer.

And then Tanner placed one hand between her legs to rub her while he pumped into her and took her mouth in a scorching hot kiss.

She was a goner and he went over the edge with her, pumping harder and faster until they both exploded with loud cries. She had never had an orgasm like that. She didn't think orgasms like that were possible.

They stayed joined for a few long moments. She felt as if all her bones had liquefied. She rested her head on his shoulder. Loving his clean, but slightly musky smell.

"Get in that bed. I wanted to have you in one since we've met, but the first time I'm with you and we wind up in a chair."

"Are you disappointed?"

"Don't ask stupid questions." He lifted her off him. "Bed. Climb in. I'm not letting you out for a long time."

She did as he asked. The bed was large and luxurious; the sheets had more threads than she had hair on her head. He got in beside her, and pulling her close, he kissed her shoulders and down her neck.

"You like to be close after sex?"

"You don't?"

"I do." She touched his face.

"Good. Because I don't give a damn if you don't. I need to be near you."

"My ex-scumbag never liked to be touched after he finished with me. I'm just not used to it."

"He was an asshole. I'm not him. If I don't want to touch you then I need to be taken out to pasture and shot."

"That's a little rough." She brought his hand to her mouth and kissed the back of it. "How are you feeling?"

"I just had very hot sex with a woman that every man in my town has dreamt about being with. I feel pretty damn good."

"How do you feel really?" She knew sex wasn't the cure-all, but she wanted to bring some comfort to him. She wanted to be closer to him today.

"Fucking miserable," he admitted and his voice was so raw in that moment, filled with such undisguised pain, that she wanted to cry. "And stupid. The thought had never crossed my mind. He was my father. That was that, but I walked in there today and took one look at him and knew that couldn't be right. There's no way I could have come from him. I'm too big. I'm too dark. I'm too different from his entire side of the family, and no one said a word."

She touched his hair that she knew was prone to curl. He was different from the man they saw today. August Brennan was the definition of WASP. Tanner wasn't. "They couldn't very well tell you that your father wasn't your father."

"They could have told me. They should have. Especially my grandfather. He knew how bad things were between my parents. I trusted him. He was the only person I trusted."

"Your mother should have told you. Not your grandfather. Not even your father. He was the one who was betrayed. Maybe it would have seemed callous to sit you down without your mother while they were married and tell you that you didn't come from him."

"Are you telling me that I shouldn't be mad at him?"

"Oh, no. I'm mad at everyone. I'm even mad at you right now. I would never tell you not to be angry, but you shouldn't be the most angry with your grandfather or even your father."

"Do you believe that he really doesn't know who she was having an affair with?"

"What's the point of lying to you? I know liars. I was married to one. I don't think your father was lying. I also think he's telling the truth when he says he loves you."

"I doubt that. How could he love another man's child?"

"You could love another man's child." She knew it was possible. She saw him with Teo. How kind he was. How caring. He had a lot of love inside of him.

"You didn't grow up with my father. There was no love there."

"Did he ever say anything mean to you? Try to purposefully hurt you?"

He was quiet, obviously thinking back to his past. "No. He didn't say anything at all. He was away on business."

"He never did anything with you?"

"Baseball. Once a year we went to a Red Sox game. Nine incredibly quiet innings of baseball witnessed from a suite."

"That sounds like an attempt at a relationship."

"Not really. I'm a Yankees fan."

"What! That's blasphemy in these parts. You might be skinned alive."

"I know." He grinned at her. He climbed on top of her, his heavy body feeling delicious on hers. The kiss he gave her was deep and so hot she started to feel the burn all throughout her body. "I promised you that I would feed you. What do you want? I can have room service send up whatever you want."

"I can't think about food when there is six and a half feet of hard man settled between my thighs."

"You want to be with me again so soon?"

"It's the only thing I want at the moment."

"Well"—he kissed the soft spot beneath her chin—"it's my goal in life to make sure that you get everything that you want."

Chapter 8

Tanner didn't think to get in his SUV and head home when he finished work the next day. He drove right to the sports fields where he knew Nova and Teo would be.

Yesterday had been one hell of a day. None of it had been planned. He started his day with her naked in her bedroom, and ended it with her naked in a waterfront hotel suite. It would have been a fantastic day if weren't for the unpleasantness in between. His biological father was a stranger. Some man his mother had an affair with. He tried not to think about the gaping hole that knowledge had left him with. He didn't know who half of him was. And maybe it wouldn't have been such a big deal if he found out he was adopted.

He knew the kind of man he had grown up to be. He was happy with the decision his grandfather forced upon him. Proud he could cobble together this existence when before he thought he had no future. It was the fact that the others around him knew and didn't bother to tell him. That was the thing that was eating at him. It tore up his gut last night and made it impossible for him to sleep. He thought about calling his grandfather, but he knew the old man would keep his lips sealed. If there was one thing his family excelled in, it was secrecy. So he sought out Nova instead.

His body had craved to be near hers last night, and when he wasn't thinking about the showdown with his father yesterday, he had been thinking of her. He wanted to have her again. Three times yesterday hadn't been enough, but it was more than that. He just liked her. He had stayed with her as long as he could until Teo had come home from his friend's house. He only left her because he knew if he stayed any longer, he would want to take her to bed again. And that was just being greedy. He was the first man to have her in so many years. She gifted him her body. He better damn well be grateful for the experience.

He spotted her sitting on the visitor side of the field again. Today was much warmer than yesterday. She must have changed when she got home from work. She was wearing a soft pink sweater. It clung to her body, forming to her breasts like a second skin. It was impossibly sexy. But it was sweet, too.

The world had so harshly misjudged her. Nova had seen a lot in her short lifetime, but there was some innocence there. He could tell by the way she made love to him. And she had made love to him, even though she would probably punch his teeth out if he accused her of it. It wasn't just sex. It wasn't the hard quick pounding of two bodies. It was unlike any sexual experience he had had when he was in the military.

When he was younger, it was a one-night hook-up with a foreign girl who didn't speak English. Or a female officer who wanted no part of any relationship, just a release and a way of reducing some of the stress of the environment. They were never experiences he craved. But Nova was one that he could see himself repeating for a lifetime.

"Daddy Long Legs," she greeted him. "I'm beginning to think you are obsessed with me or something. You keep showing up."

"I keep showing up." He nodded. Maybe he was a little obsessed with her. His days seemed emptier when she wasn't in them. "It's your big mouth. I've grown accustomed to your flapping gums. It's too quiet without them. I can only equate it to being at war, and after being shot at and nearly being blown up every day, when the silence does come, it is deafening."

The sassiness dropped from her expression and she looked up at him with concern. She reached for his hand and tugged him down on the stands next to her. "Why the hell do you have to say stuff like that, Brennan? It makes it hard for me to insult you."

"Sorry. I thought I came out relatively unscathed, but sometimes things sneak up on me. Right after I got out I realized I had been walking into places and surveying everyone in there to see who might have a gun, or a bomb hidden in a backpack. My grandfather suggested I see someone. It was the first time I took his advice with no argument."

"I'm sorry. I can't imagine what that must have been like."

"Don't apologize. It's no worse than what you went through."

He saw her guard fly up immediately, and he knew there was something big there, some deep dark secret that had changed her. "How do you know what I went through?"

"I don't." He smoothed his hand down her back to calm her. "Not for sure, but I'm hoping you'll tell me one day."

"What makes you think you deserve to know?"

"You know my deepest darkest secret," he countered.

"I didn't weasel it out of you. I just happened to be there when the shit hit the fan." He grinned at her and leaned over to kiss her face and then the side of her neck. At first she relaxed into his kisses, but her entire body grew tight and she pulled away from him, smacking his chest in the process. "Don't kiss me." Her brow creased into a deep frown.

"Why not?"

"I don't want people thinking we're together." She looked across the field to where the other parents stood.

"They already think we're together. Why else would I show up to a kid's soccer practice if I wasn't seriously interested in one of the mothers?"

"Because you're a weirdo. We're not together, Brennan. Get that through your thick skull right now."

"What was yesterday then?"

"Sex," she said as she looked away from him.

"Just sex?" He wasn't buying her bullshit. Nobody could classify what they went through yesterday as just sex.

"Okay. It was damn good sex. I might even let you have it with me again, but don't go around thinking this is something it isn't. Don't go around thinking I'm your woman and don't you dare fall in love with me."

He would have argued with her but he saw Teo running across the field toward them. Tanner would be lying to himself if he didn't come here for Teo, too. Teo was a cool little kid.

"Mr. Tanner!" He leapt into his arms when he reached him. Tanner hugged him back. He had never seriously thought about becoming a father until recently. He knew it was hard work. He knew he couldn't pull good experiences from his own childhood with his father to model, but he was beginning to think he would like the chance. Because having a child love you, and giving unconditional love to a child, seemed like the kind of thing that would give his sometimes miserable life meaning.

"Hey, buddy. I think it would be okay, if you dropped the 'mister' and just called me Tanner."

Teo looked up at him, his face solemn. "Oh, no. Uncle Wylie said kids don't call adults by their first names because it's disrespectful."

"Your uncle is from the South and they really don't like it down there. But I think you can call me by my first name because I said it's okay, and if your uncle has a problem with it, he can take it up with me."

Teo's eyes widened. "Do you think you could beat Uncle Wylie up?"

"Teo!" his mother hissed.

"What?" He turned to look at her. "Mr. Tanner is a giant, but Uncle Wylie said marines can kick anybody's behind. Especially army guys."

"Your uncle is talking trash, huh? Marines always think they're the strongest, but army men are the smartest and you can tell him I said that."

"I don't want you to fight. Mommy said that men shouldn't hit, even if they don't really mean it."

He looked at Nova. She told her son these things almost as a kind of warning. She wanted him to avoid the things she had faced. Tanner disagreed with her. Sometimes there were good reasons to hit and he would beat the hell out of anyone who touched her. She might want to deny that they were an item, and maybe they weren't. Maybe she wasn't ready for that kind of step, but she had given a piece of herself to him yesterday and he wasn't ready to give her up yet.

He ruffled Teo's jet black ringlets. "Where should we go for dinner tonight?"

"I want steak."

"You want steak?" his mother asked.

"I like steak. You made it for me that time. London boil."

"London broil, you mean."

"I liked that. I want to eat that."

"Then steak we'll have." He stood up, holding Teo with one arm as he reached for Nova with the other. "Come on, Mommy. Let's go eat steak."

Nova snuck out of her apartment and made her way to the diner where she still worked an occasional shift.

*She probably didn't have to sneak. Elijah was a lot of
things, but he didn't seem to care where she spent her time
during the day. But this time she left the house as quietly
as possible while he lay passed out in their bedroom. She
knew he wasn't going to like what she was about to do. He
didn't want her working. He said that it was a husband's
job to take care of his wife, and when they first started
dating the idea of that sounded nice. She had this crazy
vision of herself being a homemaker, taking care of a cute
home, cooking and cleaning and being normal. Her childhood had been so nomadic that the thought of staying in
one place for over a year seemed heavenly. While she was
dreaming about that version of heaven, she had forgotten
about her original dream. She had wanted to go to college.
She wanted to be something. Yes, she had been in the same
spot for over a year now. Yes, she never had to worry about
where her next meal would come from, but that was it. She
had nothing to do. Nothing to look forward to. She felt like
she had failed. Thrown away everything she had worked
so hard for her last year in school.*

*But what was her other option? Staying behind in
Texas? She had stabbed Archie. Left him on the floor there
to die. Abandoned her mama when she was at her sickest.
And it made her feel lower than shit.*

*She walked into the diner where she had met Elijah over
a year ago, dressed in her uniform. She picked up shifts
sometimes when they needed her, and even though she was
just serving people greasy hamburgers and wiping down
tables, she enjoyed it. Getting out of the house. Earning
something.*

*And today she had arrived at work extra early for a spe-
cial reason. She said her hellos and walked into the break*

room, heading straight for the phone. Calling collect, she prayed the charges would be accepted.

"Nova?" Mansi answered the phone and Nova could hear the worry in her voice. "Is that really you?"

"Yes." The tears immediately came to her eyes. It was so good to hear her grandmother's voice. Mansi was her safe place. She was the only person who had loved her the way she needed to be loved. "How are you, Mansi?"

"I'm still in the same place I've always been. Where are you? I haven't been able to find you in three years. Do you need me to come get you?"

She wanted to say yes, but the word stuck in her throat. "I'm fine. I left Texas about fifteen months ago. I got married. To a Native man," she added, hoping that would fool her grandmother into thinking she had made the right choices in her life.

"I know you had to leave your mother. I know how bad she was. Wylie tracked her down and dragged her to rehab. But he couldn't find you."

"Wylie came? What did he find out? What did he say?" Did he know about the thing she had done? Had Mama told him why she ran?

"He called here looking for you a few times. He's worried about you."

"Tell him I'm fine. Tell him I got married."

"You're so young." The disappointment was clear in Mansi's voice. "Is he a good man?"

"The best," she lied, but the words nearly choked her. "He has a good job. He makes sure I have everything I need. He cares for me."

He steals. He brings drugs in the house. He says I can't leave him.

"Are you sure? You can come to me. I'll take care of you. I'll help you. Everything that is mine is yours."

Nova knew Mansi would move the earth for her. She knew she could go back to Martha's Vineyard, but she was too ashamed to face her. Too worried that Elijah would follow her and ruin the peaceful life that Mansi lived there.

"I don't need anything, Mansi. Do you know where Mama is? Have you spoken to her? Did she say anything about me?"

"Oh, sweetheart. You don't know. Your mother has been gone for about six months now. She was at the end stages of liver failure when your brother found her. He got her cleaned up enough to have her diagnosed. There was too much damage to do anything for her. She had been sick for years, Nova. It was the drinking that did her in."

Nova's hands started to shake, so much so that she nearly dropped the phone, but she somehow managed to keep it to her ear. She had known the moment she left that her mother would be dead. There was no one there to take care of her. No one there to haul her to the hospital when things got really bad. By running away that night and not calling for help, not calling for Wylie or Mansi or anyone to take care of her, Nova had all but killed her mother. And that was something she would never forgive herself for.

"Was Wylie there when she passed?"

Mansi paused for a long moment. "No. She left the hospital when Wylie went back to his hotel to shower and change. She was found three days later in a motel room."

"With a bottle of booze in her hand." It wasn't a question. Nova knew her mother too well. She was too addicted to stop even when she was already facing death. And as heartbroken as Nova was in that moment, she was mad *as hell. Mad that her mother chose alcohol over everything else that mattered. She had died alone because of it. A former beauty queen found dead in a dingy hotel at the age of forty-six. It seemed like such a waste.*

"Come to me, Nova. I think you need to be with your family right now."

Nova touched her belly, feeling the life that was growing inside of her that only she knew about. She didn't know what she was going to do about it. Every day Elijah got a little bit worse. A little more demanding. A little meaner with her. A little more brazen with his crimes. How could she bring a baby into that mess of a life? But then again, how could she think about sending that little life away? Especially now. Especially since the person she had loved the most was gone. It was too tough of a decision to make.

She needed time. She needed a plan. She needed to think.

"Nova?"

"I will see you again, Mansi. Please, don't worry about me." She hung up, too emotional to speak, and as soon as she set the phone down a sob tore from her throat.

"Mommy?"

"Yes, baby?"

Teo stood beside her at the bus stop nearly a week later. It was a chilly spring morning, but Teo looked especially cute bundled up in his down vest and bright blue scarf. He was dressed better than any other kid on the island and she wondered if he would still look so sharp in comparison to the kids in Boston.

She hadn't decided to go yet. She hadn't thought

much about it since she had left the salon. But the option was there. For once in her life, she had choices. And as much as it was freeing, it scared the hell out of her.

"Will you have another baby?"

She jerked at the question. "What?"

"A baby? Are you going to get pregnant?"

She blinked at him, almost too horrified to function. He couldn't know about Tanner and her. There was just no way. "Why are you asking me that?"

"Aunt Cass is going to have a baby soon. I wanted to know if you was going to have one, too."

"Just because Aunt Cass has a baby, doesn't mean that I'm going to have a baby, honey. I love Aunt Cass, but we don't do the same things."

"You'll *never* have another baby?"

"Well, I won't say never. But not anytime soon. I would have to be married to have another baby and your mama isn't looking to get married again."

"Oh." His little face fell.

"Do you want me to have a baby?"

"That might be nice."

"I'm sure that would be nice for you. You would get to be the big brother and I would be the one who has to feed it and change its diapers."

"I would help."

"Would you? Okay, if I have another baby, you have to get up at one o'clock in the morning to feed him or her."

He frowned. "Babies eat in the middle of the night?"

"More than once. But you can help with that.

You're young and you don't need as much sleep as I do."

"Maybe a dog would be nice."

She laughed. "We're not allowed to have pets here, but I think I would like a cat instead. I like cats, you know. I used to have one for a short while when I was a little girl."

"What happened to it?"

"I don't know," she said feeling a little sad. "We lived in a farmhouse for a few months and I loved it there, but my mama didn't like it because it was so far away from stores and other people, so we moved to a new place and I couldn't take my cat. I think he was fine. He sometimes stayed in the barn with the other cats that lived on the property. I just left him there with his cat family." And she had sobbed the whole two-hour drive to the next place.

"What was his name, Mommy?"

"Mr. Kitty."

"What did he look like?"

Tanner's SUV pulled up then, distracting Teo from his question. His face never failed to light up when he saw Tanner. The man was slowly becoming a fixture in their lives and that was the last thing she needed. But she still wanted him. And her heart lifted a little whenever she saw him show up. There were so few people in her life who were always there for her. She was starting to think she would start depending on him. That was dangerous because as soon as she allowed that to happen, he would let her down. It was inevitable. It had happened with every man she ever let get close to her.

"Good morning, Teo. Good morning, Nova." He hopped out of his car and came to stand with them.

"Good morning," Teo said, cheerfully.

"Hey," Nova said.

"Hey, yourself." He touched Teo's curls and then placed his hand on the small of her back. "How are you this morning? It's kind of cold today."

"We don't mind. Mommy likes to stand outside when it's cold. She said it makes her feel alive."

"Does it, Mommy?" he asked with that delicious grin of his.

"I spent most of my life in the unrelenting heat and humidity of the South. I've grown fond of the cold air."

"We were talking about Mommy's cat," Teo informed him. "She don't got him no more. She had to leave him when she was a little girl. His name was Mr. Kitty." Teo looked back at her. "You didn't tell me what he looked like yet."

"Oh, he was very handsome. He was gray and orange and white and he had the most soulful eyes. You know I only adore the most handsome things. That's why I'm so glad you are a very gorgeous boy, although I would probably still adore you even if you weren't."

Teo grinned at her. "You're funny, Mommy."

"You think so?" she asked just as the bus was pulling up.

"Yeah. Have a good day." He lifted his face for her kiss and offered Tanner the same treatment like it was the most natural thing in the world. And what kicked Nova in the gut was the fact that Tanner kissed his cheek like it was normal, as if he did it every day, before he sent him to school.

Teo had asked her if she was going to have a baby. She hoped he didn't think that that was going to happen with Tanner.

The bus pulled away and Tanner took her hand without saying a word to her and pulled her toward her apartment. As much as she wanted to send him away, she wasn't going to. He had awakened something inside her. She thought about him and she started to throb. She heard his voice and her nipples tightened. She smelled his scent and moisture formed between her legs.

It was bad. She avoided all men because she hadn't wanted this, but now that it had happened, she didn't know how to stop.

He waited quietly as she took out her key and unlocked the door, and as soon as they stepped over the threshold he shut the front door and pushed her against it, his mouth crushing against hers, his tongue sweeping inside.

She went limp. She opened her mouth wider, kissing him back, sucking him in. His hands wandered over her body, touching her breasts through her shirt. She was suddenly too heated, wearing far too many clothes. He must have sensed that because his hands went to her jeans, unzipping and shoving them down to her ankles. Her underwear went next, tearing as she ripped them from her body.

There was urgency in every move, a kind of frantic passion that she didn't think was possible. He removed his lips from her and it was a tremendous loss. She wanted his lips back on hers, his warmth pressed against her. But he went to his knees and removed the flats she had been wearing. She thought he was coming back up after he finished, but he didn't. He pushed her legs apart and then with his fingers pushed her lower lips open. He blew on her. She jumped. Not expecting that, not thinking it could ever feel so good.

"I've been thinking about doing this to you for days." He licked the length of her, one long slow lick that made her knees buckle. "You taste good," he moaned. "You're sweet."

Her husband liked to talk in bed, and she had never liked it. There was something vulgar about it. But Tanner was different; the sound of his voice hypnotized her. His words were like honey to her raw soul. She wanted more of them. But he stopped talking because his mouth was busy giving her the kind of pleasure she had never experienced.

Her fingers curled into his hair as she moved against his mouth. She was approaching orgasm fast. They always came fast with him, but she wanted to slow down so she could savor it, or at least experience it with him.

"Stop it." She pushed his head away. "I want you inside of me now."

"Let me make you come," he said, placing his mouth over her nub and sucking it into his mouth. She yanked on his hair, not knowing if she did it because she wanted him to stop or if she wanted him to keep going.

"Now." It came out as a sob, but he listened and stood up, removing himself from his jeans. He pulled a condom out of his pocket. He ripped open the packet with his teeth and quickly rolled it on, before he lifted her up and shoved himself inside her.

It was a hard thrust, but she loved it. She wrapped her legs around his waist and bit into his shoulder, spurring him on. He was so big, and powerful and raw. He filled her up. He made her feel wanted. She could get addicted to this type of sex.

"Please, come for me, baby. I need you to come." He switched up his rhythm, longer, deeper strokes. She was crying out, mumbling incoherent words. She was no longer in control of her body. He was. And he was propelling her toward the most intense climax of her life.

He covered her mouth with his, and slammed into her. She couldn't see for a moment, the buildup was so intense. The orgasm was so big that her entire body seized up and so did his. He roared with release. His arms tightened around her. It felt possessive and primal and it was something she never thought she would like. But she did.

He held her wrapped around him, his cock buried deep inside her for a few moments, but then he let her feet touch the ground. Her knees were weak and she stumbled, but he didn't miss a beat. He picked her up and carried her all the way to her bedroom.

He set her gently on the bed before he took a step back and removed the rest of his clothing. She followed suit and stripped off her remaining clothes.

He looked at her and she looked at him. He was such a beautiful man. They had barely finished and yet she wanted more of him.

"Come here." She extended her hand and pulled him down next to her.

His warm naked skin against hers was incredible. She wanted to burrow inside him.

"I didn't come here just for this. I swear."

"I would be okay if you did. I quite liked it."

"I didn't get carried away?"

"You were just right. Do you have to get to work soon?"

"I'm not going in today."

"This is two weeks in a row you took off the same day as my day off. I think my brother is going to get suspicious."

"I don't care if he does. I'm not trying to hide this from him."

"You should. I don't want him to know I'm sleeping with his best friend. He'll skin me alive."

"I think it's me who should be worried about the skinning."

"No. He thinks you're good and noble and trustworthy. He'll think I seduced you and made you come over to the dark side."

"Your brother knows me too well to think that. And he probably doesn't know you at all if he does."

"He saw me talking to Leonard Briggs last year."

He made a disgusted sound. "That guy is a creepy asshole."

"I know. Wylie said I must have LOSER MAGNET tattooed on my forehead because I seemed to attract every slimy shithead in a ten-mile radius. Like I could have stopped him from flirting with me."

He cupped her cheek, gently stroking it with his thumb. "How old were you when you got married?"

"Eighteen."

"Did you have a boyfriend before your husband?"

"No."

"And after?"

"I went on a few dates when I first got here, but nothing that went anywhere."

"You haven't slept with anyone since your husband, have you?"

"I got close once. I went away to New York City with my cousins and we met some of their friends down there. There was one guy. He was in finance. He was really handsome and things got pretty hot and heavy, but I just couldn't go through with it. He called me a bitch and a cock tease and stormed off."

"He was a prick. I don't know why you let everyone keep this bad girl image of you. You're one of the most innocent women I know."

"Bullshit. What makes someone a bad girl? Sleeping with a lot of men? What I choose to do with my body is my choice. And as long as I'm safe it's no one's business what I do with it. Men are allowed to sleep with whoever the hell they want. Droves of women and no one thinks twice about it. They get congratulated. Liking sex doesn't make you a slut. Being sexy doesn't make you a bad person."

"I didn't say it did. Do you think I give a shit how many people you slept with? I would still be here if you slept with a hundred men. I would still want you."

"Then why did you ask?"

"Because I knew you weren't whom everyone perceives you to be. Why did you answer if you didn't want to tell me?"

"I don't know. Now tell me about your sexual history. Starting from the moment you lost your virginity."

"I was fourteen. But I was six foot two so I passed for a lot older. The woman I was with was older. Beautiful. And I gave her the two best minutes of her life." He chuckled. "I'm so glad I never saw her again. I was an awkward fumbling teenager, pretending to be a man."

"You've gotten better. I would give you a solid B minus."

"A B minus!" He climbed on top of her, mischief in his eyes, and nibbled her neck, causing her to giggle. She couldn't remember the last time she had done that. She couldn't remember the last time anyone had made her feel this good.

The landline on her nightstand rang. "I should get that. It might be Teo's school. They are usually the only ones who call the house."

"You answer the phone. I'll keep doing this." He slid his lips down to her throat.

"Hello?" she said, trying to keep the lust out of her voice.

"This is the office of Dr. Andrea Curtis. She would like to make arrangements with you to do the hair and makeup for her daughter's upcoming wedding."

The name sounded familiar but Tanner's warm lips closing around her nipple distracted her from connecting the dots.

"Wait a minute. Are you talking about the wife of the vice president?"

"I like to think of him as the husband of the head

of the sociology department at Juniper University, but yes. My husband is indeed the vice president," a different voice said.

Tanner's tongue flicked across her other nipple and she shoved him off her and sat up. "Is this a joke? I can't take this if this is a joke. I told my brother I voted for your side because you were wearing really gorgeous leopard print heels and I've never seen a politician's wife dress so damn hot, but I didn't really mean it. Well, I did. I loved those shoes, but I knew all about the plan to revive the economy, and if Wylie is pulling some kind of joke on me, I am going to knock him in his big old jarhead."

The woman laughed. "I like you. This is not a joke. Our daughter is getting married in Nantucket and we would like to fly you over so you can do all of our hair and makeup for the rehearsal dinner and the ceremony. Word about you has been traveling. We would like to book you, if you are free."

"Would you mind if I checked my schedule and called you back later today?"

Nova exchanged the information with Dr. Curtis and then hung up the phone. Tanner was frowning at her.

"What was that all about?" Tanner was sitting up on the bed naked as the day he was born. He was frowning.

"That was Dr. Andrea Curtis."

"As in the Second Lady of the United States? You can't be serious."

Nova nodded, not sure she could process what was happening. Was it a dream? It could have been a dream. She just had really amazing sex and then got offered the job of a lifetime. Nothing this good ever happened to her. Nothing even came close. It was too surreal. "Her daughter's getting married on Nantucket. She wants me to be their hair and makeup artist. She said they'll fly me there. I can't believe it."

"Believe it. You're that good. Congratulations, Nova. This is going to be big for you."

"Don't speak so soon. I haven't accepted the job yet."

"But you're going to."

"I'm not sure I am. It might be too big of a job. What if I screw up? What if the concealer I use causes the Second Lady to break out in a hideous rash? What if I burn her daughter's hair off with a curling iron? They'll execute me."

"The United States does not execute people for crimes against beauty."

"I'll be the first!"

"You are being ridiculous."

"I'm scared," she admitted to him. "I wanted a chance to get out of here, a sign that I was good enough."

"If this isn't a sign, I don't know what is. Stop being scared."

"Easy for you to say. You used to jump out of planes as part of your job. I get so flustered around wealthy people. I don't belong around them."

"Do you feel out of place with me?"

"No. But you're a freak just like me."

"Rich people are freaks, too," he whispered. "Just as fucked up as everyone else."

"Let's talk about you. When the hell were you going to tell me about the money? If I had known, I would have stayed the hell away from you."

"Why do you think I didn't tell you? Besides, I work hard for my money. What my family has doesn't have anything to do with how I conduct my life now."

"You're from old money. You grew up wealthy. I bet you have a trust fund," she accused. He had probably never worried about where his next meal was coming from. He probably never had to sneak out of a motel room in the middle of the night to dodge an angry manager. Most people hadn't, but he had always had unimaginable wealth at his fingertips. He had been educated by the best and with the best. He probably looked around her simple little apartment that she worked so damn hard to get and thought he was slumming it.

"No self-respecting Brennan leaves home without one. But if it makes any difference to you, I live off of what I earn. I share a yacht with another family to keep costs down, and instead of eating off of solid gold plates, I settle for plain old china."

She grinned at him. She couldn't help it. "I find myself liking you. More than I should. Don't tell anyone that."

"I'm telling everyone that. In fact I'm taking out a billboard."

"You keep your mouth shut, or I'll have you

singing soprano. I don't want anyone knowing we're together."

"So now you're admitting we're together?" He grinned at her and gently pushed her back on the bed.

"No! That's not what I meant. We're hooking up. Just having sex. No strings attached. No expectations."

He let out a short sigh and shook his head. "Okay. We're not together." He kissed her shoulder. "You need to call back and tell them you're taking that job. I'll go with you if you want. We'll make a weekend out of it."

"You're not trying to push this couple thing on me, are you?" She lost her train of thought as he continued to kiss down her shoulder. "Because I won't have any of it. No commitments. No falling in love."

"Okay. I'll just continue to use your body for sex and save all the money I would have spent on you if you were my girlfriend and spend it on myself."

"Good. That's what I like to hear." It was what she needed to hear from him. She had to give up on her dreams when she fled Texas, and for a long time she thought she would be stuck, but she had clawed her way up again. She had new goals, new dreams, and she was so close to reaching them she could almost taste it. Men had derailed her in the past. She was never going to let that happen again.

"Call them back right now. Tell them you're taking the job."

"I can't." She swallowed hard as his hand traveled down her side.

"Stop being chicken shit and take the job."

"It's not that. I have to get dressed before I call back. I can't believe I got offered the job of a life-time with a naked man all over me."

"Oh, honey, didn't you know that's the best way to receive a job offer?"

Chapter 9

The next afternoon Tanner sat in the waiting room of the maternity ward of the hospital. Cass had gone into labor that morning. Tanner had been with Wylie when he got the call. The man lost all color in his skin and stood there for a moment looking like he was scared witless before he snapped into marine mode, barked out orders to them, and then rushed off the job site like a bat out of hell to get to his wife.

It was Tanner's job to go get Mansi. She was Nova's grandmother, but she had become Wylie's family too since he moved here to be near his sister. The old woman moved faster than he had ever seen her when he told her the news.

"Hurry up, Stretch," she said as she rushed out the door. "If we get there fast, maybe they'll let us name her."

Cass was still in labor when they arrived and after an hour of waiting for news of the baby's arrival, Mansi went to another floor to see her friend who was also in the hospital. When Tanner took the job on the island, he had no idea that he would be here, sitting in a hospital, waiting for someone else's baby to be born. He sure as hell never thought he would be excited about it. Life had changed so much since he'd left the military.

At first he never thought he would get used to the silence. The inaction. The safety.

He never thought he would have close friends he would see every day. People who would be such a big part of his life. In the army, people got deployed, people got stationed all around the world. People died. Tanner got used to saying good-bye and not expecting to see people ever again. He had gotten numb to the deaths after a while. He had lived enough life for three men, but today he was about to experience something new. Being there when a life was being brought into the world, being able to say hello to someone for the first time instead of good-bye for the last time was refreshing.

"You look like you are deep in thought." He heard Nova's voice and looked up to see her standing just a few feet away from him. He hadn't expected to see her so soon. He had spent all day with her up until the moment Teo came home. He hadn't wanted to leave then. He liked her kid. He liked eating dinner with them. He liked hearing about Teo's day. She liked being with him, too. He could tell. It was more than just sex, but she was still keeping him at arm's length. "I'm not sure that a brain the size of yours can handle all that thinking. It might explode."

Her refusal to get closer made him think back to all the little things she had said to him; they were little snapshots of the life she had before she came here. Someone had hurt her when she was a kid. Her husband didn't want to be close to her after he'd been intimate with her. Life with her mother had been a wreck.

She hadn't been loved properly. She didn't know how to be loved properly. Not that he loved her. He liked her. A whole hell of a lot. But he didn't love her.

Somebody should.

Tanner wasn't sure he was even capable of loving someone that way. His childhood had been a wreck, too. In a much different way, but there was something missing inside of him, that thing that made people want to connect to each other. A scarred single mother was the worst possible woman to get involved with. He should find some sweet girl with no baggage and no demons.

And she should probably find a man who had always been stable at love and knew which path he wanted his life to take.

He stared at her for a moment. Her long thick hair was bone straight and cascading down her back. She was dressed in all black again. Tight black skinny jeans. Tight black short-sleeved shirt. Sky-high leopard print heels. His damn heart beat a little harder. His nerves began to tingle.

Yes, they should find other more normal people to be with, but those people wouldn't be able to light the spark that burned inside each of them. If there was one thing that he and Nova had in common, it was that neither one of them ever took the safe route.

"Big life events make you think about shit, you know?"

She sat down next to him. He cursed the arm-chair he was in because he couldn't feel her pressed against him. "I know. Teo asked me if I was going to have another baby. He says he wants a sibling."

That made Tanner's brows go up. "Do you want another baby?"

"I was firmly no on the subject. I was too much of a mess to have one kid much less two. But if some-how I had another kid, I wouldn't be upset. I took one look at Teo and my heart kind of exploded. It's the only way I can describe it. I made something so perfect with so much potential and it scared the hell out of me because I knew I could screw him up. It's crazy to know that you have that kind of power."

His hand had somehow merged with hers. "I think Teo would be a good big brother."

"I told him that maybe we could get a pet. A cat to be precise."

"Ah, that's how the cat conversation started."

"My lease says no pets, but I'm wondering if my landlord will let me. I don't want to promise Teo something I can't deliver. I hate letting him down."

"What time does he get out of school? He's going to want to see the baby."

"Three-fifteen. I can't bring him here tonight. There's some kind of icky kid germs going around the school and he came home yesterday all snotty and congested. I have to dip him in disinfectant first."

"He's going to be disappointed."

"No kidding. He told me he didn't want us to move because we had to be here to meet the baby."

"You told him you were moving?"

He was there when she got the job offer, and there when she got the phone call of a lifetime, but thinking that she was actually moving away bothered the hell out of him. Things had just started up between them. He didn't want to think about the ending so soon. It shook him a little more than he wanted to admit.

"No. He's a smarty-pants and he overhears conversations. If we do move, I definitely have to get him a pet. It will take away a little of the misery I'll be inflicting when I tear him away from his uncle."

"Then don't take him away from his uncle." *Don't take yourself away from me.*

"You know I can't improve his life and my life for that matter if I stay here on the Vineyard. My kid is going places. I'm going to give him the opportunities I never had."

He knew that. It was absolutely true that she could make a bigger mark on the world if she was out in it instead of on this tiny island. She had to go. She had to lead the life she wanted for herself.

They were in search of different things. He had come to this island in search of a quieter, simpler existence, and she wanted to leave it to find bigger and better things, to lead a more exciting life.

"I don't like the thought of you being somewhere away from your family."

"I've relied so much on them these past few years. But things are changing. Mansi is getting older. Wylie and Cass are starting a family. I'm going to have to do things on my own again. I've spent so much time trying to get myself together that I left my kid with other people. If we move, then he'll have only me. I can get back some of the time I missed with him." She shook her head. "I need to shut up. Why don't you tell me to shut up, Brennan?"

She might be able to give her son more, but Tanner knew that it wouldn't make Teo happy. Tanner had everything a kid could ever dream of and it didn't make him happy at all. What he craved was a real family. Teo had that, even if it wasn't the definition of perfect.

"Give me a kiss, Nova."

"No!"

"Yes." He leaned over and placed his lips on her ear. "I think about your mouth more times a day than one normal man should. I've started to think that every woman should wear red lipstick because all lips should be that color. But then I realize how stupid that would be because all other lips pale in comparison to yours. They can't look like yours. They can't taste like yours. They can't feel like yours. And the knowledge of that makes me want to feel them against mine even more."

"I'm not going to kiss you," she said softly after a long minute. "Because if I do, I'll want more than a kiss from you and frankly we don't have time for what that entails."

He smiled and leaned in to kiss her cheek. His lips lingered there, taking in her scent, which was surprisingly sweet for the bold woman.

"Excuse me," they heard and looked up to see

Wylie standing there with a tiny pink-wrapped bundle in his arms.

Nova jumped up. Tears came to her eyes immediately. "She's here. I'm an auntie."

Wylie grinned at them. Tanner had never seen a smile so wide. "Come meet Sunny."

"Sunny!" Nova approached. "How incredibly perfect."

"You like it?" Wylie asked her. "Cass and I went back and forth over names. We wanted something with meaning, but then we saw her and it just popped out of Cass's mouth."

"I'm so happy for you, Wylie."

"Stop crying and hold your niece."

"You trust me with her?"

Wylie handed his new daughter over. "I'm sure you have had more practice with this than I have. Cass asked to see you. Why don't you take her back to her mama?"

"I love you, Wylie James." She kissed his cheek.

"I love you, too. Just make sure you don't trip walking down the hallway in those monster heels."

"Do you think I'm some kind of amateur?" Nova disappeared down the hallway with an extra swish in her step.

"Congratulations, man!" Tanner walked over to him and slapped him on the back. "She's gorgeous. Looks just like her mother."

"Thank you. She's about the most perfect thing on the planet. Cass and I are so happy."

"Mansi went to visit her friend on another floor. Do you want me to try and find her?"

"I'm sure she'll be here soon. I have a question

for you, though. What the hell is going on between you and my sister?"

Tanner knew this was going to come up eventually. He couldn't stay away from Nova, and he didn't want to; he just didn't know how to tell his friend. "I'm not sure what's going on with us. Can you ask Nova and then tell me what she says?"

Wylie didn't look impressed with his answer.

"I want to be with her. There is no other way to say it. She drives me absolutely insane and half the time she makes me want to bash my head into a wall, but I want to be with her."

"She's been hurt. I think it goes without saying, but if you do anything to my sister to cause her pain, I'll murder you and have your body spread around this island in so many pieces that they'll never be able to put you back together."

"Understood." Tanner nodded.

"Good." He smiled. "Let's go see my kid."

Nova pulled into the parking lot of the coffee shop where her appointment was taking place and sat in her car, unable to make herself get out. Elijah had just given her this car. He actually bought it. It stunk of cigarettes and had already broken down twice this week, but it was hers. A little piece of freedom he had gifted her because he knew she was growing increasingly unhappy. He had actually cleared the apartment of all his friends and sat down to tell her that he didn't want her to leave him.

She wondered why. He used her body for sex. He liked her cooking, but that was it. He didn't spend any time with her. It's not like it used to be when they were dating. She was sure that any woman could step in and take her place. She was sure that he would be happier with a quieter woman. One who didn't question him, or yell at his friends for being too rowdy.

She was positive that he would be much better off with a woman who didn't mind that he had started using hard drugs. She hadn't seen him do it yet. She had banned drugs in the house and surprisingly enough, he and his friends had listened, but that didn't mean Elijah wasn't using. He would come home too amped up, fast talking, almost manic. She told him that she would leave him. He told her that he would follow her, that he would find her and make wherever she went a living hell. She believed him. He was insanely jealous. He broke the nose of one his best friends for looking at her behind. He smashed the windows of another man's car after he learned that the man kept asking her out. She couldn't imagine the kind of destruction he would bring to Aquinnah, to the quiet town that Nova had longed to go to. When she got in the car today, she imagined taking off for there, leaving Florida and the life she'd foolishly locked herself into behind.

But her car would never make it. She only had twenty bucks on her and she was serious about making this appointment she had set up.

A knock on her window jolted her from her thoughts. She looked up to see a young couple standing there. She had recognized their faces from the pictures they had e-mailed her.

"Nova? Is that you?"

"Yes," she said, her voice cracking.

"I didn't mean to scare you. I'm Chris and this is Kelly. We're excited to meet you."

Nova opened the door and got out. She couldn't say she was excited to see them. In fact she had been dreading this day since she first arranged this meeting. "It's nice to meet you."

"You're very beautiful," Kelly said. "Even more so than your picture. I don't think I've ever seen anyone who compares."

"Thank you." Nova shut her eyes and leaned against the car. "I know we're supposed to go inside, but do you mind if I stand here for a few moments. I'm feeling a little queasy." It wasn't a lie. She was feeling queasy and light-headed and disgusted with herself. She had known the moment that she had gotten pregnant that she couldn't bring a baby into this world. For a moment she thought about ending the pregnancy, but it was only for a moment. She knew that decision would haunt her. She had gone to the library and researched adoption. There were thousands of couples who couldn't conceive, looking for a baby to love. They had money and stability. They could raise her baby to be happy and healthy.

Her unborn child would have the shot she never did, a life that would help the baby grow into something special. But being there, seeing the hope on these people's faces, had the exact opposite effect on her than she had expected. She was feeling selfish. She wanted to see her baby's face. She wanted to watch her infant grow up. She wanted someone she could love unconditionally.

This baby was her little gift and the thought of giving it away was making her ill.

"Of course. Stay here as long as you need to. We can go get you some water."

"No." The tears began to stream down her face. "My husband doesn't know I'm pregnant," she blurted out. "I never told him."

She had told him that she was going to the clinic because

she had been having stomach issues. He had encouraged her to go.

See if that has anything to do with you getting fat.

She was unable to bring herself to tell him, but she was in her second trimester now. How much longer could she keep it up? How could she prevent him from finding out?

"He could contest the adoption," Chris said.

He would raise holy hell. Their baby would be Native American, which would make adoption even trickier. She couldn't agree to give him or her to a non-Native couple. And she had known that the entire time. She knew this endeavor would be impossible. She had wanted it to be impossible because as bad as she knew life could be with Elijah, she still wanted to raise his child.

"Maybe if you tell him and he meets us, he'll see that we're good people and he'll agree," Kelly said hopefully.

"Maybe," she said, knowing it was impossible, but not wanting to break the woman's heart. "I have to go. I'll be in touch if he agrees."

She got back in her car and sped away, knowing that she would never see them again.

"I know I said I would give you as many kids as you wanted, Wylie," Cass said to her husband from her hospital bed, "but you think we could wait a couple of years before we try again? It will take me at least that long to forget about how much this hurt." She looked exhausted, but she grinned at him and then glanced down at the newborn baby in her arms.

It was so different from when Nova had been in the hospital with Teo. She had been alone the entire time. Elijah had gone off on some mission and had been missing for three days. She didn't have a car seat to get the baby home in. She had been terrified out of her mind about how they were going to get through it.

But one of Elijah's friends showed up at the hospital out of the blue with his sister and baby supplies. He figured out that she must have gone into labor when he couldn't find her at home. She had wept when she saw him. He had shown her more kindness that her husband had.

"You were in pain!" Wylie said. "I almost died watching you go through it. I don't think I can do it again, Cass." Wylie sat beside her on the bed and kissed her forehead. "I'm sorry for putting you through it."

"Your unit was hit with an IED," Tanner started. "You had shrapnel lodged in your ass, but seeing your wife go through labor is the thing that makes you cry uncle? I never thought I would live to see the day."

Wylie grinned at Tanner. Nova would have never described her brother as a happy person. He didn't smile much. She couldn't remember a time she had heard him laugh before he got together with Cass, and now that their baby was here, he seemed different. She had seen him the day before but there was a definite difference in him today. It wasn't that he was a new man, but he seemed like he was a better man for having love in his life.

Nova used to be so angry with him for having it better than she did, for escaping the chaos, but it was a wasted emotion. He may have had a calmer life, but he didn't necessarily have a happier life.

"Come hold her, Tanner." Cass motioned him over with a nod of her head.

"Me?" He looked befuddled and Nova found it adorable.

"Yes, you. Get over here."

"But I've never held a baby before."

"Are you scared?" Cass teased. "You were an Army Ranger. I heard you trained other people to jump out of planes, because you were so good at it. A little baby should be nothing."

"This is scarier. And I haven't jumped out of a plane in two years. I might have lost my nerve."

"We'll go for your birthday," Cass told him. "I've always wanted to try it."

"No, we won't," Wylie said. "You wait till we have a kid to decide to be a daredevil?"

"I pushed a human out of my body. I'm tough as hell."

"Damn right," Tanner agreed. "How do I do this? I don't want to hurt her."

"You won't. Just make sure you support her head," Nova said to him, speaking directly to him for the first time since they had been in the room. She was in a dangerous mood. She was feeling things. She could probably blame it on hormones. Newborn babies must have something in their scent that made otherwise normal, levelheaded women turn into piles of sappy goop. But she was feeling things as she looked at Tanner holding that baby. Big goopy dangerous-to-her-heart feelings. He had spent hours waiting in the hospital for a baby that wasn't his. Her husband couldn't be bothered to show up at his own son's birth.

"She's so tiny," he whispered. "Her eyes opened," he said in awe. "Hello, Sunny. You're beautiful like your mother."

Nova walked over to Tanner, looking down into his arms so she could see her niece's eyes. They were huge and alert and a soft brown like Wylie's.

"Most newborn babies are ugly," Mansi said coming back in the room after a trip to the gift shop. "But this one is beautiful. You should get her on the TV."

"Most newborns aren't ugly, Mansi." Nova shook her head at her grandmother. "Teo was gorgeous."

"Maybe, but most of them are ugly with misshapen heads and scrunched faces. You were, little one." Mansi patted her cheek. "Very ugly and you used to cry like a banshee."

"You were there when I was born? I didn't know that and hey! I'm sure I was a lovely newborn."

"You weren't, but you grew up to be almost as beautiful as I was in my youth, so it worked out. And of course I was there when you were born. I had to make sure your mother was sober those last two months. I kept her locked in the house. Your father was on the straight and narrow at that time. He helped me keep her in check."

Nova felt gut punched then. Her mother had been a drunk her entire life, but knowing that she could barely keep sober while she was pregnant with her hurt. She knew it was a disease and that it was serious. Logically she knew that, but the little kid inside her felt like her mother didn't even try, couldn't even be bothered to give a damn that she was poisoning her unborn child.

"Give me this baby," Nova said to Tanner, trying to distract herself from her annoying feelings. She felt dangerously close to tears again. All of this was bringing up her past again. No matter how hard she tried to forget it, it wouldn't go away. And it was bringing back that extreme guilt again.

She had tried to give Teo away.

Tanner gently placed the baby in her arms and then kissed the side of Nova's face. For a moment she forgot that she was surrounded by her entire family and leaned in to his kiss, wanting his lingering lips to stay as long as possible. But then she remembered where she was and what she was doing. Only Tanner could make her forget the world.

"Ew, Tanner. Don't kiss me."

He tipped her chin up and kissed her lips. As annoyed as she was with him for it, she couldn't deny the tingles rushing through her body. She couldn't deny that his kiss made her feel better. She had wanted to kiss him as soon as she had seen him today. She had missed him yesterday after he had gone home. She went about the rest of the day like she normally would have. She helped Teo with his homework. She cooked for him. She read him a story, but she felt alone when she was doing it.

Tanner was getting too close to her, too into her head. She needed to put some space between them. But it was hard when he was everywhere she turned.

"Stop it," she whispered. "I'm serious."

"Hey, Nova. We've been found out."

She frowned up at him. "What are you talking about?"

"Wylie knows."

"How?"

"You two were holding hands in the waiting room and Tanner had his lips pressed against your ear. I'm not an idiot. I figured it out. Plus the reason he keeps showing up to soccer practice has nothing to do with the love of the game. I think I'm not the only one who knows."

"You're together?" Cass cried. "I'm so happy for you."

"It's about time," Mansi huffed. "The way you two look at each other, I'm surprised your clothes don't burn off. You've been single since Teo was a baby. It's time you got some steady loving. A woman needs that. She'll go insane without it."

"Mansi!"

"What? Stretch looks good at it. Everything is so long on him."

Nova felt her face burn. Wylie and Cass were laughing. Tanner just looked at her, his expression almost sympathetic. "We're not together," she said firmly.

"Why not?" Cass asked seriously.

"Because it's not what I want."

"It's what I want for you," her brother said. "If you're worried about what I think, don't be. I would rather you live in a convent, but if my little sister is going to be with somebody, I want it to be with a man who doesn't make me want to punch him on sight. And I don't want to punch Tanner on sight. Maybe after a few hours. But not on sight."

They all laughed. Maybe not Tanner, but she couldn't tell because she wasn't looking at him. She was feeling overwhelmed. She couldn't put into words why she was feeling that way. She should be happy. Her brother clearly didn't care that she and Tanner were together. Mansi loved him. Cass seemed elated over the news. But this changed things. This put pressure on them. Everyone knew. Everyone was watching him. She could no longer justify in her head that they were just sleeping together. Their relationship felt bigger than that. It had always felt bigger than that, but she could deny the truth to herself—that when he wasn't with her, she wished he was.

"I've got to go get my kid from school." She finally looked up at Tanner who wasn't laughing. There wasn't a trace of humor on his face. "You'll make sure Mansi gets home okay?"

"Don't go," he whispered.

"I have to." She handed the baby back to him, kissed Cass and her brother good-bye, and left the room. She needed space, from all of them, but especially him. The last thing she needed was to fall in love.

Chapter 10

Nova walked into her kitchen as she always did after she put Teo to bed to make his lunch for school the next day. But she realized that she didn't have to. Spring break had arrived and as much as she loved the thought of having her little boy with her all week, it worried her.

What was she going to do with him for the next five days? Before, he used to spend huge chunks of his time at Mansi's house. Before Christmas, if he had a day off from school, he automatically went to her. After school had been spent at her house. Weekends when Nova had to work Teo went there. Nova had been absent from his life. Yes, she was working. Or taking classes. Studying up on the latest techniques. She was desperate to give him a better life than she had, especially since she had gotten pregnant with him at the worst possible time. But it had caused a rift between her and her son, a distance that she sometimes thought she would never be able to seal. He thought she didn't want him. He had said the words out loud, and knowing that almost killed her. She had made an effort to change that day. She was going to spend as much time with him as possible. This week she was going to be with him.

Time was what she'd wanted with her mother. Sober, clearheaded time. It was what she'd wanted from her own mother and never got. Nova had thought about her mother a lot lately. She wondered what the woman would think about how she turned out. Would she have been happy with it? Nova hadn't accomplished any of the goals they had made for her. Her life had gone so off course at the age of seventeen it was nearly unrecognizable from the dreams she had once had. But it wasn't a bad life and there were moments when Nova had happiness. Teo made her happy. Being around her family made her happy.

Tanner . . . Well, she wasn't sure he made her happy. He made her . . . feel something. Sometimes she thought she was numb to anything other than anger and bitterness, but Tanner made her feel things she didn't know how to put into words.

The landline in the kitchen rang and she picked it up without bothering to look at the caller ID. It was usually Mansi at this time. Telling her to turn on some show so that they could watch it together, or asking her to pick up some item from the store. Since Nova left Teo at Mansi's house less and less, she was seeing less of her grandmother. She missed the old woman.

How the hell could she seriously consider moving to Boston, if not seeing her grandmother every single day of the week made her sad? That was something she was going to have to face. She had accepted the job for the Second Lady. The wedding was in a couple of weeks. She had already spoken to the bride three times and sent over her ideas. Her career was growing. It was getting too big for the island. She would have to grow with it. She would have to leave to complete her journey. The longer she stayed, the harder it would be to go.

"Hello?"

"Nova?"

She didn't immediately recognize the voice, but it sounded familiar. Slightly accented, but she couldn't tell from where.

"Yes?"

"It's Winona."

Nova immediately felt her knees begin to buckle and she grabbed hold of the counter with her free hand to keep herself from sliding to the ground. It was Elijah's mother. She hadn't heard that voice in over four years. It was she who had given Nova the money for the bus ticket to escape Elijah. Winona had saved her life.

"How are you?"Nova asked, when she wanted to demand how she got her number. It had been un-listed. She hadn't had a landline until Teo started at the elementary school last August, and she rarely gave it to anyone. Especially anyone who could be linked to her past.

"I'm fine. But I can tell by your voice that you're wondering how I tracked you down."

"That thought had crossed my mind."

"Even though you never put a return address on the packages you send to us, it's not exactly like you're in hiding. You've amassed quite a following on social media. I saw you have over one hundred thousand Instagram followers. Congratulations. You are very good at what you do."

"What do you want, Winona?"

"You know what I want. To see my grandson. It's not fair that we are robbed of him."

"Not fair? Not fair! It wasn't fair that your drug-abusing son is a criminal. It's not fair that he beat the shit out of me when I refused to look the other way while he planned violent home invasions. It's not fair that I had to spend months in hiding with my baby."

"But Jerry and I didn't do any of those things to you. Why are you punishing us?"

"I called you from the hospital when he was born. You didn't pick up. I was there alone with a baby, and no matter what Elijah had done to you, Teo was innocent. You made it clear that you wanted nothing to do with him that day. And as the grand-parents, you have no legal right to him. Even less so, now that Elijah's parental rights have been terminated. I paid you back for the bus ticket with interest. As far as I'm concerned, I owe you nothing. The pictures I sent to you were a very generous gift."

"Our grandson deserves to know us. Deserves to know about his heritage."

"He does know about his heritage. He is being raised with my father's people. He knows he is Native. My grandmother makes sure he is proud of who he is and where he came from."

"But your tribe is different from our tribe. It's a

different background. Different history. I am a professor. Who better to teach him?"

"Elijah is dead to him. I made that decision. I can't go back on it now."

"But Elijah is *not* dead. He's alive and he asks about his son."

"That's too damn bad. He hurt my baby. He was so high when they picked him up, he didn't even know he had a son. He had no idea what he had even done."

"We're sorry he did that to you and to Teo. If we had known sooner . . ."

"You would have done nothing. I had to steal his drug money to buy formula and diapers. I had to beg social services for help. Do you know how humiliating that was for me?"

"We're sorry."

"Your sorry came a little too damn late. Do not contact me again. I made a new life. I refuse to look back into my old one."

She hung up the phone, made her way to the kitchen table, and sat down heavily. Her heart was pounding so incredibly hard it hurt. Elijah was speaking to the parents that cut him out of their life. Elijah was asking about her son. Four years in prison must have given him time to think. He didn't want Teo. He incessantly complained about him when he was a baby. And now he was so concerned? There would be no contact. He brutalized them. She shut her eyes trying to shut out the memories of that time.

Her hand was trembling. She hated herself for getting this worked up, this scared over something that was out of the realm of possibility. If she was a drinker, now would be the time to pour herself a large glass of wine. But she wasn't a drinker. She never kept the stuff in the house. Never ordered it when she went out. Because she was afraid it was hereditary. That she could have an addictive personality, that she could turn into her mother. She refused to do that to her kid.

But right now she needed something to calm her. She picked up the phone, her fingers dialing, her mind not thinking.

"Hello?"

"Talk to me, Tanner. Just talk to me."

As soon as he heard Nova's voice come through the phone he knew that something had gone wrong in her world. He was about to get ready for bed, but he changed his direction, shoved his feet back into his shoes, and headed for his SUV.

"What do you want to talk about, baby?"

"Anything." She sounded breathless. He knew better than to ask her if she was okay. She would avoid the question, pick a fight, do anything other than admit she was feeling vulnerable, but that's what she was. She was strong as hell. Probably the strongest person he knew, but that didn't mean that she didn't need taking care of. It didn't mean he wouldn't try like hell to be the one to do so.

As he drove, he told her about the first time he had jumped out of a plane. It was before his army days. He had been sixteen and he had forged his father's signature on a bunch of paperwork. He had made her laugh a couple of times and he had stretched out the story long enough to last him until he pulled up in front of her apartment.

"Thank you for telling me that story."

"You're welcome. Now there's something I want you to do for me," he said as he climbed the last few steps to her apartment.

"What's that?"

"Open your door."

A few seconds later she was there, barefoot and barefaced, looking relieved and devastated at the same time.

"I needed to see you," he said, slipping his phone back into his pocket. It was true. He hadn't seen her since the day Sunny was born. It had been almost a week. He missed her, but he knew her well enough to know that he had to give her a little space.

He shouldn't have kissed her in front of her family even though he knew Wylie was aware and cool with the relationship. She had felt cornered and if he wanted to keep her, he couldn't force this. He had to let her come to him, even if the wait had nearly killed him.

The tears started to stream down her face and he closed the distance between them and wrapped his arms around her.

"My sweet girl." He lifted her into his arms and kicked her door closed before taking her into her bedroom. He unbuttoned her jeans and pulled them off, before pulling her shirt off over her head, and finally he removed her bra, revealing her perfect teardrop-shaped breasts. She sat there quietly, looking up at him with almost a serene expression.

He was feeling the opposite of serene, like there was some raging beast inside of him roaring at him to strip off his clothes and bury himself inside of her. But he ignored that primal side of himself. Warned his erection to calm the hell down. He turned away from her, to her funky painted dresser and pulled out a nightgown. It was anything but seductive. It had yellow ducks printed on and looked like it would fit someone double her size.

"I don't own many sexy things to sleep in, but I do own something sexier than this," she said to him as he handed it to her.

"Put it on."

She obeyed without another objection and he sat on the side of her bed and began to remove his shoes and shirt, before he stood up and took off his pants. He folded everything neatly and pulled down her big fluffy bedspread. "Get in."

She looked at him curiously, but climbed beneath the comforter. He got in beside her, pulled her close, and placed his lips on her neck.

"Tanner?"

"Yes."

"What the hell do you think you're doing?"

"Waiting for you to tell me what's wrong."

"You don't want to have sex with me?" He felt her hand stroke down the front of his underwear. His manhood twitched, asking to be freed, but Tanner removed Nova's hand. He had to be stronger than his desires.

"I think about having sex with you eight hundred and forty-seven times a day. But right now I'm more interested in finding out what's upsetting you."

"I'd rather have sex."

"No," he said firmly. "Talk."

She sighed. "Teo's grandmother called me tonight."

"I'm guessing you didn't want to hear from her."

"No. It scared me. They want to see him."

"Why won't you let them? It seems natural for grandparents to want to see their grandchildren. Especially if their son is gone."

"They've only seen him twice before. It's not as if I tore him away from them. When I was married to their son, they wanted nothing to do with us. They wouldn't even come to the hospital to see him."

"Did they hate you?"

"I don't think so. But they had washed their hands of their son. Elijah was a drug addict. I should have recognized the signs when I had first met him, but I was kind of blinded by him. He was charming as hell and manipulating as the devil, which is why his parents wanted nothing to do with him. He stole rare artifacts from them and sold them for a tenth of what they were worth. I think they thought that he was using my pregnancy to get back in their pockets, and maybe he would have, and maybe they were right not to trust him, but I did have a baby and I did need their help and they completely ignored me. I had my baby alone in the hospital. No one was there, not even Elijah. I had called them. I had asked them to come, but they refused."

"Oh, God, Nova. I'm so sorry. You didn't deserve that. Where was your husband?"

"I still don't know for sure. Doing something illegal somewhere."

"Why didn't you call Wylie or Mansi? They would have come for you."

"Wylie was in Afghanistan. I didn't know how to reach him and I was too embarrassed to call Mansi. She is so strong and I didn't want to show her how bad I had let things get. She was not a fan of me marrying a man I barely knew at eighteen years old."

"It sucks when the people who know you best, know what's best for you, doesn't it?"

She nodded. "I'm mad, Tanner. I'm mad at my mother for putting me into a position where I was forced to flee. I'm mad at Elijah for manipulating me into thinking that I needed him to survive. I'm mad at his parents for not helping me when I needed it the most, but most of all I'm mad at myself for not making different decisions."

"If you had made different decisions, you might not be the person you are now. You might not have Teo and you would be miserable without him. You need him."

"Oh, shut up." She shut her eyes and inched closer to him. "I'm not in the mood for you to be supportive and understanding. You were supposed to screw my brains out and then leave."

"Don't say things like that."

"Why not? I'm vulgar. Don't you know who you're trying to get involved with?"

"I'm not going anywhere. It's not going to work. You're not going to push me away."

"You should run." She opened her eyes and when she looked into his, there was something in the darkness of her eyes. Something he couldn't describe, but it was beautiful and haunting.

"I don't scare easily. I jumped out of planes for fun. Dealing with you is almost as big of a rush."

She gave him a small smile and then pressed her lips to his. "You really are crazy, aren't you?"

"Yes. Tell me one more thing. Why did you have to flee your mother?"

"No." She shook her head. "You don't want to know."

"I do."

"Too damn bad." She kissed his lips once again. "You didn't try to offer me advice on what I should do about my former mother-in-law."

"If you want my advice, I'll give it to you, but I didn't come here to give you advice."

"And you didn't come here to have sex with me."

"No."

"We can if you want to. We just have to be quiet."

"Not tonight. Soon, but not tonight. You're tired. Go to sleep. I'm not leaving."

She did fall asleep, her back toward him, but her body snuggled into his. He couldn't fall asleep as easily. Two hours later he was still wide-awake. He was sleepy. He was comfortable. How could he not be in a soft bed with an even softer woman who smelled delicious? But his mind wouldn't shut off and all of his thoughts were about her. If he were smart, he'd put his clothes back on and hightail it out of there, but he had never been known for making rational decisions.

He moved her hair and kissed the back of her neck. She didn't even stir. The light was still on, making the entire room bright, but it didn't seem to bother her at all.

She claimed that she didn't want this, but he knew she did. That she needed this as much as he did. They had been thrown together for some reason and they owed it to each other to see how things played out.

"Excuse me, Mr. Tanner?"

He looked toward the door to see Teo there, his face full of curiosity. "Hello."

They had been busted and he knew that a huge part of Nova's reservation was what to tell her son about them. She was right not to want to bring men into her son's life. He had the feeling that her mother had brought far too many men into her young life. It was Tanner's job to prove to her that she could trust him.

"What are you doing here?"

"I couldn't sleep so I came to see your mother. Did you need something? Did you have a bad dream?"

"I had to go to the bathroom. I saw the light on. I just wanted to make sure Mommy was okay."

"She's fine."

"Sometimes she gets sad at night."

"Oh?"

"Mansi says Mommy needs someone to take care of her. Mommy says she doesn't need no stinking man."

Tanner grinned. "Your family tells you a lot, don't they?"

He shrugged. "Mansi says I need to stay out of adults' business. She says I listen to things not meant for little boy ears."

"I was the same way as a kid."

"Are you Mommy's boyfriend?"

"I want to be," he answered honestly. "I don't think she wants you to think that you aren't the most important man in her life though. She always wants to make sure you are happy first."

"I like you. You could be her boyfriend if you want to. Mommy likes you, too. She don't like anybody, but she likes you."

"I like you too, Mr. Teo. But we're going to have to let your mother decide if I get to be her boyfriend."

"I'll talk to her for you. Sometimes she listens to me. She says I'm like a wise old man."

Tanner just smiled at him again. He couldn't disagree about that. "I think you should go back to bed, wise old man."

"Okay. Are you going to stay tomorrow? I didn't get to see you at practice this week."

Tanner knew he shouldn't promise things without clearing it with Nova, but he nodded. He'd missed Teo this week when he hadn't made his weekly trip to the fields. He was becoming more and more attached to this little family. It was hard to imagine his life without them.

Nova woke up the next morning feeling better than she had in years. She'd slept the entire night. No tossing and turning. No fitful bouts of unrest, just deep uninterrupted sleep. The warm heavy giant who had her protectively encased in his body probably had something to do with that. She wished he hadn't. She wished she could feel secure without him, but the truth was that the week without him had been a lonely one. It had been her doing. She had told everyone close to her, including him, that they weren't together, and yet still she had watched for his SUV to arrive at the Little League fields. She had been more than a little disappointed when he hadn't shown. She had felt guilty when she had to explain to Teo that Tanner was busy and that they couldn't always expect him to be there. But he could have been there. She had pushed him away. She knew if she didn't she would end up hurt in the long run, but if she did she would end up hurting now. Which was better?

She was going to move away from this place eventually. Maybe in the fall, just before Teo had to go back to school. It would be a natural time for a break. It would be easier to end things then. She wouldn't have to worry about running into him everywhere she went in their small town.

For now she could enjoy him. Enjoy the spring and summer with him however long this lasted. She was just going to have to make sure she shielded what was left of her heart.

He had already snuck inside. She just had to make sure he didn't run away with it.

Tanner moved her hair and kissed the side of her neck. She shut her eyes and let herself relax into the sensation of being kissed by a sexy slightly bearded man. "Did you sleep well?"

"I did. Very well. Which is surprising. I usually only sleep like that after hours of mind-numbing sex."

"I don't know if I can arrange hours of sex today, but if you're a good girl, I can arrange twenty minutes of quiet sex tonight."

She rolled over and smiled at him. "I don't hate you for showing up at my place uninvited."

"You're welcome. I will show up uninvited more often." He pressed a slow kiss to her lips. She went all liquidy again. She could strip him naked right now, but she knew she didn't have time. Teo would probably be up soon.

"You have to go."

"Why?" He frowned at her.

"My kid is going to catch us if you don't."

"We're not doing anything wrong. I didn't even get to have sex with you."

"You could have. Your loss." She tried to roll away from him, but he wouldn't let her go.

"Not my loss. I missed you, Nova Reed. I know I must be insane to miss a prickly, big-mouthed pain in my ass, but I missed you this week. I don't plan on missing you again."

"Shut up," she said without heat. She didn't want him to go. "Just go home, get changed, and come back here. Teo is on spring break. I took some time off. We can do something."

She heard her bedroom door open and her mouth dropped open when she saw Teo walk in fully dressed.

"Good morning, Mommy. Good morning, Mr. Tanner. Can we go to the diner for breakfast? I want chocolate pancakes."

"Hey, Teo!" Tanner rolled out of bed and picked her son up, ruffling his hair. "I like your dinosaur shirt."

"I picked out my clothes all by myself. Do I match? Mommy said it's important for clothes to match."

"You match. Let's make Mommy some coffee. We'll go to the diner as soon as she finishes getting ready."

"Don't take too long, Mommy," Teo said as they left the room. Nova stared at the door for a long time. She couldn't wrap her head around what had just happened.

Chapter 11

"Damn it," Nova cursed and slammed down her phone. "Damn it, damn it, damn it."

"What's wrong?" Tanner put down the newspaper he had been reading and walked into her tiny kitchen.

"Mansi can't babysit for Teo tonight. She told me weeks ago that she couldn't and I forgot. I can't ask Wylie and Cass to do it. They just had a baby and her parents are there. I know they would do it, but I can't in good conscience ask them to." She put her head in her hands. "I don't know what I'm going to do."

"Where do you have to go?"

"It's Thursday. I'm going where I always go on Thursday."

Ever since he had known her, she had been disappearing on Thursday evenings. She said it was her date night. He once heard her tell her brother that she had gone out with a different guy every week, but he knew that it had all been bullshit. He had let it go, but tonight he was going to get at least this secret out of her. "You mean to tell me you have a date?"

She blinked. "Yes."

He had been here every day with her and Teo since the kid started spring break. He knew there was no one else. "Give it up."

"Okay. I'm not seeing anyone else. But I need my alone time. Thursday is my night to have it."

He shook his head. "Try again."

"It's true!"

"You look like you're in a panic. If it was just alone time, you could reschedule it, but you're afraid of missing something. What is it? Don't keep this from me, Nova. You know I'm a Ranger. I'll track you down if I have to."

"I'm afraid to tell you." She actually did look nervous.

"You're stripping at the Kitty Kat across town."

"We both know that there is no strip club on this island!"

"Ok, so you're going off island to do it. It's okay, baby. If I looked like you I would charge money for people to see me naked, too."

"I ran away from home my senior year and never finished high school," she said so quietly he had to strain to hear her. "I was so close to finishing. I even had my college picked out. All I had to do was send out the application. I hated that I never got a diploma so I enrolled in night school classes. I've been going every Thursday for the past year and I'm only allowed to miss twice or I won't be able to graduate at the end of this semester. I already missed once because Teo was sick. I worked so hard for this. I know it's stupid, but it's what I want more than anything right now."

Tanner stood up and pulled her out of her chair and into his arms. He kissed her. He had to. He had thought he wanted her before, but he didn't realize how bad it had gotten. He didn't realize that he could feel so much for one woman. "I'll take care of Teo."

"What?"

"I'll watch him. I'm a little annoyed that you never even considered me, Reed."

"But . . ." There was a little fear there. It was more than uncertainty and he wondered how many times her mother had left her alone with some man who was up to no good.

"I know it's hard, but you're going to have to trust me with him." He kissed her forehead. "You're going to have to trust me with yourself."

"Okay." She exhaled. "If you . . ."

"No ifs. Trust me."

She nodded and he kissed her again. "Teo!" He let her go and walked toward the boy's bedroom where he was playing with the toy soldiers he had bought for him. "Pack a bag. We're going swimming at my house."

"It's too cold to go to the beach," Nova yelled as she came rushing from the kitchen.

"I have a pool."

Teo came flying out of his room, his face full of excitement. "We get to go to your house? Mommy, Mr. Tanner has a huge house."

"And a pool apparently."

"It's a little pool, but it's inside. I never seen a pool inside of a house before."

Nova's eyes widened as her nostrils flared a bit. He picked Teo up and went into his room and grabbed a handful of clothes out of a drawer. He knew he had to get the hell out of there before Nova went all squirrelly on him. "Come over after you're finished, Mommy. I'll text you the address."

He made his escape with Teo before she could say another word.

"Mr. Tanner?" Teo called him from his kitchen table. Tanner had let him play on his laptop while he cooked them dinner. It wasn't much, just spaghetti, but that's what Teo requested when Tanner asked, and Tanner knew it was something he could handle. It was nice to cook for someone else. It seemed like a waste to cook for himself most days. But tonight he had a guest in the house. It was nice to have it not feel so empty.

"What did I tell you about calling me Mister? We're buddies."

"I like to call you that. Mommy says it's a sign of respect."

Tanner bent over and kissed Teo's forehead. "You're a good boy, Teo. What can I help you with?"

"I'm trying to spell words. Where do you type?"

"You can play any game you want, but you want to write words?"

"Yes. I like to type. Mommy can do it really fast."

"What does your mommy type?"

"Her homework."

"Did you know she was going to school?"

He shrugged. "She didn't tell me. But she does homework."

He scooped Teo up and sat in his seat placing the boy in his lap. "Let's get you typing. Maybe you'll be a famous author one day."

His video chat notification popped up. It was his grandfather. He had been ignoring his grandfather's calls and e-mails for the better part of the month. He had nothing to say to the man who kept such a big damn secret from him. Nova told him not to be angry at him, not even to be angry at his father. But his anger was too large just to focus on his mother. It was her fault, but it wasn't only her fault. He had always felt like an outsider in his own family. He would have understood himself more if one of them had just given him a clue.

"What's that?"

"Video chat," Tanner answered. "It's like a phone call, but you see the person."

"Who's calling you?"

"My grandfather, but I can talk to him later."

"Can I meet him? I don't have a grandfather."

Teo did have a grandfather, but Nova didn't want him to know that. A part of Tanner thought she was wrong to keep his family a secret, but he might feel the same way she did if they had abandoned him when he needed help the most.

"Okay, but only for a little while. Dinner is almost ready."

He accepted the call and saw the surprise on his grandfather's face when he saw Teo there with him. "Hello, Captain."

"Tanner . . ." He used his name instead of his rank. "I've been wanting to speak to you for quite some time."

"I've been busy. This is my friend Teo. Teo, this is my grandfather, Captain Edmonds."

"Are you a captain like on *Star Trek?* Uncle Wylie took me to the movies to see that."

"No, son." The captain smiled. "I'm a naval captain. I was in charge of a very large ship."

"That's cool. Do you still have your ship?"

"No. I'm retired, but I'm sure I could arrange for you to tour one."

Teo looked at Tanner. "Can we go? Will you take me?"

"Yes, but we have to ask your mom first. Go wash your hands. I think the sauce is ready."

"Okay. It was nice to meet you, Captain."

"It was nice to meet you, too."

Teo hopped off his lap and hurried off to the bathroom.

"He's a nice boy."

"He is. As you can see, I'm entertaining tonight and don't have time to talk."

"Why are you avoiding me?"

"Why didn't you tell me my father wasn't my father?"

His grandfather went pale. "How did you find out?" he asked softly.

"I figured it out. I should have twenty years ago."

"It wasn't my place—"

"Save it. You were the only one I could count on and you let me down. I've got to go. I don't have anything else to say to you."

* * *

A loud crack of thunder made Nova jump as she walked up the steps to Tanner's front door. Even if the threat of a torrential downpour wasn't there she would have been jumpy. Teo hadn't been exaggerating. Tanner had the biggest house she had ever seen. She never got to this part of the island. Tanner's house was in Chilmark. The part where all the superwealthy lived on their beachfront estates. It seemed like another world to her, but there she was, about to go inside to get her kid. She had forgotten how different Tanner was from her.

She had seen small signs of his wealth when they went to Boston, but she could put it aside, because that was just the one time. But now it was right in her face and she couldn't ignore it. It made her feel like she didn't belong here, that she had no business in being involved with a man who never knew what it was like to be without.

He opened the door wearing the same ratty jeans and T-shirt she had last seen him in. He reached for her hand and she felt the roughness of his calluses. He knew hard work. And the doubts she had got pushed down again. "Come inside, princess. I've got dinner waiting for you." He treated her well. "Teo's in my old bedroom. I made him brush his teeth and all that mom stuff you make him do before bed. He asked me to make sure you told him good night when you came in."

He was good with her kid. She may not belong here in this house with an heir to a fortune, but she couldn't walk away. He was too good to pull herself away from. She reached up and kissed his cheek. And then she smacked his arm. "Why the hell didn't you tell me your house was the size of a football stadium?"

"It's not my house. It's my grandparents' house, but they haven't used it in years and they are letting me use it so it doesn't sit empty."

"It will be yours one day. The entire empire will be yours."

"Don't sound so . . . so . . . foreboding. It's too big for me. It's too much. I was thinking about moving into a little house near Mansi's on the outskirts of town."

"And give up this view?" She walked through the living room and into the kitchen, which had a full-sized deck overlooking the ocean. Lightning flashed across the sky, lighting up the deck and displaying the ocean and the small beach before it.

"My current view is far better." She felt his lips on her shoulder and then on her neck. "Come on. Let's go say good night to Teo."

He took her hand and led her down a long hallway to a bedroom that was twice the size of her own. It was a little boy's room done in a nautical theme. There was a captain's bed built into the wall and ships in bottles, oars tacked to the wall. It was one of the most beautiful rooms she had ever seen. "He's never going to want to come home after being here."

"I'll still come home," she heard his small voice say from the middle of the huge bed.

"You will?" She kicked off her shoes and climbed onto the bed with him.

"I have to take care of you." He nodded.

"Yes, you do. I don't do well without you."

"Mr. Tanner told me that you go to school on Thursdays."

She glanced up at Tanner who was standing near the door. "I do."

"Why didn't you tell me? I knew you didn't have dates."

"How did you know? You told Aunt Cass that I do."

"Ladies take a lot of time getting ready for dates. You just said you needed a sweater because the building gets cold, and you took books with you."

"You're very smart. I can't get anything past you."

"I know. I will help you do your homework now."

"Thank you, sir. I'm going to need all the help I can get."

"You spend more time with me." She was trying. She was happy that he knew she was trying.

"I think I'm finally getting the hang of this motherhood thing."

He nodded. "You're doing a good job."

"Why, thank you." She kissed his cheeks.

"You didn't ask if you could kiss me," he said with surprise.

"I'm sorry. I forgot."

"I like it better when you don't ask me." He grinned at her.

"I'll remember that. Good night, Teo."

"Good night."

She left him, grabbed her shoes, and went to Tanner. He kissed the side of her face and wrapped his arm around her, leading her to the other side of the house and into a bedroom that was bigger than her entire apartment.

"My God, look at the size of this master bedroom."

"This isn't the master," he said to her as he locked the door. "This is the guest suite. My grandparents' bedroom is the master, but I couldn't bring myself to sleep in there."

"Why not?"

"Just in case I brought a girl home." He took her shoes from her and tossed them aside before he unbuttoned her jeans and pulled down the zipper. "I don't think I could make love in their bed."

"You brought a lot of women back here, have you?"

"Only you." He planted a kiss on her throat and tugged her jeans down from her hips. "This house is a magnet for gold diggers."

"What makes you think I'm not a gold digger?"

"Because you looked more horrified than impressed when you came in."

"A little." He slid his hands up her back unhooking her bra, but he made no move to further undress her; he just kept rubbing her back in slow gentle circles. It was more arousing than any overtly sexual thing he might do. "Are you honestly telling me that you haven't had sex since you've been on the island?"

"Just because I haven't brought any women home doesn't mean I haven't had sex. My backseat is pretty spacious. I'm fond of doing it in alleyways behind bars."

"I don't believe you."

"You shouldn't. I haven't been with anyone since

I left the army. I had an understanding with another officer. She wanted to get serious, I didn't."

"Why not?"

"If life had gone according to plan I might have settled down with her. She was smart. She was attractive. She loved the army as much as I did, but one of my men died during a training exercise I was in charge of. It happened right in front of my eyes. His parachute malfunctioned and I watched him plunge to his death. He was twenty-two. He was supposed to be heading home for leave a few days after that. Instead I was the one to show up at his mother's door to notify her. It fucked me up, Nova. I kept seeing his broken body in my dreams and then all the other shit from war that I've been putting out of my mind came flooding back. I wanted to get away from everything that reminded me of it. I came here."

"And had the misfortune of running into me."

"I should want to get the hell away from you, but the only thing that comes to mind when I'm with you is getting closer. I want to keep you with me."

His words scared her. He hadn't even scratched the surface of her past. He'd be running for the hills if he really knew all about her. About what she was capable of. "What did I tell you about being sweet to me?"

"You're not the boss of me," he said just before he kissed her.

"I'm sorry that you lost that young soldier. I wish you hadn't had to be a witness to that."

"Me too, but if it wasn't that, it would have been something else. It was time for me to get out. The army taught me to be a man. It was time for me to see how that man functioned outside of it."

She stepped away from him to remove her shirt and the rest of her clothing. "Can I spend the night?"

"Did you think I was letting you out of this bedroom tonight? It's raining now and it's dark and I can't let you drive all the way back to your house in these conditions."

"And will you make love to me tonight?"

"If I have to," he said with a grin.

"I would like it to last for two hours. More if you can manage it."

"I'll see what I can do." His eyes ran up and down her body slowly. She grew so aroused she was shaking with need. But he didn't touch her. He knew her body too well. He knew if he did, things would heat up much too fast and she would explode as soon as she felt his hands on her skin.

They hadn't been together in over two weeks. He had seen her every day. There were a few times he slept in her bed at night, but mostly he was just there with her, for her. He had gone grocery shopping with her and to the movies. He had fixed stuff around her house. He had just been there and it made her want him even more than she had.

He was trying to make her fall in love with him. It was the exact opposite of what she wanted but it was working. He was masterful at it.

"I promised you dinner. I made spaghetti. It was a big hit with Teo especially when I covered it with cheese."

"Sounds delicious."

"Get in bed. I have wine. Red and white. Which one do you want? I can bring you both."

"I don't drink."

His eyes widened slightly. "Now that I think about it, I've never seen you even take a sip."

"No. When both your parents had substance abuse issues and you married a drug addict you tend to avoid anything that can be addicting."

"Does it bother you when I drink?"

"No. You don't have a problem. I've never seen you have more than one or two."

"So, it will be okay with you if I lick wine off your body?"

She wrapped her arms around him. "Just take me to bed now."

"I'm not going to be able to last two hours if I take you to bed now."

"I lied. I don't need it to last a long time. I just need you."

He nodded and lifted her up, depositing her on the bed with a bounce. She sat up, and crawled toward him. Not content to just sit there and watch him strip, she undid his jeans, pulling his erection out and placing it into her mouth. He shut his eyes briefly and moaned, but then pulled away. "Oh, no, you don't. I can't deal with that right now."

"You like it when I do that."

"Of course I do, but I'm too far gone." He peeled off his shirt and shoved his pants down his legs and came to lay on top of her. She loved this feeling of skin against skin, the way her nipples rubbed against the hair of his chest. He licked across her lips and kissed her in a slow, deep, unhurried way that caused her to burn up.

"I've been thinking about this moment for the past two weeks," he said when he lifted his mouth to kiss down her body. "I don't know what it is about you, but I can't seem to function unless I'm with you."

"It's . . ." She lost her train of thought when his mouth closed around her nipple. "It's probably because you haven't had sex in over a year."

"It's not that." He looked up at her. "It's not the sex. It's you. I want to be with you."

"Okay. Okay. You win. Make love to me."

"I need to get a condom."

"Wait." She grabbed his shoulder. "I went back on birth control after Boston. You don't have to go."

"I don't have to go. You're sure?"

This was a big step for her. She was letting her guard down. She was trusting him with more and more of her as the days went by. "I'm sure. Are you sure?"

"I've never been with a woman without protection."

"It's okay. We can use protection. There's nothing wrong with wanting to be safe."

He wrapped one of her legs around his waist and pushed inside of her. She gasped, was shocked by the intrusion, but it was a good kind of shock. "I'm sure."

He started to move inside of her, deep, long, slow strokes. He took his time. He ran his hand down her body. He kissed her face. He was making love to her. This was no longer sex. He was the first man to ever make love to her and she was starting to think that he would be the last. Because after this ended she wouldn't be able to give this much of herself to another man. There wasn't another man alive who would be as worthy of it.

Tanner watched Nova as she gazed at her tiny niece with adoration. She was prickly and could be standoffish and with her long nails and glamorous façade, she looked like the last person who would be maternal, but she looked so natural with a baby in her arms, and just for the briefest of moments he wanted to make her a mother again. He thought about seeing her with his child in her arms.

It was an outrageous thought. It was probably something primal. Something to do with phero-mones and men wanting to spread their genetic seed around. It sure as hell wasn't a rational thought. She would probably bash him over the head with a cast iron pot if he ever mentioned it, but he couldn't ignore the fact that the thought was there and fully formed.

"What's it like being a father?" he asked Wylie who was standing next to him outside of his house. It had warmed up a lot. April on the Vineyard was a beau-tiful time of year and they were taking full advantage of the weather and having a small get-together with Cassandra's family in order to celebrate the birth of little Sunny.

"I thought Cass was the love of my life. But my

kid, man. I keep looking at her and thinking, I made that. In reality I know that Cass has done all the heavy lifting and to Sunny I'm nothing more than another set of arms when her mama needs a break, but still, I love it."

"That's good. You're my first friend with a kid. I guess that means no more late nights on the town for us."

"We never had late nights on the town. Everything closes around here before eleven."

"I know. I guess that's why I came here after I got out. I needed to calm down. There was a time when I didn't think I was going to make it more than a week here. Over a year later I can't seem to get my ass to go off island anymore."

"You went to Boston. You took my sister. Both of you have been pretty closemouthed about that trip. I didn't know until Mansi told me about it. Nova didn't even tell Cass, and she tells her everything."

Tanner glanced over to Nova again. Teo was at her side; he was touching the baby's hand and looking at it with awe. The kid would be a good big brother. "Hey, Teo. Your uncle and I are going to take a walk. You want to come?"

"No, thank you. I'll stay with Mommy."

"Okay." Tanner motioned his head toward the path that led to the beach. It might have been a mistake to head that way because he couldn't think of this beach without thinking of Nova. It had been a sort of breakthrough for them and he didn't think he would ever get the image of her topless in the moonlight, looking up at him with that expression of naughty innocence that only she had.

"If you wanted to speak to me in private, why did you invite Teo?"

"I knew he wouldn't want to leave the baby, but I don't want him to feel like we're leaving him out."

"He's growing attached to you."

"I'm growing attached to him."

"His father is dead. Nova is an adult and I don't want to get in your business, but unless you plan on sticking around it might not be such a good idea to get so involved in their lives. I don't want to see Teo hurt when you decide that a family is too much for you."

"It won't be me who ends it," he said with certainty. "I have no idea what's going on in your sister's mind."

"You know she doesn't tell me anything."

"And yet she cares so much about what you think."

"No, she doesn't. I think she does the opposite of what I say just to annoy me."

"Do you know where she goes on Thursday nights?"

"I thought she might be seeing someone who lived out of town, but with you two together I don't know what to think."

"She's going to night school. She's getting her high school diploma. She's graduating in June."

Wylie stopped in his tracks and stared at Tanner for a long moment. The shock on his face was clear, which was odd for a man who used to be so unreadable. "Why the hell didn't she just say so?"

"She's ashamed that she never finished, but from what I can gather, something happened to make her run away from home. Her not finishing wasn't her fault."

"My mother was bad off then." He rubbed his head. "That's bullshit. My mother was always bad off, but when I tracked her down, she was unrecognizable. She was in extreme liver failure. Her skin was yellow, her body bloated and misshapen. There were bottles of gin everywhere. She didn't even recognize me. She thought I was there looking for sex. Do you have any idea what it's like for your own mother to proposition you? I can't imagine what it had been like for Nova. I hauled her ass out of there and put her in rehab, but she died soon after."

"Where was Nova?"

"I don't know. I couldn't find her. I wish she would have come to me instead of marrying that loser."

"She was ashamed. It's the same reason she never told you she was in school."

"I would have supported her. I would have done anything to make it work for her."

"In her own stubborn way she wants to prove to you that she doesn't need you anymore. She wants you to be proud of the things she's doing on her own."

He nodded. "She's been better about Teo. There was a time when I thought she didn't want him. Cass and I were ready to take him."

"I think she's afraid of turning into your mother."

"Why the hell can't she tell me any of this? I would have understood. I wouldn't have been so hard on her."

"The last thing your sister wants is your pity."

"She's planning on moving away, isn't she? That's why you went with her to Boston. I thought it was just something she was thinking about, but she's really ready to do it."

"She's still thinking about it. Her career is blowing up. But that's not why we went to Boston. We went because I asked her to come with me. I had some family business I had to take care of."

"Are you leaving here, too? You don't say much about it, but I know that you are one of those Brennans. Your family has enough money and power to buy up this entire island."

"Ah, but that's what I went to take care of. It turns out that I'm not one of those Brennans. My mother had an affair. My father isn't my father."

"What?"

"They've been lying to me my entire life."

"Who is your biological father?"

"I don't know. My father claims he has no idea."

"What did your mother say?"

"Nothing. I'm too damn mad to speak to her. I should have known. The signs were staring me in the face for years. In a way what she did to my father was cruel. She would throw my existence in his face. She used to like to tell me how tall and handsome I was getting and that I must have gotten that from my father's side of the family."

"Damn." Wylie shook his head. "And I thought only poor people were this messed up. It seems like rich people are just as trashy as the rest of us."

Tanner laughed. "Damn right. Even trashier at times. Makes you feel better about life, don't it?"

Chapter 12

Nova went down her mental checklist for about the hundredth time that morning. She couldn't forget anything. She didn't want to look like a fool in front of one of the most powerful political families in the country. As it was, she was working on two hours of sleep. She went to bed early, even tried to send Tanner away so she could get a full night's sleep, but he wouldn't go. And she ended up being glad he didn't. He was the only reason she got any sleep at all. After putting up with hours of her tossing and turning he had made quiet love to her. It calmed her. She was annoyed that he knew her body so well. Knew that that was what she needed to get any rest.

They had been together every day. Going back and forth between each other's houses. They saw each other after work. They texted throughout the day. He was a part of her life. There was no doubt about it. A big part of it and the worst thing about it was that he never once forced his way in. He pushed her without it hurting. He merged his life with hers so subtly she hadn't noticed. She was starting to depend on him. She was starting to fear being without him. It was the same thing that happened with her and Elijah. She had stayed for so long because the thought of being completely alone in the world had terrified her.

Rationally she knew this time was different. Tanner didn't slap her around. Tanner didn't screw around on her. Tanner didn't steal. He didn't use drugs. And Nova was different now. She had a skill. She had her family back in her life. She had choices. She knew she was strong and that she could stand on her own.

But she was afraid that she might choose not to stand on her own, that being with him would become too addictive. That she wouldn't be able to pull away and follow her own dreams because her life would be too attached to him. She would hate herself for that. When she was old, she would hate herself for giving up everything to stay here with a man.

"The last suitcase is in the back of my car." Tanner walked through her door and eased himself down on the couch next to Teo, who was playing on the tablet that Wylie got him for his birthday. She didn't let him have much screen time, but she felt guilty for leaving him for nearly four days, so she was letting him take it with him to Mansi's house. "You should have taken them up on their offer to ship your supplies to Nantucket. All of that stuff weighs a ton."

"Why do you think I'm taking you with me? I can't entrust thousands of dollars' worth of hair and makeup supplies to some shippers even if it is the Secret Service."

"You trust me." He gave her that cocky grin she was growing so damn fond of. "I'm honored." He knew he was getting to her. He knew the number he was doing on her heart.

"Oh, shut up, Sasquatch."

"You know I like it when you get all salty with me, Nova. It makes me feel alive."

She tried to stop herself from smiling but she couldn't. He made her smile. He always made her smile. She looked at her son. "Time to turn off the tablet, Teo. We've got to get going."

Teo said nothing. He continued to play the game, completely engrossed in it.

"Teo," she said, a little louder this time. "Screen time is over for now. Turn it off."

"But I just want to finish this level. Why can't I play it in the car?"

"Young man," Tanner barked in a voice he must have used with the men in his unit, "your mother told you to do something. She should never have to repeat herself. Give her the tablet."

Teo dutifully shut it off and handed it to her. "I'm sorry, Mr. Tanner," he whispered.

"Don't apologize to me. Apologize to your mother. What she says goes. You have to respect her. She's the most important person in your life and always will be."

"I'm sorry, Mommy."

"I forgive you. I think the tablet is staying here though." She scooped him up. "I'm going to miss you this weekend. I'm coming back though. I promise. When you get home from school on Monday, I'll be here."

"I know you're coming back. I'm not worried."

That was new. He used to be worried about it. Afraid that she was going to walk away from him and never come back. She felt guilty all over again. "I'll call you every day."

Teo nodded and rested his head on her shoulder for a moment. "Is Mr. Tanner going to call me, too?"

Tanner got up and took Teo from her arms. "Of course I'm going to call you. Probably more than your mother. I'm going to be bored when she's working." Tanner smoothed his hand over Teo's curls. "You don't think I'm mad at you, do you?"

"I don't know."

"There will be times when I get tough with you, but that doesn't mean I'm ever going to stop liking you. But you've got to listen to your mother."

"Uncle Wylie yells at me all the time when I don't listen. I'm tough. I can take it."

"I never doubted it." He kissed Teo's cheek. "Now let's get going. We don't want Mommy to be late."

Nova felt odd about what had just happened. Tanner hadn't done anything wrong. He was firm with Teo and then sweet to him. It was very . . . fatherly.

It was one more reason why this thing with Tanner scared her so much. She had already disappointed her kid so much in his short life. She couldn't allow him to get so attached to this man if she knew it was going to end before winter.

After they dropped Teo off they took the ferry over to Nantucket instead of flying. It was just easier with all of her supplies. Tanner hadn't arrived in the SUV he drove around the island; instead he showed up in another black luxury model sports utility vehicle. When she looked at him questioningly, all he said was that he wanted her to arrive in style. He must have known that that's what the superwealthy would arrive in because nearly every car she saw in the parking lot was sleek and black and cost more than she made in the last three years. The nervousness set in as the valet came to take their car away. Bellmen in crisp white uniforms carried their belongings to their room. She spotted Secret Service men in the lobby and her voice shook ever so slightly as she gave her name to the woman at the front desk when they checked in.

Tanner's hand settled on her back, a gentle reminder that he was there.

A woman in a gray, no-nonsense skirt suit walked over and handed her a thick leather folder. It was an itinerary for the weekend with Nova's role and schedule broken down for her. They had rented out the hotel's salon just for her use. She was to report at four to do the hair and makeup for the rehearsal dinner. Until then she could relax in her room. She just nodded as the woman told her these things. Her tongue felt too heavy to speak and she was afraid if she attempted words, the wrong ones would come out and she'd make them realize how in over her head she was before she even started.

When she was finished with her briefing, they went upstairs to the room they had assigned her. It was lovely with a view overlooking the harbor.

"It's nice," Tanner said, going over to the window. "I haven't been to Nantucket since I was a little kid."

"I've never been before."

"My parents had friends who summered here."

"Summered." She smiled. "I don't think I've ever heard anyone actually say that word. I think it must be a word only rich folks use."

"My grandmother used to say it all the time." One side of his mouth curled into a smile. "I think you must be right." He turned away from the window and walked to her, but he didn't touch her. He sat on the edge of the bed instead. She studied him for a moment. She hadn't noticed what he was wearing when he got dressed that morning because she had been too preoccupied with this weekend's events, but he looked like a different man. Well, maybe not different. He was still impossibly tall and handsome. He still looked at her the same way. He still made her smile, but there was a sharpness to his dress today. No old jeans. No worn shirt. He wore a soft pink button-down shirt that fit his muscular body perfectly and made his slightly brown skin look even more beautiful. Over it he wore a gray cotton blazer complete with a navy pocket square that matched his pants perfectly.

He looked like he fit into this environment. A young businessman on vacation for the weekend. She stood out. Her nails were too long. Her heels were too high. Her look too ethnic. She didn't want to change any of that about herself. It took her too damn long to like the person she had become. But she wasn't sure she could be who she really was here. And she wasn't sure she could fake it long enough to get the job done.

"You look really handsome today," she told him. "If you weren't with me I would be checking you out. I didn't know you had this sense of style in you."

"I don't. I knew we were coming here and I didn't want to embarrass you. I went into one of those fancy boutiques in Oaks Bluff and bought some stuff. Of course nobody makes clothes in giant size so I had to get everything altered."

"It's funny that you think you could embarrass me. You summered on islands as a kid. I lived in roach-infested motels. Your father is a billionaire."

"And I am an enlisted man. I went to war. I slept in the dirt and on military bases. I get my hands dirty every day. I am not my family."

"No." He was right. He was just a man who worked hard and treated people right. A man she never would allow herself to have fallen for if she knew where he had come from. It wasn't fair. "Ignore me. I'm in a funky mood."

"Did I overstep with Teo today?" His question surprised her. She had felt funny about this morning, but she wasn't sure how much it had to do with Tanner.

"I think I turned a corner in my relationship with my kid. He used to be so afraid I was going to leave him that he never acted up. Now he trusts me enough to be a pain in the butt."

"That's a good thing." He squeezed her hand.

"It made me feel guilty. I don't think I'll ever stop

feeling guilty. I think they must install a guilt chip the moment you get pregnant."

"Everything you did was to better his life. Everything you are continuing to do is for him. So stop acting so damn nervous. I know you, Reed. You're acting like these people are better than you. I've lived with them and I'm here to tell you that they are just as fucked up as the rest of us. You're here because you deserve this job. Start acting like it."

"Sir, yes, sir." She saluted him.

"I like having you obedient. Makes me feel like I'm wearing the pants in this relationship for a change."

"Hey! I'm not in charge. I compromise all the time."

"But you don't have to." He stood next to her and kissed her cheek. "We both know I would do anything you wanted."

"Lucky for you I'm easy to please."

"This weekend will be about pleasing me, woman." He grabbed her hand and pulled her to the door. "When you're not working we're going to go where I want to go and do what I want to do and I don't want to hear any back talk or sass from you."

"What happens if I get sassy?"

"You will be spanked."

"I think I might like that."

"I think you know that I'm hoping you fight me at every turn." They left the room and ended up leaving the hotel through a door that led them out to the beach.

Tanner had suggested they head to a little bistro

a few minutes' walk from the hotel and Nova was just about to agree when they ran right into an elderly man.

"I'm sorry!" Nova cried.

Tanner remained silent. His jaw went tight. His nostrils flared a bit. There was anger in his eyes.

"Senator Edmonds," he said when he finally spoke.

"Tanner. I'm glad to see you."

"You don't look surprised to see me. You knew I would be here."

"The vice president has been my friend since my first term in senate thirty-six years ago. Of course I was invited to this wedding. Of course, I knew you would be coming. Why do you think I'm here?"

"I don't have time for this. I'm not here to rehash some family drama. I'm here for Nova and I'm not going to let your personal agenda distract her from what she has to do."

"I'm sorry, dear girl." He looked at her with sincerity in her eyes. "My name is Bryce. It's lovely to meet you. I spoke to your son. He's a handsome, well-mannered boy. You should be proud."

Nova shook her head. "First of all, thank you. I am proud of him and it's nice to meet you. Secondly, you're a senator. I'm not calling you by your first name. I just can't. Lastly, when did you speak to my son?"

"I was calling to video chat with Tanner. Teo was with him when he answered."

"You're the captain?" It dawned on Nova at that moment. "That means you're Tanner's grandfather. He keeps talking about you."

"I'm assuming you mean your son. Tanner probably hasn't mentioned anything to you about me."

"He neglected to tell me you were a senator."

"It's not important," Tanner interrupted. "We've got plans for lunch and then Nova has to get ready for work."

"Maybe we could have lunch together," his grandfather said.

"Maybe we should have lunch apart. Excuse us." He took hold of Nova's hand and led her away. Nova looked back at the senator who was clearly disappointed with the encounter. She never thought she would experience this, but Nova actually felt bad for a politician.

Tanner tried to remain as inconspicuous as possible as he walked through the hallways toward the salon that the Second Family had secured for Nova to use. It was hard to not be seen when you were the tallest person in the room no matter where you went. He recognized a lot of the people who were starting to fill the hotel. It was one of the pitfalls of belonging to a wealthy political family in New England. He had gone to school with so man of the guests. Attended polo tournaments w them and gone on lavish ski vacations with them didn't want to see a single one of them. They happy memories that came up when he back on that time. That had been anothe he had been a different person then, a unhappy one. All because his family secret that ended up tearing them ap

He should have realized that befo come here, but as he walked th

doors he knew it didn't matter if he had realized that. He had come here for Nova. She had gone down earlier than she was expected to report. She told him that she needed to set up. That a good stylist always had their tools set up as soon as the client walked through the door.

She had changed her clothes and was wearing her signature black stylist's uniform. But this time instead of tight black pants or a dress that hugged her body, she was wearing a long loose fitting sack with some sort of kimono-like silk short-sleeved jacket on top. There was no sign of red high heels; even her red lips had been changed to a more neutral color. Her beautiful thick black hair had been ruthlessly pinned up, held back from her face with a headband. She didn't look anything like his Nova. It was like she was trying to hide her beauty. But she was being foolish. She would still be the most beautiful woman in the room, no matter what she did to disguise it.

"You look different since the last time I saw you. I didn't realize you had changed," he said.

"You were on the phone with the town of Chilmark when I left. I didn't want to interrupt you."

"You didn't want me to see you," he accused. "You 'ook like a nun."

"I do not!"

"A very beautiful nun, but still a nun. Where's ur red lips? Where's your hair? Where are your ·ls?"

' always dress like this when I am doing weddings

like these. Besides, I thought you said you would be attracted to me no matter what I wear."

"I will be. But this makeover is not for yourself. It's so you don't stick out. I thought we talked about this, Reed. You are here because you are damn good. They aren't going to send you away for being more beautiful than the bride."

"I'm not more beautiful than the bride."

"Yes, you are. You're sexier than every woman you work with, and they hire you because they pray that you'll make them look a fraction as good as you do."

"Only you could manage to annoy the hell out of me and make me feel good at the same time."

"Well, if you got your head out of your ass I wouldn't have to be here annoying you."

"I get hit on at these jobs. Groomsmen. Brothers. Uncles. Even a father of the bride or two has tried it with me. The baggy clothes help a little."

"Anyone try anything with you tonight and I'll break their damn face," he said seriously.

"I don't think you should do that. Secret Service is here."

"That's why I didn't say I would kill them." He winked at her. "Show them how sexy you are. Show them the girl I'm crazy about."

"Fine." She ripped off her headband and pulled out the elastic tie that was keeping her hair up. It came tumbling down her shoulders in a wavy black waterfall. "Better?"

He nodded. "Red lipstick."

"You know this is the color-stay kind of lipstick. I can't just wipe it off with a tissue."

"You have three thousand dollars' worth of makeup with you. I think you can find the right thing to take it off."

"You're being a bossy pain in my ass," she said as she took a cotton pad and some sort of liquid and scrubbed the bland color off her lips.

"You like it. You would never be with me if I were some sort of wimpy guy."

She put on her signature red lipstick and then faced him, her hands on her hips. "Happy now?"

"Take the jacket off."

She removed it to reveal bare shoulders and arms and then turned in a slow circle. The dress was sexier than it first appeared. There were laces in the back, giving it a little bit of a daytime dominatrix feel. "Okay? I'm done now, Your Royal Highness."

"There's my girl. Sassy mouth and all." He closed the distance between her and hugged her. "Damn, you're short without your heels. You want me to go get them?"

"No." She smacked his shoulder, but smiled at him. "Why did you come down here anyway? You told me you were going to take a nap."

He pulled out his phone and handed it to her. "Play the first voice mail."

It was Teo. "Mansi said not to call Mommy when she was doing the rich people's makeup, so I called you. Can you tell Mommy good luck and that I hope she gets a big tip. And ask her if she'll make waffles for dinner when she comes back. That's it. Bye."

Her eyes went watery. "You're determined to crack through my hard shell, aren't you?"

"I didn't leave the message. Your kid did, and I'm

going to get through the shell. But it's the gooey stuff on the inside I'm after."

She stood on her tiptoes and kissed him. He wanted more as soon as she did so. She had that effect on him. He would have to wait until tonight to have her again. She was addictive. One taste and he was in search of his next fix.

"Get out of here." She stepped away from him. "They'll be here soon."

"Okay." He kissed her cheek. "Dinner as soon as you're done. There's a little lobster place in town that I think you'll like."

"I'm looking forward to it."

"I'm looking forward to after dinner," he said with a grin. He squeezed her hand and then turned to walk away when he saw a woman he recognized walk through the door.

"Tanner! I haven't seen you since high school. It's great to see you." She hugged him. "I knew your grandfather was coming, but I never guessed I would see you here."

"I'm actually here with the woman who is going to make you even more beautiful."

"Hi, Molly," Nova said with a wave. "Tanner is my boyfriend."

It was the first time she had called him that, the first time she admitted that this was more than just a fling. It was greedy of him, but he wanted more than just the label of "boyfriend." He had girlfriends before; somehow this felt bigger than that.

"I can see why Tanner would want to be with you. You're even more gorgeous in person. But Tanner here was the wildest, craziest kid in our class and we were sure he was going to end up in prison."

"I almost did." He smiled, but thinking back to the angry kid he was, he didn't find any humor in it.

"He turned into a decorated war hero and leader." Nova spoke up. "He's one of the most dependable people I know and I have a hard time imagining him as the boy he used to be."

"I've heard wonderful things about you," Molly said to Tanner. "My father told me how proud he was to give you your Medal of Honor."

"Thank you, but we're not here to talk about me. Nova has to get you ready for your rehearsal dinner. Congratulations, Mol. I'll get out of your hair."

"Come to the wedding. Both of you." She looked back at Nova, then turned to Tanner again. "You were at my fifth birthday, my sweet sixteen, and graduation party. You might as well be here for this milestone."

"I couldn't impose."

"You wouldn't be."

He glanced at Nova who looked a little afraid. He knew she was nervous enough about being here. He knew the last thing she wanted to do was mingle with everyone. And the last thing he wanted was to be constantly reminded of what a screw-up he had been.

"We didn't come prepared to be wedding guests. Especially at such a high-profile wedding. We can grab a drink sometime though and catch up. I'm living on the Vineyard. Just stop by the next time you're in town." He looked back at Nova and then kissed her cheek again. "Bye, baby. I'll see you tonight."

He walked out of there before Molly would try to convince them further. He was ready to head up to his room, when he spotted his grandfather sitting in the lobby. Tanner couldn't avoid him this time. He had no excuse. "Come on, Captain. If you're this determined to speak with me, you're at least going to buy me ice cream."

"What?" Bryce looked surprised.

"I want ice cream from that stand in the center of town. You're my grandfather. You're going to buy it for me."

"I was thinking more along the lines of Scotch, but if that's what you want."

"It is. Let's go."

They were silent on their walk through town. He couldn't recall the last time he had been alone with his grandfather. The captain was the person in his family he spoke to the most and yet he rarely saw him. Rarely spent any time with him.

All those years he knew. He knew why his parents fought. Knew why Tanner felt so out of place and he had remained quiet.

His grandfather walked up to the stand and ordered the same thing that Tanner had always ordered when the two of them used to take their summer trips alone into town to get ice cream. Chocolate soft-serve ice cream. Chocolate shell. It was nice to know that he still remembered. For himself he ordered a root beer float.

"Let's go sit." They picked a picnic table in a shady spot and for a moment they just ate. Not saying anything to each other. Tanner was waiting for his grandfather to speak first.

"I'm waiting for you to let me have it," the captain said. "Go ahead."

"Don't take the fun out of it." He shook his head. "I'm pissed. I'm so angry that I feel it boiling beneath the surface. I feel like I did when I was a kid. Pissed at the world. Only now I can't crash cars, or vandalize an abandoned building. I can't get high or drunk, or be a rebel because you forced me to grow up when you made me join the army. And you knew. You knew the whole time why I was so damn mad and you never said a thing."

"You weren't mad. You were hurt. And you're right. I never said a thing. I couldn't."

"You could have. You could have prevented it all, by just telling me the truth."

"I gave your mother my word."

"Damn your word. I felt like a stranger in my own family."

"I know and I'm sorry. But your word has to mean something. If a man doesn't have that, he doesn't have anything. And when was I supposed to tell you? When you were five and wondering why your father never showed up at your school concerts? Or when you were twelve and starting to look more and more like the man you never met? How would you have taken it if I sat down and told you? Be honest. Think about the boy you were. Think about the man you are now. What would you have said to me?"

"I would have wanted to know why Mom didn't tell me."

"You're damn right. So why the hell are you so mad at me?"

"Because I need to be mad at someone and you're the only person in our family that I'm speaking to."

"You could be mad at your grandmother. She knew, too."

"But that woman is an angel. I could never be mad at her."

His grandfather smiled. "I really am sorry, son. I begged her to tell you the truth. You should have known. You shouldn't have had to grow up as a pawn in their sick game."

"Who is he? Dad said he didn't know."

"I don't think he does."

"But you do."

He frowned deeply. "I don't know for sure. Your mother has never told me, but I have had my suspicions."

"Tell me who he is."

"Your mother needs to tell you. You need to have a face-to-face conversation with her. Now that you know, I don't see the point in keeping it from you."

"Maybe she doesn't want me to go looking for him. Maybe he doesn't even know I exist."

"You might be right, but there's only one way to know for sure and that's for you to speak to your mother. I can arrange a meeting that she won't be able to flake out of. You can make it a little trip. I told your little boy that I would arrange for him to go on a tour of a battleship. Let me make it happen."

"I would have to check with Nova, but I think he would love that."

"Nova," he said. "You wouldn't have found a woman like her if you'd continued in our social circle."

"I guess that's one of the benefits of having been to war. You meet other veterans with single sisters."

His grandfather nodded. "Eat your ice cream. It's melting." They were both quiet for a moment as they ate. "She is one of the most beautiful women that I've ever met."

"She's talented, too."

"I know. How much do you know about her?"

"A lot. She's had a tough life, but she's a hard worker and a good mother."

"You know she had to have her background investigated in order to get this job."

Tanner stiffened. "What did you find out? That she has some sort of petty theft in her past? If she ever stole anything it was to feed herself. Her mother was an alcoholic. She had to run away from home at seventeen."

"I'm sorry to hear that. Her record is clean. Her ex-husband's is not."

"He was an addict."

"He's more than an addict. He's a criminal who deserves more than to be locked up for five years. Most of the charges got dropped due to a technicality, but he was the mastermind behind a string of high-profile home invasions in Mississippi. People were killed. He should be in prison for the rest of his life."

"Wait a minute." Tanner was having a hard time processing what he was hearing. "Nova told me her husband was dead."

Bryce's eyebrow rose. "She probably wishes he were. She's the reason he got as much time as he did in prison. He's the kind of scum that shouldn't be walking the earth."

"She never said a word about any of that to me."

"If you're planning to get serious with this girl, and I think you are, you need to find out the truth from her."

"I will."

Tonight. He wasn't going to leave Nantucket without answers.

Chapter 13

Nova shut her eyes and slumped down in her seat a little. She was exhausted from the weekend, but overall proud of the work she had done. The bride had given her free rein to do what she wanted to do. At first she had been terrified, but she embraced the opportunity. Molly may have been from society but she was a romantic bride, and instead of the sleek classic styles Nova was so used to doing, she had done intricate braids, combined with soft romantic curls and precisely placed flowers in her hair. She had done versions of that for the entire bridal party. She kept their makeup fresh, lots of peaches and pinks. They all looked like goddesses in their long gowns.

The ceremony had been held outdoors, the ocean serving as a backdrop. She had been so worried about failing but she had done her job well. She was pretty sure she could conquer anything now. She would do just fine in a high-end salon in Boston. In the back of her mind she had thought so, but the doubt had been so strong in her she was afraid to make the next move.

"Nova?" Tanner placed his hand on her knee as he drove off the ferry and toward her apartment. He was the reason there was some doubt in her mind, too. He had been there for her this weekend in a way that no one else could have been. No one had cheered her on like he had and it made her wonder if she would be so confident without him.

"Hmm?"

"My grandfather likes you."

"I like him, too. He makes me nervous but I like him." They had had dinner with him last night. He had stayed the extra night just to be with Tanner. He kept him occupied on Sunday while Nova was working, doing the hair and makeup for the photo shoot the immediate family had the day after the wedding. She could tell that Senator Edmonds loved Tanner a great deal. She was glad to see that because the more she learned about Tanner's childhood, the more she knew how miserable he had been.

"You don't have to be scared of him. He told me the Secret Service investigated us before we were approved to go to the wedding."

The hair on the back of her neck stood up, and her heart rate immediately shot up and made her a little breathless, but she forced herself to remain calm. She already knew she was subject to a background check. She knew she had never been wanted. She didn't know what happened to Archie after she plunged the knife into him, but no one pressed charges. It seemed that no one was looking for her at all. And it made her want to know even more what had happened after she ran. "That makes sense."

"You had to know they were going to find out about you."

"What are you getting at?" She looked over to him.

"Your husband. You've been telling everyone he's dead."

She turned away from him. "He is dead."

"He's in prison." She could hear the disapproval in his voice, the disappointment. She had lied to him. She lied to everyone.

"He's dead to me."

"Not even Wylie knows the truth."

"And I plan on keeping it that way."

He stopped in front of her apartment. She got out of the car without saying another word to him and began to pull her bags out of the car. They were heavy and weighing her down, but she moved as fast as she could, away from Tanner and his disappointment.

She didn't like to think about Elijah, even though he popped into her thoughts more and more often, but she sure as hell didn't want to talk about him, to be reminded of how stupid she was to get saddled to another addict, to someone else who was a drain on her life instead of an asset.

"Nova." He followed her up the stairs.

"I don't want to talk about this."

"Well, we are going to talk about this. You owe me some sort of explanation, damn it."

"I don't owe you shit, Brennan. I'm not your

property." She unlocked her door and let herself inside her apartment.

"Didn't you think anyone was going to find out? What happens when he gets out of jail? What happens when he wants to see his son?"

"That's not going to happen!" She was terrified of that. Sometimes it kept her awake at night. He was furious with her when she had last seen him. Rail thin. In detox from whatever drug was his choice at the time. She closed her eyes, trying to shut out the memories that were starting to invade.

"You don't know that."

"His parental rights were terminated. I have a restraining order. He can't come here."

"What happened to you?" He sat down on her sofa, looking more tortured than she had ever seen him. "Just tell me what he did to you."

"He nearly beat me to death." She went over to the decorative chest in her living room where she had kept little sentimental things that she had managed to keep with her throughout the years. Her father's necklace. Letters that Wylie had sent to her when they were kids. A lock of Teo's hair. And pictures. One of her parents. Some from her time spent on the island with Mansi and the ones she kept buried at the bottom of the box. The ones she never looked at, but kept there as a reminder to never get caught in a man's trap again. "Look." She shoved the pictures at him.

She heard the air wheeze out of him.

"Fractured my cheekbone. Busted my lips so hard I needed stitches. Broke my rib. Dislocated my shoulder. Should I go on?"

"No." He shut his eyes and tossed the pictures on the coffee table. His hands were shaking.

"You want to know why I tell everyone he's dead? It's because I wish he was. I wish he would have gotten hit by a truck, or burned alive in a fire. And it's not just because he beat me for telling him I was going to go to the police if he went through with the home invasion he was planning that night. It's because he did it in front of Teo. And when Teo wouldn't stop crying he flung him across the room. Teo was six months old. If he hadn't landed on the couch, he could have died that day. And every time I look at my kid I feel an overwhelming guilt because I could have prevented that. I could have given him up for adoption to a wealthy young couple. I could have saved him from being exposed to drug and guns. I could have done more."

"You should have called Wylie. He would have helped you."

"I was ashamed, damn it! How many times do I have to tell you that?"

"He beat you to a pulp. Somebody needs to beat him to a pulp."

"Wylie would have killed him. He would have found a way to kill him and he would have thrown away everything he had ever worked for. Wylie was the one who was given a shot. He was spared from life with my mother, and even though I was so jealous of him sometimes it made my stomach hurt, I didn't want him to throw any of that away for me. I wasn't sure if I could ever be anything but trash, but I knew he would make it and I couldn't have interfered with that."

"He's going to be mad as hell when he finds out that your ex is alive."

"He doesn't have to know."

"He'll find out! I found out. And your son will find out. If anyone needs to know about this it's Teo and he needs to hear it from you."

"Hear that his father almost killed the both of us? Are you insane? No child needs to know that."

"He may not need to know the details but he needs to know that his father is alive and that you left him for a good reason. Because there will be one day when Teo gets a letter or a phone call from his father and you won't be able to do anything about it. He's not going to think that you kept the truth from him to protect him. He's going to see it as a lie. That you intentionally lied to him."

"I'll cross that bridge when I get to it."

"It's not fair to keep this from him! He asks questions about him? He wants to know who he looks like. He wonders about the other side of his family. Identity is important. Knowing the facts about yourself is important, and you're doing your child a disservice if you keep this from him."

"You're just a guy that I'm sleeping with. You don't get a say in how I raise my kid."

"Don't go there, Nova," he warned.

"Don't go where? Just go home, Tanner, and stay there until you can learn how to mind your own damn business."

"You want me gone? Fine. Right now I don't want to be near you either."

He stormed out, slamming the door behind him so hard that two pictures fell off the wall. She knew she had pushed him away, but it was for the best. After this weekend she was pretty sure she had fallen in love with him, and she had promised herself she would never let herself fall in love again.

It was a promise she had intended to keep.

"Tanner!"

Tanner shook himself out of his fog and looked over to Wylie who was sitting across from him in the office space they had secured in town. They were branching out. Tanner was going to be in charge of the government project in Chilmark and Wylie was going to head up the new part of their business. They were going to do construction on the island for the locals. The young men from Mansi's tribe who had worked with them on the last project were going to stay on full-time.

Tanner was putting down roots, it seemed. He hadn't been sure he was going to last here, but when he agreed to take on this bigger role, things had been going so well with Nova that he was thinking about her when he was thinking about those roots. But he had been premature with those thoughts. He hadn't seen or spoken to her in nearly three days.

He kept thinking back on their fight. He wanted to say that it was stupid, that he was wrong, but he couldn't do that. He stood by what he said to her. Even if her ex was a degenerate dirtbag who should have the shit stomped out of him, Teo deserved to know that he had a father. One who might try to contact him one day. It made sense now why she was so afraid when her former mother-in-law called out of the blue. Teo's father probably wanted contact with him.

If Tanner were Nova he wouldn't want that man anywhere around his kid either. But as a man who didn't know where he came from, Tanner knew it was important for Teo to be told about the other half of him.

"Yeah?" he answered Wylie.

"I've been trying to talk to you for the past five minutes. You might as well be off the island, you're so far away from here."

"I'm fine."

"Listen, you know I'm not one to get in your business, but you're definitely not fine. You've been in a funk ever since you came back from Nantucket, and don't get me started on Nova. She's been quiet and there's nothing worse than a quiet Nova."

"You need to ask her about it."

"I'm not asking her about it. I'm asking you about it."

"It's not my secret to tell."

"Is she pregnant again?"

"No. I would be happy about that."

"Would you?" Wylie sat up straight. "You've only been together for a little while."

"I think it was about just as long as you and Cass were together before she got pregnant."

"That's different. We had history."

"Yes, and that history included you two breaking up and her marrying another man who happened to be your best friend."

"If we could get through that, we can get through anything." Wylie grinned. "Just call Nova and tell her you're sorry. You've been walking around the past few days like your dog died."

"I'm not apologizing to her. I didn't do anything wrong."

"You know she's not going to come to you. Nova is the biggest stubborn pain in the ass on the planet. She's got a hell of a lot of pride. She didn't want to let anyone know how bad things got with my mother. She didn't want to let us know how her husband was treating her. If it weren't for Teo she never would have come back here and let us help her."

"That's what the fight is about."

Wylie nodded. "It makes sense. It's your relationship. It's up to you how you handle it, but you can either be miserable or you can go see her. Call a stalemate. It's the only way you're going to survive life with my sister."

Tanner wasn't sure how he was going to handle things with Nova. He wouldn't back down just because she didn't agree with him. He would lose respect for himself if he did. He left work early that day. Their new project didn't break ground for another month. He returned to his huge empty house. Teo had left his lunch box there. There was a Chapstick of Nova's on the kitchen counter. A sweater of hers was in his bedroom. There were little signs of them all over the house.

He got out of the army because he needed to clear his head, because he needed space to think, but now he wanted something more to fill up his days other than his work.

His cell phone rang and he pulled it out of his pocket to see that his father was calling. To say

Tanner was surprised was an understatement. He had never heard from August even when he didn't know that the man wasn't related to him. He really didn't expect to hear from him now that the truth had been revealed.

He answered, curious about why he called. "Dad?"

"You're still calling me that?" he asked softly.

"Would you rather I not?" It was a serious question. They hadn't left things in a good place. Tanner hadn't left things in a good place. He walked out on him. He was too overwhelmed by the depth of his anger to stick around that day.

"You're my son. You can know the truth, but as far as the rest of the world is concerned you are my only child. You will inherit everything that I own. You will bear my name."

He wanted to say he didn't want any of it. But he couldn't give back the Brennan name, even if he felt detached from the family who gave it to him, it was his name. It was part of his identity. Besides, he didn't have another one to replace it. "Okay. What can I do for you?"

"I was calling to see what I could do for you." He paused. "I spoke to your mother. I told her you knew. She thinks I told you. She's furious with me."

"With all due respect, Dad, how is that different from any other day?"

His father laughed. "That's true. I never understood what I had done to make her hate me so much."

"You stayed. She wanted you to be the one to break it off so that she could play the victim. She's used to getting what she wants and you didn't give that to her."

"That's a harsh assessment of your mother."

"She didn't happen to tell you who he was, did she?"

"No, but I think it was someone who worked for your grandfather. Have you asked him?"

"He says he doesn't know for sure and to ask my mother."

"He would say that. I think it's someone who worked for him during his reelection campaigns."

"Why do you think that?"

"Because she was so involved in them. She would spend hours at campaign headquarters. She would find excuses to be there. She would go on the road with your grandfather to make campaign stops and she would be so secretive."

"She's never devoted that much time to anything in her life."

"I know and it happened twice. Six years apart. Once before we got married and right around the time you were conceived. And then it never happened again."

"Do you think she just ended it?"

"Something happened. He moved away or got married. Something. I'm sure if he had asked her, she would have run away with him. Your mother's always wanted the grand romance that I didn't have in me to give to her."

"She was always addicted to the drama. I hated that you were so distant when I was a kid, but sometimes I hated the fact that she was too much, too damn draining, too over the top even more."

"I never knew you felt that way. I always thought

you had put her up on this pedestal. That you thought she was this perfect human and I was an evil creature, just here to punish you when you stepped out of line."

"If it makes you feel better, I thought you were both awful," Tanner said.

His father laughed again. "I'm glad we're talking like this."

"Why is it easier now than before?"

"Because there is no secret hanging between us. No fear that it's going to slip out."

"You should have told me years ago."

"But we didn't and I'm sorry and there's nothing I can do to change it. So you can accept that and move on or you can go on hating me forever," he said sternly in that voice that took Tanner right back to his teenage years. "But I hope you won't hate me."

"It takes too much out of me to hate you."

"That's why your mother and I are getting a divorce. It takes too much out of me to continue to fight."

They were silent for a long moment and then his father spoke again. "If you want to know who your biological father is you need to find out who was working for your grandfather's election the year before you born and the six years before that."

"Stop hogging the baby, Nova!" Mansi swatted Nova on the behind, in an attempt to make her hand over Sunny, but Nova didn't want to let her go.

"Buzz off, old woman. It's not your turn." She was

perfect. Gorgeous brown skin, a head full of black curls, and big almond-shaped eyes that were the exact color of her father's. "She smells so good. I used to sniff Teo all day. I can't do that anymore unless I want a whiff of stinky little boy."

"Teo's not stinky," Cass said from the couch. She looked exhausted but happy. The way all new mothers should look.

"That's because I make him take a bath every single night. You should smell those feet after a soccer game."

Cass laughed. "His clothes always smell so clean. You're going to have to teach me how to do laundry. I've watched you but I can never get our clothes to smell as good."

"Nova does do good laundry," Mansi agreed, still hovering around Nova for her chance to hold the baby. "She missed her calling. She needs to forget about hair and makeup and open up a laundry service. Or better yet, just come over here and be my servant."

"Nova's never going to have to do her own laundry again," Cass said with a grin. "Pictures of the wedding you did are all over the Internet. The bride's face was on the cover of three magazines when I went to the supermarket. Your phone is going to be ringing off the hook for the next five years."

It already was, but she didn't tell them that. She had gotten a call from an actress who was getting married in New York in September. She wanted Nova for it. There had been full-time job offers, too. Two high-end salons, and the hair and makeup department from the highest rated talk show in the country had called. Their head makeup artist was retiring in the fall and they wanted her to replace him. The salary was huge. Four times what she made at the little shop in town. But she might be able to make more money as a traveling stylist. People were offering her thousands of dollars for one day of work. But in the end she had to what was best for her son, and what was best for him was to be with her.

"It was a good weekend," she admitted.

"Then why did you come back so miserable?" Mansi asked her.

"I'm not miserable." She handed the baby to her in hopes that would stop the questions sure to follow.

"Hello, precious," Mansi cooed at the baby. "You are the luckiest child on the island. You have so many people to love you." She sat down on her love seat, cradling the baby in her arms.

"You're right about that," Cass said. "This place does something to people. If Wylie hadn't brought me here and introduced me to you all, I don't think I would be alive today. This placed squeezed all my broken pieces back together."

Cass couldn't have been more correct, and that's what was troubling Nova. If she hadn't come here when she did, she was sure she wouldn't have made it to her next birthday, but Mansi had cleaned her up. Healed her wounds and put her on a path to pull herself out of the hole she was in.

How could she leave here? But with so many opportunities coming her way, how could she stay? It would almost seem like an insult to everything

Mansi had taught her if she didn't go out and show the world what she could do.

She sat on the love seat next to Mansi and rested her head on her Mansi's arm. "Don't worry, Nova." Mansi kissed her hair. "I still love you a tiny bit more than everyone else."

"You'd better."

"Tell me what happened with Tanner to make you so sad."

"What makes you think something happened?"

"I saw him. That's how I know. The man looks pathetic."

"He does not. It's only been three days."

"What happened?"

"My stupid ex-husband happened."

"He's dead." Cass frowned. "What could have happened?"

"He's not dead," Nova admitted out loud for the first time. "He nearly beat me to death when he was high and now he's in prison. He hurt Teo too, which is the reason I left. Tanner thinks it's wrong of me to tell Teo his father is dead, but if Elijah comes anywhere near my kid, I'll kill him. His rights were terminated. The only thing he gave Teo was some of his DNA. I don't want him to know what a terrible person he is."

"Does Wylie know about this?" Cass was alarmed by the revelation.

"Of course not."

"He would kill him for you so you wouldn't have to worry about telling a lie anymore."

"Do you think what I did was wrong? How the hell am I supposed to tell Teo about his father?

He's a criminal and an addict and an abuser. How do I explain to a kindergartner that his father almost killed him and that's why he's not allowed to see him?"

"You don't," Mansi said firmly.

"What do you think, Cass?"

"I don't know. I have no idea what I would do in that situation. I agree with you. If someone hurt my baby I would want them dead. But I can see Tanner's point as well. As long as your ex is alive, there's a chance that he could contact Teo, and you don't want your son to blame you for keeping such a huge secret from him."

She didn't, but Teo was so innocent and she wanted to keep him that way for as long as she could.

She left Mansi's house, picked up Teo from school, and then took him to his soccer practice. She was sitting on the other side of the field in her usual spot away from the other parents. She had sat here alone plenty of times before but this week it was lonely.

Teo had asked her if Tanner was coming this evening. He had asked her about him a half dozen times since she had gotten back from Nantucket. He missed him and that was going to be a problem, a big one if she moved them to the other side of the country. It was her fault. She should have prevented them from getting close. She should have kept her and Tanner's relationship to sex only, conducted in secret. There should have been no dinners. No sleepovers. No extra time spent together. She couldn't take it back now and a huge part of her didn't because she believed that knowing Tanner enriched Teo's life. He saw firsthand how a man was supposed to treat a woman. It was something he would have never learned from his father.

She heard heavy footsteps behind her and she turned to see him standing there. His clothes looked a little better than the work clothes she had gotten so used to seeing him in.

"Why don't you look like a bum?" she asked him, instead of saying what her heart wanted her to. *I missed you. I'm glad you're here.*

"More new clothes." He sat down next to her and all those silly girlish feelings returned. It was like the first time she had seen him. So strong. So tall. So damn handsome. It didn't matter that they had been together before. The rush was still there. The fluttering heart. The butterflies in her stomach. She had a weakness when it came to him and she found it incredibly annoying. "The sales guy suckered me in when I went to get clothes for the trip."

He was wearing colors that were a change from his normal set of dark blues, black, and grays. "I like this color green on you. It looks beautiful with your skin tone." She brushed her fingers up his arm. His skin was growing darker, more olive. So vastly different from his grandfather and father who were as about as dark as milk.

"What do you think I am?" he asked her.

"A very tall man. Or maybe an alien that they disguised to look like a man."

"I meant my ethnicity. My mother's side is English. So there's no color there. I don't think I'm just white."

"Do you have a problem with that?"

"No." He kissed the side of her face. "I've never been attracted to those waspy girls I grew up with. There's something about brown skin and dark hair that makes me unable to think straight."

"I've always been drawn to incredibly beautiful men. That's why I get in trouble so much."

"Do you think I'm trouble, Nova?"

"The worst kind of trouble." She turned her head to kiss his lips. "I'm scared to death of you." It was the truth. She was scared of what feeling this much represented.

"Do you want to talk about what happened?"

"No. I'm not apologizing to you."

"I'm not apologizing to you, either. I meant what I said, but it doesn't mean I want to be away from you."

They were never going to agree on this. He would always think she was lying and she would always think that she was protecting her son. "I want to sleep in the same bed as you tonight."

"Stay at my house. It feels empty without you and Teo in it." He wrapped his arms around her and hugged her. He was so open with his feelings. He was able to say so much more than she could. How was it so easy for him?

"Maybe things are moving too fast. Maybe we're seeing each other too much."

"Who cares? We like being with each other. We don't like being apart. It's a no-brainer. You're just afraid of falling in love with me."

"Oh, shut up. I wouldn't love you if my life depended on it."

"Keep up the trash talking, Reed. It only makes me more determined."

"Mr. Tanner!" Teo came flying toward him, leaping into Tanner's arms. "You came. Mommy said you weren't, but you came. I missed you."

"My boy." Tanner wrapped him in a hug and kissed the side of his face. It was another very fatherly thing to do. It was natural and sweet and made her heart hurt and it also made her worry about what it would do to Teo if he never got to see Tanner again. "I'm going to take you and Mommy out for dinner and then we are going to sleep at my house."

"Is the school bus going to find me there?"

"I'll take you to school. You don't have to worry. Go finish your practice. I'll see you soon."

"Okay." He ran off and not two minutes after he was gone, one of the mothers came over to them.

"Hi, Nova. I'm Jackie. I don't know if you remember me."

"I do. You're from New York. You moved here just after Christmas. I cut three inches off your hair in February. You were afraid of the change, but you look hot."

"I think so." She grinned. "I just came over to tell you that you did an amazing job with the vice president's daughter. You turned a plain girl into a princess and that must have taken some work."

"It was a fun job. She let me do what I wanted."

"Do you have any appointments available anytime soon? I think it's time for another visit."

"I don't have anything free at the shop this week, but I can come to your house tomorrow after Teo gets home from school. I'll do it for free if you give me free rein to do what I want and then let me put your picture in my portfolio."

"It's a deal. Bring your son. And you can come, too, Tanner. My husband just bought a smoker. He needs a manly man to talk about meat with and drink beer."

"Okay." He grinned. "Your husband is Bobby, right? I met him at the hardware store last week. He's a funny guy."

"Mr. Fix It." She shook her head. "We've spent more money repairing the things he broke while fixing. Maybe you could give him a few pointers."

"Happily."

"Why don't you two sit with us in the bleachers?"

"The other mothers think I'm going to steal their husbands."

"You mean the robot wives with the two percent body fat and the twin sets?"

"Yup."

"Screw 'em. I need a friend up here in the land of the yuppies. You come and sit with me."

"Come on, Nova." Tanner bumped her shoulder. "Let's go sit with the other parents."

The other parents. He was including himself like he was one. Like he wanted to be one. And the scary part about it was that she could see him being a good father. A very good father to her son.

Chapter 14

Tanner came up behind Nova in his kitchen and wrapped his arms around her as she was making Teo's lunch. It was nearly the end of May and more nights than not Nova and Teo stayed over at his house. They had never talked about their disagreement since that day. He was pretty sure he would be wasting his breath trying to convince her to tell her son the truth. But in reality he had no right to say anything to her about how she dealt with her son, because Teo was *her* son. Not his. Not theirs. But he loved the kid. Missed him when he wasn't around.

It was beginning to get hard to imagine a life without them, and that meant they had to move forward. He was just too damn crazy about her not to. But he wasn't sure how she felt about things. He knew he couldn't rush her, because she would close herself off, pull away. He kept reminding himself that she had been hurt before. Too many times to count. He just had to be there for her. Show her that she could trust him to always be there for her.

"How's your grandfather?" she asked him.

"He's fine." He kissed the back of her neck. She had her hair piled high on the back of her head in a messy bun. Her feet were bare. Her face clean of all makeup. "You look so pretty tonight."

"Do I? My hair is a mess and I just washed my face. It must be the lighting in this kitchen. Remind me to take all my selfies in here."

"I like the freshly scrubbed look."

"I thought you liked me in red lipstick and high heels."

"I like you like that too, but this is the side of you only I get to see. I get a part of you no one else does."

"Stop being sweet to me. You know I don't like it," she said, but she leaned her head back to rest on his chest for a moment.

"What are you making this boy for lunch? You've been in here for twenty minutes."

"I do these bento box things for him a few times a week. Half the time he wants to buy lunch in school, but at least twice a week Teo gets the most elaborate time-consuming lunch I can make him."

"The sandwich is in the shape of a frog's head."

"And he's wearing a little crown."

"How did you make it green?"

"It's made from lettuce. He won't eat anything green unless I make it look cool. I'm making a beaver sandwich next time. It's going to have the cutest little cheese teeth."

"I hope he appreciates all the work you put into this."

"I do it for me more than him. I'm just hoping when he's an adult he remembers that I made these lunches and not just all the times I had to be gone for school or work."

"He'll remember this. My mom never made me a damn thing. I wish somebody had loved me this much to make elaborate lunches for me when I was a kid."

"I'm sure other moms who don't do this love their kid just as much as I love mine."

"I'm sure they do, too. Do you think you could take a long weekend for Memorial Day? My grandfather arranged it so that Teo could get a private tour of a battleship."

"I had already planned to take off a couple of days and maybe take Teo down to Boston."

Boston? Was she planning to take Teo there to show him where he would eventually be living? Or just for fun? He purposely didn't bring up their future plans because he didn't want to rush her, but he was thinking maybe he should. He didn't think she would make plans to move away without telling him, but maybe she would. Maybe this was one-sided.

But it couldn't be. He saw the way she looked at him. She was happy. There was no denying it.

"The ship is in D.C. There's some fancy fund-raising thing my mother will be in town for."

"Ah, the showdown with your mother is finally upon us. You know I have to be there for that. The fancy fund-raising thing you can count me out of. You know the thought of hanging out with all those rich people gives me hives."

"Aw, come on, baby. You know the only reason I

date you is to show you off to my friends." He kissed her cheek.

"Well, that's too damn bad." She sighed. "I'll go if you need me to, but you know how I feel about stuff like that."

"I'm kidding. I'd rather eat live bees than go to one of those things. But you wouldn't need to feel uncomfortable. You're just as smart as everyone else there. I wish you would stop thinking about yourself that way."

"I'll feel better once I get my diploma. At least I can say I finished."

He let go of her and leaned against the counter beside her. "Let me take you on vacation this summer to celebrate. Take two weeks off. We can take Teo to Disney and then we can hop on a plane to the Keys. Or we could head out of the country. Maybe to Europe."

"You know I'm trying to save up. I can't afford to go to Europe."

"Do you think you would have to pay for a single thing while we were away? I would take care of everything."

"I should pay half. It's only right."

"You should pay for nothing. I invited you. I want to take you away. I would pay."

"I feel bad enough when I let you buy us dinner and pay for all the groceries."

"We've been through this before. I make good money working with Wylie. Enough to take you on vacation. And there's the other money. Just tucked away. You would never have to work again."

Her expression changed and he saw anger flash

in her eyes. "I like working. I love my job. It's the only thing I've ever been any good at."

"I know you love working. You're amazing at your job."

"Are you suggesting I give it up and let some man take care of me?"

"No, of course not. I was just letting you know that I have the ability to take care of you. That you don't have to worry about money. I want to do things for you."

"I had to stay with my husband because he was taking care of me. I'll never put myself in that kind of position again. I swore the day I divorced him that I would never let another man take care of me again."

"That's crap. He wasn't taking care of you. He was abusing you."

"But he had the apartment and the car and all the money and I had nothing. No way out. No way of escaping him."

"I'm not him. And this situation is different. Taking care of a person is not just about the money and you know that. It's about wanting the best for them. Trying to make them happy. Being there when you need them."

"I want to do that for you," she yelled at him.

"And I want to do that for you, but you won't let me."

"You knew what you were getting into when we started this. You know I wanted to leave this island and start a new life."

"I'm not asking you to change the course of your life for me. I'm just asking you to go on vacation."

"Okay," she relented. "We'll go. Wherever you want. I'll shut up and be happy about it."

He nodded, but her agreement didn't feel like a victory. Instead it felt like the crack between them got bigger. He knew if he had such a hard time convincing her to go away with him, he was going to have a hell of a time convincing her to spend the rest of her life with him.

"I feel human again." Cass was admiring herself in the mirror and smiling. Nova had loved her sister-in-law immediately when she had met her. Cass was calm, levelheaded, and effortlessly pretty. She had a serenity about her that could soothe even the wildest of beasts, and that's why she was perfect for her brother. "Thank you for cutting my hair. I looked like a hot mess, but your brother is a big fat liar and will only tell me I'm beautiful."

"You popped his firstborn out of a very sensitive place. If that man calls you anything but beautiful, you kick him in his man parts. Better yet, I'll kick him in his man parts."

"You don't know how many times I have wished you were a boy instead of a girl." Wylie stood in the doorway, their daughter in his arms.

"Is it because if I were a man, you would punch me?" Nova asked with a grin.

"You got it. I guess you've got some brains in that big head of yours." He kissed Sunny's cheek.

"She's bathed and changed. I think she wants her mama now."

"Are you hungry, little one?" Cass got up and collected her daughter, looking so naturally maternal that it pained Nova a little. Cass was born to be a mother. Maybe it was why she chose to be a kindergarten teacher before she came here. Nova was an uneasy new mother. Nothing felt natural. She never felt she was doing anything right.

"Take a walk with me on the beach, little sister."

Wylie was looking at her. There was concern in his eyes. She could take annoyance from her brother, even anger, but she didn't like it when he looked at her the way that he did at the moment.

"Are you going to drown me, big brother?"

"I wouldn't admit that in front of Cass. I don't want any witnesses."

"I'm your wife, baby. They can't make me testify against you in court."

Nova gasped. "You're supposed to be my best friend."

"He's a good kisser." She grinned at him. "Go for a walk. I'm going to feed my baby."

Nova went with her brother, leaving her heels on the path that led to the beach. It was getting much warmer. She and Tanner and Teo were set to go to Washington, D.C. that Friday afternoon. She was nervous about the trip. She still hadn't been able to shake off the argument she'd had with Tanner.

He wanted to get serious. And she was finding herself falling into the same pattern that she'd had with Elijah. Moving way too fast, too soon. She had to break that cycle, because this time when things fell apart it would be much, much worse.

"Why did you want to take a walk, Wylie?"

"We haven't talked in a while."

"We haven't talked ever, you dumb jarhead."

"That's because you have such a big damn mouth that I can only tolerate very short interactions with you. If I'm near you longer than five minutes, I want to shake the hell out of you."

"Well, you had better talk fast. We're nearing the time limit."

"I want to know about Teo's father."

"Cass told you, huh?" she asked quietly.

"You knew she would. Why didn't you tell me?"

"What would you have done if I had?"

"Don't ask questions you know the answer to."

"That's why I didn't tell you. Besides, you were overseas when it happened."

"If he comes near you, I'll kill him. Although Tanner might beat me to the punch."

"You talked to Tanner about this?"

"Tanner's family has a lot of power. I think if he wanted to arrange for a man to be roughed up in prison, he could do it."

She stopped walking. She wanted to shrug off the idea as just talk, but Tanner had a dark side. He had been to war. He had done things that most people were never forced to do. "I wouldn't let him do that."

"Because you still love Elijah."

"Hell, no. I never really loved Elijah. I loved the idea of having a husband. I loved the idea of someone finally taking care of me. I wanted that so bad growing up, and when Elijah came along offering it to me, I jumped on the chance. I don't want Tanner to have Elijah hurt because I wouldn't do something that makes him go against everything that he has ever stood for. He's a good man with strong morals. And Elijah is my mistake to fix. Not his."

"He would do anything for you. I see it in his eyes."

"But violence? You're being crazy. I don't believe he would ever do it."

"I think he would get more satisfaction from beating the hell out of him himself." He shook his head. "He said those pictures of you haunt him at night."

"He's never said anything to me."

"How would you react if he did?"

She opened her mouth to respond, but then snapped it closed. She couldn't answer that question.

"You're so goddamn secretive, Nova. You go around letting me think you're some kind of selfish drama queen. Going out with a different guy every week, when the whole entire time you've been in school. Why the hell didn't you just tell me? I've been mad at you before, but this is the worst thing you have ever done."

"It was none of your business if I went out with a different man every week. I'm an adult. I wasn't hurting anyone."

"No, you were taking math classes! And I'm your big brother. I don't even want Tanner to touch you, and he's the guy I want for you. Of course I don't want you dating a dozen different guys."

"You're always so quick to think the worst of me."

"You're always so quick to let everyone think the worst of you. Tanner has been schooling me though. He tells me things about you that sound like a completely different person than the little sister I know."

"He should shut his big mouth."

"He's happy. You make him that way. Teo makes him that way. He's serious about you. I don't think he's planning on letting you go."

She looked out at the ocean before them. Aquinnah was so different from the touristy parts of the Vineyard. There was a rough beauty here. It was even different from where Tanner lived in Chilmark. There were cliffs ahead of them and lush greenness behind them and then there was the ocean and its sweet-flavored air. This felt like home. This was home. There were some days when she couldn't picture leaving it and there were other days when she wanted to run like hell.

"I'm getting job offers from all over the country," she admitted to him. "Good ones. Huge ones. I can give my kid the kind of life I always dreamed of giving him. He could go to a fancy private school. To any college he dreamed of. He could make a real go of it."

"That's true, and if you want to follow your dreams, I would never say anything to stop you. But if you're thinking about going for Teo's sake, don't. He's happy here. He's loved here. Tanner loves him. And if you let Tanner, he could give you both the world."

"I don't want Tanner to give me the world. I want to earn the world for myself."

"Fine. Go out there. Prove yourself. Get a fancy

job and show all those people who thought you were trash that you're not. Do it for Mama. But don't do it all and sacrifice having love in your life."

"Who says there's love?" She tripped over the last word. She was having a hard time denying to herself how she was feeling.

"Don't, Nova. Don't deny it with me. Tanner looks at you and sees the future. Why do you think he's taking you to meet his family?"

"He wants to talk to his mother."

"He could have gone by himself. He wants them all to know you and your son."

"Don't say that! It's too much pressure." She dragged her fingers through her hair. "We're together because we're in proximity to each other. I'm one of the only single women in the town and he was lonely. I'm the last person he really wants to be with. A divorcée with no high school diploma, a kid, and an ex in prison. He's worth millions. As soon as I leave here he'll find another woman. A better woman."

"He might find another woman, but he won't find a better woman. You're right for him."

"How the hell do you know that?"

"I know because I'm right for Cass. On paper we should never be together. She's the daughter of a doctor who was born in one of the wealthiest towns in Connecticut. I'm the son of a farmer who could barely read. From Alabama. She's black. I'm white. But we fit. You and Tanner fit. You're both misfits in a world that has done nothing but shit on you. But someone or something put you in each other's paths and you'd be a fool not to realize that what you have is something special. It's something that can last for a lifetime."

"Wylie," she whispered, feeling overwhelmed suddenly. "I never want to get married again. I'm just learning to be a good mother to Teo after almost six years. How can I do it all over again? I see Tanner. I know he wants kids. I know he wants to create a family of his own. He deserves to have a family of his own. I'm just not sure I can be the one to give it to him."

"Then you better tell him now. Don't drag this out. Don't hurt my friend."

That was the last thing she wanted to do, but she was afraid she wasn't going to be able to avoid it.

"This is a hotel room, Mommy?"

Tanner bit back a smile as he saw Teo question his mother with a frown on his face. They had flown down right after Teo had gotten out of school. It was Teo's first time on an airplane. He had been excited but scared, and as soon as the pilot told them it was okay for them to remove their seat belts, Teo climbed into Tanner's lap and rested his head on his chest as he looked out of the window. By the time Tanner was Teo's age, he had been on four continents. He had taken so many things for granted as a child. It was nice seeing something through a non-jaded little boy's eyes. He wanted to show Teo as much as possible, if Nova would let him.

"This is more than a room, little man," she said to him. "It's a suite. Bigger than our entire apartment."

They were staying in an historic hotel in the

Georgetown section of town. Not far from his grandparents' town house.

"I never stayed in a hotel before," Teo said more to himself than anyone. "I like it so far."

"You get your own room," Tanner told him. "Just right through that door."

"Can I go look?"

"Of course you can."

As soon as Teo stepped through the door, Nova slid her hands along Tanner's cheeks and kissed him gently on the lips. "How are you feeling?"

"I'm a little tired."

"I meant about being here, but I think you already knew that."

"I'm fine. I'm half expecting her to bail on this."

"And if she does?"

"If she does, I'll have a nice weekend with my family." Nova looked uneasy for a moment and he knew why. He'd said "family." He wanted to say that he meant his grandparents, but he hadn't. Somewhere along the way he had started thinking of Nova and Teo as his family.

"But I thought it was important for you to find out who your biological father is."

"It is, but there are other ways to find him, and if she won't tell me, I'm just going to have to do a little digging of my own."

"I love digging up dirt. Can I help you?" She wrapped her arms around his waist.

"Do you think you have any other choice? No one is better than a woman at digging up dirt."

"What a sexist thing to say." She sounded outraged but her lips curled into a smile. He was addicted to that smile, to the sound of her voice, to the way that her body felt pressed against his.

He had been nervous about coming here. There was much about himself he didn't know and his mother was holding the knowledge prisoner. He was glad Nova and Teo were with him. Glad he had somebody standing behind him when he felt so isolated in his family for all those years. "Thank you for coming."

"Don't thank me. I feel like you're getting the short end of the stick. I get a weekend in D.C. at a ridiculously expensive hotel and you get a hair-dresser with a five-year-old to entertain."

"He's easy to please."

"And the fact that you made him do extra chores around the house this week to earn this trip just about made me swoon."

"You're easy to please, too."

"I'm not and we both know it." She kissed his throat. "I'm very annoyed that you spent so much money on this suite. We would have been fine in a less luxurious hotel. Hell, we would have been fine in one room with two double beds."

"Nova, I spent nearly my whole military career, nearly fifteen years at war and in foreign countries, sleeping in the most cramped places with nothing but the smell of other unwashed men. I ate bad food. I roughed it and now I'm home. And I'm treating myself. I got myself a sexy girlfriend and I'm sleeping in a big comfortable room. This has nothing to do with you. The choices I make are selfish and all about me."

She kissed him along his throat. "You say things

like that and it makes think I won't ever be able to leave you."

He leaned back and looked down into her eyes. "You're thinking about leaving." It wasn't a question; it was a statement. He knew then that the thought was there in her mind.

Her eyes grew wide for a fraction of a second and then Teo walked back into the room. "My stuff is already in there," he said, sounding awed. "That man in the uniform must have put it in the room."

"He did, baby," Nova said, picking him up. "That's his job. Are you hungry?"

"Yeah. Where are we going to eat?"

"Anywhere Tanner wants to go. Mommy is paying tonight. Go wash your hands and face before we go."

She set him down and he scampered away, leaving Nova and Tanner alone once again.

"I'm here, Tanner." She rested her head on his chest. "I don't want to leave you. I'll never want to leave you."

He believed her, but what she didn't say was that she wasn't going to leave. And he wondered if there would ever be anything that he could do to change that.

Chapter 15

The next morning they arrived at Tanner's grandparents' D.C. townhome for brunch. Nova was once again dazzled by the wealth of this family. The Martha's Vineyard home was worth millions alone and now this town house in a very posh section of D.C. was worth a fortune. She had never been to brunch before, never even stayed in a hotel before the one she had stayed at in Boston with Tanner. She'd only been to motels that were populated with drug addicts and women who earned their livings with their bodies. Nova was supremely uncomfortable in these rich settings, feeling like she could never get rid of the stink of her childhood. Tanner had tried to assure her every time that she belonged. That she was just like him, but she knew she didn't. Tanner was part blue blood, despite his paternity. Despite his time in the service. He had grown up in homes like this, attended functions with the country's most powerful. He knew which damn fork to use at the table.

But she tried to squelch her nervousness and be

present for him. He had been quiet most of last night and all of this morning. She knew he was thinking about seeing his mother again, but she also knew that she had hurt him last night. It was unintentional, a stupid choice of words, but it revealed her thoughts. She had to tell him what was on her mind. The beautiful thing about being with Tanner is that they never talked about them, about where their relationship was ending up. They were just together. It was easy to be with him and that's how she had gotten in so over her head with him.

They weren't supposed to be presenting as a family. He was just supposed to be a man she dated before she moved away. In her head, she tried to think of him as a lover with whom she could have a relationship through the spring and summer, but in her heart he felt more like a partner she could be with for the rest of her life—and that scared her.

He was not in her plans. Love was not in her plans. And yet it was right there in her face, making her want to throw away all she had worked for during the past four years, all that she had dreamed about for herself when she started on this career path.

She rested her head against his arm as they waited in the foyer of the house after the housekeeper admitted them. They had dressed up for the occasion. Teo was in a soft blue blazer with a white button-down shirt, camel colored pants, and the most perfect plaid bow tie she had ever seen. Tanner nearly matched him. He didn't wear a tie and kept a few buttons open at the neck, which she liked.

Nova wore a formfitting white top and a floral printed midi skirt. Her hair was up in a sleek ponytail. It was far from what she normally wore. It was sweet and she liked it more than she thought she would. She still kept her lips red. It was part of her identity now. Tanner was right to push her away from wearing another color. She could still remember the first time she painted her lips red. She felt powerful. She felt sexy. She felt like a woman in charge of her own body for the first time in her life. Wearing it daily reminded her of that. Being with Tanner taught her a lot about herself.

She leaned up and kissed his cheek. Her arm looped tightly in his. Even Teo seemed to sense that there was something off in him. He came over and wrapped his arms around Tanner's leg and rested his head on his thigh.

Tanner lifted him into his arms and kissed the side of his face twice. It made Nova feel dizzy. This man had shown much more love to her son than his own father had. "What's the matter, kid?"

"Are we going to meet the president?"

"You'll have to settle for a senator." Senator Edmonds came from down the hallway with an apron tied around him. "Hello, my young friend. Do you remember me?"

"You're the captain." Teo lifted his head off Tanner's shoulder. "It's nice to see you again."

"What good manners you have." The senator took Teo from Tanner. "A sign that your mother is doing a great job with you."

"She tries real hard, sir."

"I'm sure she does." He walked over to her and

kissed her cheek. "Hello, Nova. You are looking too beautiful to grace us with your presence. My grandson is going to have to take you out and show these stuffy Washington insiders how it's done."

"Hello, Senator. It's good to see you again."

"Call me Bryce." A very beautiful, very proper woman walked into the room. "Mariam look who has returned." Tanner's grandmother had shockingly white hair and dark brows. Her features were refined. She held herself with dignity. She looked as if she could eat nails for breakfast all the time, but she smiled so warmly at Tanner, Nova liked her immediately.

"My boy." She kissed both his cheeks. "You look so handsome. I thought I would never see the day. You're also on time, which is something you never were when you were a teenager."

"You can thank Nova for that. She was up at six-thirty making sure we were all dressed."

"Ah, Nova. So you're the woman my husband is so taken with. He's right. You certainly are striking in person. And you do good work. I have heard nothing but wonderful things about you. If you ever decide to move to the D.C. area, you would have a hundred women waiting for an appointment for your services."

"I have been offered a job here, Mrs. Edmonds. As the head stylist at the Ian Michael Studio."

"And about a hundred other places I'm sure." She nodded knowingly.

"Yes, ma'am. It's so nice to meet you. Tanner has nothing but wonderful things to say about you."

"Thank you, dear." She turned to her husband

who was still holding Teo. "You must be Teo. You're the young man who we are going to take on a battleship today. My husband has been going on about it for weeks. He has wanted another boy in the family to show off all his ships to."

"What about Mr. Tanner?"

"He's too old now. Young men are the best to show them to. You're very handsome, Teo."

"Thank you. My mommy says so, too."

Mrs. Edmonds's face bloomed into a smile. Teo had that effect on a lot of women. "Come into the dining room. We've been preparing a feast for you." She looked back at Tanner. "Your mother is here. She's still upstairs getting ready. She's brought her new beau with her."

Tanner simply nodded and Nova could feel his body getting tighter. She slipped her hand into his. He squeezed it and led the way to the formal dining room. There was a maid there, complete in a uniform and white apron.

Nova felt odd to see her. Nova worked in the service industry. She had scrubbed toilets in a motel when she first arrived in Florida, before she got hired in the diner. It was strange to be on the other side being served.

Even though they were now seated, Tanner still held her hand. He was always in tune with her moods and he looked into her eyes with curiosity. This trip wasn't about her, so she just leaned over to kiss his lips. She knew as soon as she had done it that it was the wrong thing to do in this setting. These people didn't do public displays of affection, but Tanner didn't seem to mind. He placed his hand on her cheek, his kiss lingering far longer than it should. It was just a little while ago she didn't want him to kiss her when they weren't in her bedroom, but now she was the one doing the kissing.

"Well, hello there." Nova pulled away and looked up to see a woman who looked very much like Mrs. Edmonds. "You must be Nova." The woman gave her a critical, but not necessarily judgmental once-over. "From what I hear, the entire beauty industry is buzzing about you. I can see that you are aptly named. A star becoming brighter before it fades . . ." She trailed off. "Well, let's hope the second part of the definition doesn't apply to you."

"Actually, I'm Native American. For us it means 'chases butterflies.'"

"Really?" Tanner asked her, smiling.

"Really." She smiled back.

"That's probably the loveliest thing I have heard all year," Mrs. Edmonds said.

"Nova, this is my mother, Catherine. Mom, this in my girlfriend, Nova, and her son, Teo."

"It's nice to meet you all." She sat down across from them. Nova knew Catherine hadn't seen her son in years, but she hadn't really greeted him. No hugs. No kisses. She treated him more like he was a familiar stranger. It made Nova sad for Tanner. Her mother was a drunk and a hot mess, but there was affection there. Her mother had loved her in her own way.

"I thought your fiancé was going to be joining us," Tanner said as they began to eat.

"You might meet him tonight. He had to go speak

to the owner of the art gallery where he is having his show next week."

"We won't be around tonight. I'm taking Nova and Teo on a night tour of D.C."

"I thought you were here to attend the fundraiser." She raised one of her sharply pointed brows.

"You know why I'm here, Mother. Let's not pretend we don't. We're all smarter than that."

"Mommy." Teo tugged on her skirt. "I thought we was here to see the battleship."

"We are, baby." She touched his curls. "You're going to have a very good weekend."

They had made it through brunch. Thankfully his grandfather was a skilled politician and could manage to talk to people for hours without ever really saying anything meaningful. Nova kept up the conversation as well. She was a hell of a lot smarter than she had given herself credit for. She asked his grandmother about their homes and how she decorated them. It was a topic his grandmother was passionate about and it made the brunch less painful.

Tanner's own mother had said very little, which wasn't like her at all. He noticed her studying Nova throughout the meal. Taking in every inch of her. His mother never liked any of his girlfriends, not that he brought many home, but when he did, she always seemed to find some kind of fault in them.

She had been incredibly possessive over him as a child. He had thought then it was because she loved him when his father didn't seem to want to, but now as he looked back, he realized what was going on.

He's my son, she used to scream at his father.

He *was* her son. Only her son.

"Let's go out for cupcakes afterward," his grandfather cheerfully announced as they got up from the table. "I know a great dessert place not far from the battleship."

"Dad," Catherine said. "I think I'm going to skip out on this battleship tour."

"You're right," he said, all traces of humor dropping from his face. "You're going to stay here and talk to your son about what you should have discussed twenty years ago."

"I don't know what you're talking about." She lifted her head in that haughty way that had always driven Tanner crazy.

It must have driven his grandfather crazy as well. "In my study. Right now," he snapped, and Tanner felt like he was a sailor on one of his ships. Both he and his mother dutifully went into the study. His grandfather shut the door behind them and said, "It ends today. You ruined your marriage and hurt your son with all your lies, and what's so bad is that I think you believe your own lies."

"You don't know what you're talking about, Father. You know nothing about my marriage."

"I know that you are still married and traipsing around the world with some other man. You have no decency or respect for the institution. If you didn't love your husband you should have ended it years ago. Or you never should have married him in the first place. But you were unhappy, so you had to spread your misery around."

"Don't act like I shouldn't have married him. I knew that it was what you wanted. Two powerful families joined together."

"You can place the blame on me if you want, but I have never interfered in your relationship with your husband. I never suggested you even go on a date with him. It was your choice to marry him. Your choice to have an affair. And now it's up to you to make things right."

"Things are right. Tanner is August's son."

His grandfather looked at him. "His name is Richard Powell. He worked for my campaigns back then. I didn't know for sure when you were a child, but the older you get the more you look like him. For what it's worth, he was a brilliant strategist and a decent man."

"How decent could he be?" Tanner asked, surprised he didn't feel something more after finally hearing the man's name. "He had an affair with a married woman."

"It's a good question." He shook his head. "One you should ask him yourself one day. As hard as your grandmother and I tried, we still ended up raising a spoiled, entitled princess who doesn't seem to give a damn about anyone else's feelings. I didn't want you to grow up that way. Acting like you could do whatever you want and face none of the consequences. That's why your father and I were both so hard on you. We wanted you to be a man who could stand on your own. And we're both proud of you." He squeezed Tanner's shoulder. "If you'll excuse me, we're going to take a very excited little boy to see a battleship. You talk to your son, Catherine. You owe him that and probably a hell of a lot more."

He walked out and Tanner was alone with his mother for the first time in as long as he could remember.

She stood there staring at him, pain in her eyes, and he wondered what exactly was hurting her. That she felt bad about keeping his paternity a secret or the fact that she was forced to come to terms that it wasn't a secret anymore.

"Say something."

"Your girlfriend is very sexy. I can see why you completely lost your head over her. I don't think she likes me very much."

"What the hell is that supposed to mean?" He shook his head. "No. We aren't going to do this your way. You're not going to try to distract me. You're going to tell me about my father."

"He's in Boston. I think he's interested in Elizabeth Platten, my old friend. He's very puritanical though. I don't think he'll even ask her out until we're divorced."

"Cut the bullshit and talk to me!"

"You watch your mouth. I'm still your mother and you will respect me."

"It's hard to respect a woman who hasn't done a damn thing I can respect."

"You're acting like this is all my fault. I thought you loved me and hated him. Why are you on his side now? He spent your entire childhood either barking at you or ignoring you and you act like I was the one who hurt you. I gave you everything you've ever wanted."

"I wanted someone to parent me. Not to spoil me. And if you loved me so much, why haven't you made an effort to see me in years? Or talk to me? Most mothers would be concerned about their kids being in combat, but I didn't even get a goddamn letter from you. If it wasn't for your father I would have felt completely alone. Hell, even Dad had a care package sent every month."

"He just didn't want to look like the cold bastard he is."

"Is that why you did it? Because he was cold?"

"You seem upset with me for cheating on your father. If I hadn't, you wouldn't have been born. Your father couldn't get me pregnant. Why do you think there were no more? I wanted a baby and I got one."

"You wanted a baby?" He couldn't believe it. "That's why you had an affair?"

"Yes, but I loved him, too. He was passionate about helping people and he was brilliant, and if I wasn't married to your father I would have married him. Societal rules be damned."

"What rules? If he was so brilliant and honorable, why couldn't you marry him?"

"Because your father is a black man. I know you think we've come a long way, but sometimes people in Boston don't have the most open minds when it comes to interracial love. At least they didn't then. How do you think you would have been treated if the world had known?"

"That's a cop-out. You don't know for sure what

would have happened. You still should have told me. I had every right to know."

"I did it to protect you."

"You did it so no one would talk about you. I don't believe you really loved him. If you had you would have tried to make it work. The only person you really love is yourself."

"That's not fair. You don't know what I went through."

He didn't care what she went through. It was clear to him that she lived her life only to serve herself. "Does he know about me?"

"Why do you care? Are you planning on tracking him down and forcing a relationship?"

"I sure as hell don't want to try to be a son to a man who doesn't want to be my father, but I need to know if he knows about me."

"He didn't at first. He knows now. You look very much like him," she admitted straightaway, which was very uncommon for her. "It's hard to look at you. I see so much of him in you."

"Where is he?"

"That I don't know." She shook her head. "I'm being honest. I haven't spoken to him in fifteen years."

"Right around the time I was going into the military."

"Yes," she whispered. "I was furious with my father for making you go. I wanted to let Richard know."

"And what did he say?"

"That it would make a man out of you. He was right. You turned out well."

"Yes, I did. No thanks to you."

He walked away from her, left the room, not sure where he was going, but he spotted Nova sitting on the floor near the door, her legs crossed. Her pretty skirt flowed all around her.

"Baby, what are you doing on the floor?"

"Waiting for you. I figured I would have the best chance of catching you if I was blocking the door."

"Why would you need to catch me?"

"I'm nosy." She reached out her hand to him. "Help me up. I'm dying to know what she said."

"Really?" He pulled her up. "That's why you stayed?"

Her expression grew somber. "I didn't know if you would need me, but I thought you might want me here."

He hugged her close to him. "I always want you with me."

"I can understand if you need to be alone. You can be honest with me if you do. I can still meet your grandparents at the ship."

"You let Teo go with my grandparents alone? You had trouble leaving him with me at first."

"I have to be able to trust someone sometime. You taught me that."

He wasn't sure when he had fallen in love with Nova. It might have been two months ago. It could have been the day he met her, but he knew right in that moment that there would never be another woman he loved as much as he loved her.

"What time did my grandparents say they would be back?"

"They said they were going to be on the ship for

a couple of hours and then take him for dessert. Your grandmother said they would bring him back to the hotel around dinnertime."

"Okay. Let's go back to the hotel. I just want to be alone with you for a couple of hours."

Chapter 16

Nearly a month later Nova had pulled up in front of Tanner's house, her diploma on the passenger side seat. She opened up the cover and peeked inside again, just to make sure that it was still there. To make sure it was real. She had finally finished. She had done well on her final exams. This was one of the last roadblocks in her way to becoming the woman she wanted to be when she started out on this journey. There were more than a few times she had wanted to quit. There really had been no point. She had her beautician's license. She had a steady job. Her career could advance without it, but she needed it. To prove to herself that she could work hard for something other than just survival.

She grabbed it and walked up to Tanner's front door, letting herself in with the key he had given her nearly two months ago. She hadn't been back to her apartment in days and just yesterday she had caught herself thinking about this place as home, which was a very dangerous way of thinking. This multimillion-dollar house didn't belong to her.

The huge kitchen wasn't hers to cook in. This life was really not hers. Tanner was trying to make it that way. He wanted Nova and Teo with him at all times.

When she complained that she was paying rent for a place she rarely slept in, he offered to pay it for her. When she refused, he packed a bag and stayed at her place without complaint even though they both knew it was silly for them all to be in the cramped apartment when he had so much space. He seemed to know that she thought that his place was too much and she caught him looking at smaller houses on the island, even though she knew his grandparents had turned over their house to him when they were in D.C.

He was thinking long term. He was thinking permanency. She still hadn't spoken to him about what she wanted because she knew it would hurt him. She knew it would end things, and truthfully she didn't want that yet. Being with him was like sinking into a bath at the end of a long day. It made her feel good all over, but it felt too good to last forever. And just like with a bath, she knew that the heat would seep away and she would have to get out eventually.

She opened the door to find a feast awaiting her when she walked into the kitchen. Mansi was there at the oven pulling out a pan of corn bread. Tanner was nearby with a tray of lobster and fresh corn. Teo was just outside on the deck that overlooked the ocean. She could see him setting down napkins and forks.

"What is all this?" she asked, making her presence known.

"Let me see it." Tanner put the tray down on the kitchen table and took the diploma out of her hands. His face bloomed into a huge smile as he opened it and Nova immediately felt teary-eyed. "I'm proud of you, baby." He picked her up and spun her around. "I'm so damn proud."

"It's just a high school diploma. It's nothing special."

"It is. I knew you weren't going to let me throw you a graduation party, so I decided on this dinner instead. Your brother wants to take us all out this weekend to celebrate and he said if you say no, he'll put you in a headlock."

"I'd like to see him try," she said, unable to muster up much feistiness. They were all so happy for her. She had such a hard time letting anyone but Mansi know what she had been doing. It had felt like failure not having finished. If she had just avoided Elijah, listened to those warning bells that went off in her head, she could have enrolled in a program and finished school so many years ago. But she wouldn't have had Teo if she had. It was time to stop beating herself up about that. It was time to put the past in the past and look only to the future.

"Mommy!" Teo ran inside and right into her arms.

"Hello, little man. You look very handsome tonight."

"Mansi made me take a bath as soon as I got home from school today. She said Mr. Tanner shouldn't

even have let me in the house and should have
turned the hose on me in the yard."

"Were you very dirty?"

"There was mud outside at recess and we had
pizza in school for lunch. It was ice cream day too,
and I got some on my clothes. Mansi said if you
made me do my own laundry that I wouldn't get so
much junk on my clothes. But I don't know why she
said that because I don't mean to get dirty."

"No. Of course not. You're like a little dirt magnet.
It just comes flying at you."

He spoke to her so easily now. His words flowing
out of him like a fountain that she never wanted to
shut off. "We got you a present, Mommy. I picked it
out, but Mr. Tanner paid for all the stuff."

She looked up at Tanner who was shaking his
head. "Teo, it's supposed to be a surprise."

"I didn't tell her what it is." He frowned. "You said
we can give it to her after dinner. You didn't say I
couldn't tell her we got her a present."

"You're right. Remind me to be extremely ex-
plicit in my instructions from now on. I can see
you when you're older telling me I didn't tell you
that you weren't allowed to take my car without
permission."

He had done it again. Spoken about the future,
about him being there always, like it was a given.
Every time she heard him do that, it made her chest
tight. It made her feel like she couldn't leave.

"Just give it to her now," Mansi said. "It's not a
diamond. I told him to give you a diamond. They
really are a girl's best friend."

She was glad it wasn't a ring. She wouldn't know

what to do if he had given her one. But she had a feeling she might say yes, because saying no to him was too damn hard.

"Go get it, Teo." Tanner sighed. "This is the last time I let anyone else in on a surprise for you."

Teo wiggled out of her arms and ran down the hallway. He returned later holding a pet carrier. At first Nova couldn't see anything inside, but then she did. It was a calico kitten with huge eyes and a sweet curious face.

"It's a boy," Tanner said softly. "We got him from the shelter in Edgartown. He's seven weeks old."

"His mommy died," Teo added. "I thought you could be his mommy now, even though you're not a cat."

She dropped down to the floor and pulled the kitten out. She rubbed her face against his soft fur and promptly burst into tears.

Tanner felt the back of his throat burn as he watched Nova completely fall apart. He knew it was a risky move getting her a cat, but just once he wanted the experience of giving someone a kitten in a box complete with a bow. Her reaction was better than he had ever hoped for. Mansi urged him to propose, but he had held off. Not because he didn't want to, but because he knew it wasn't the right time. It would send Nova running for the hills.

"Don't cry, Mommy." Teo sat on the floor beside her and patted her knee. "What's wrong? You don't like him?"

Nova made some incomprehensible noise.

"You want us to take him away? Maybe Mansi will take him home with her. She says he's sweet."

"Your mother likes him. Those are happy tears," Tanner explained. "At least I'm hoping they are, because I'm going to be really scared of shopping for you at Christmastime if they aren't."

She nodded. "He looks just like my old cat."

"You won't have to leave him behind this time," Teo assured her.

"Thank you, Teo." She put down the kitten and grabbed her son up in a fierce hug. So much had changed with her in the past few months. She used to ask permission before she touched her son. They used to struggle to connect, and now they were just like any mother and son. Well, not any. Not like Tanner and his mother. The interaction between them still rolled around in his mind. It had been a month but it still bothered him. If it hadn't been for Nova and Teo, he was not sure how he would have reacted. If he was still a kid, he would have done something stupid. Drank himself into a stupor. Crashed his car into a wall. Picked a fight with someone just to release some of the wild anger he had been feeling. But being with them tempered all the wildness inside of him.

Being with them filled him up in a way that made him realize how empty he had been all those years.

"Thank you, Tanner." She let go of her son and wrapped herself around him. "This means a lot to me."

"It was a cheap gift, too," he said into his ear. "Thirty bucks for the adoption fee and another twenty for some cans of cat food and some litter. And to think I was going to buy you diamonds?" he joked.

"How about a diamond cat collar? He would be very handsome in that."

Tanner laughed and kissed her forehead. "Let's go eat. The food is getting cold."

Two days later Nova was in her own kitchen packing Teo's last lunch of the school year. She and Tanner had to work late tonight, so Wylie was taking him. He had called her just to ask if he could have him overnight. She thought her brother would be too busy, or too preoccupied with his own child, to want to take Teo on. But he missed him. And now Teo had two men in his life who really loved him.

The other one was walking into the kitchen. Her heart lifted when she saw him. She should be over it by now. He had slept in her bed last night. She had already said good morning to him. But seeing him walk into the kitchen, his hair still damp from the shower, made her feel a rush of something powerful.

"The kitten is asleep on your ottoman. I think he likes it here better."

"I wasn't expecting you to bring him when you showed up last night."

"I didn't want to leave him by himself overnight and I didn't want to sleep by myself overnight."

"You're clingy, Brennan," she told him, giving him a kiss. He wasn't, really. He would give her space, let her read a book, or play on social media or watch hours of YouTube tutorials.

But he did want to be with her in bed at night. She wanted that, too. She loved it best when he would throw open his bedroom windows and the cool ocean air would flow in and she would listen to the sound of the waves as they crashed against the shore. She would fall asleep with his arms wrapped around her, and it was so good and sweet that she never wanted to lose that feeling. But then she would pull herself back to reality, not wanting to get swept too far away.

The cat had been a smart move on his part. She would never be able to look at the kitten and not think of him.

"How are you feeling today?" He had seemed a little down since they had come back from D.C. She had wished she could fix it for him, take away that heaviness that he was carrying with him, but she couldn't.

"I found him."

She didn't ask who, because she knew. He didn't talk much about what was said that day, only that he got a name and that his mother had tried to deny her affair up till the very end.

"I didn't know you were looking. You never told me."

"I wasn't looking. This morning when you were in the shower I Googled his name and he came right up. He lives in New York. He works for the governor. I had wanted to know so bad who he was, but then when I got a name I was afraid to look, afraid to confront the other part of my DNA. He's married.

His wife is a doctor specializing in pediatric oncology. He has twins. One is in college. One has special needs. He has spent the last twenty years advocating for better services for people with disabilities. He seems like a goddamn saint."

Nova grabbed his hand. "It seems like you inherited some of that from him. Who else could put up with me?"

He flashed her a quick smile. "What do you think I should do next?"

"Let me see what he looks like. I'm dying to know."

He pulled his phone out of his pocket and showed her a picture. Tanner had forgotten one detail when he was describing his birth father to her. "You look like him. He's a beautiful man. A beautiful black man. You didn't tell me."

"Does that bother you?"

"Don't ask stupid questions." She looped her arms around his neck. "My brother married a black woman. I think we both have similar taste in partners."

"You never told me what you thought I should do."

"I'm not going to tell you what you should do. You can try to contact him and meet him or you can spend the rest of your life wondering about him. It's up to you, but you have to live with your choice, and when you're an old man, are you going to be able to look back on your life and be happy with the decision you made?"

"When you put it that way, I don't think I have much of a choice."

"No." She turned around and retrieved a large paper bag off the counter. "I made you lunch today."

"You didn't have to do that."

"I wanted to." She kissed his lips. "Feed Cornelius the cat for me. I'm going to run Teo to school."

"I hate that name." He shuddered. "I knew a kid in school with it. He was an asshole."

"Teo named him that. It stays."

"I get to name the next one."

They said their good-byes and Nova dropped Teo off at school. She had an early appointment at the shop. But she still had some time to kill before she had to be there.

She sat in her car in the parking lot and went through the mail that had piled up in her mailbox this past week while they were staying with Tanner. It was mostly junk mail, some bills, but one envelope stood out and made her heart stop beating for a moment. It had originated at Mississippi River State Correctional Facility. She didn't want to open the letter. Her hands shook as she held it, because she knew who it was from. He had never written to her. Never reached out to her. The last she had heard from him was the day he was sentenced, when he was screaming that she was a bitch and he was promising retribution. She tore it open, even though she didn't want to know what it said.

Nova,

It's not right what you are doing to my parents. They deserve to know my son and I deserve to know him, too. I don't care what the courts say. You can't keep him away from me. I'm going to see him.

E

Nova crushed the letter between her fingers. He had found her. Found them. Prison must have given Elijah plenty of time to think, because before he never had time for Teo. He was an annoyance. Another mouth to feed. Something that just cried and made it less fun for Elijah's friends to hang out at their apartment. But he hadn't wanted to give him up for adoption when she had mentioned it to him.

We don't give up our kids, he'd said so passionately that she had liked him in that moment. He had conned her again those last few months of her pregnancy. He had been kinder to her. He stayed home more often. He told everyone he knew that he was going to be a father, and that little glimmer of hope that she had when she first met him had brightened again. She thought they were going to be a real family. She thought he was going to straighten up like he promised, get a legitimate job. But he disappeared right before she gave birth and she knew then that he was never going to do the right thing.

There were so second chances with her. She might have felt guilty if he had apologized in his letter. Or mentioned Teo by name. Or said that he thinks about him every day. Or . . . something to show that Teo was more important than Elijah's own pride. He was still a self-centered asshole and she would be damned if she was going to let him try to bully or scare her into doing what he wanted.

She was going to make something of herself and by the time he got out of prison next year, she would be so far away from here that he wouldn't have any idea where to find her.

Chapter 17

Tanner looked up from his work computer to glance around the room he was in. It hit him, probably for the first time, that he had an office and a desk. He had a normal job. No explosions. No guns. No foreign lands. He left the house at the same time every day. He went home on time every night. He was a partner in a successful business. It was the thing his father had always wanted for him and the thing he rebelled against the most.

But he kind of fell into it. When the town of Chilmark approached him and Wylie to plan a similar community to the one they had done in Aquinnah, it seemed like a no-brainer. The young men of the tribe needed work. They were a great crew and it wasn't as if Tanner had another job waiting. There was no home to return to.

And when Wylie asked him if he wanted to branch out into general contracting, Tanner agreed without giving it much thought. They had people in the community lining up to ask them to do it. They had enough men to handle it. When the office space came up for lease at a really cheap price, Wylie asked him if he thought they should go for it. It made sense to get it, instead of working out of Wylie's kitchen. They needed a place to plan all the projects they were taking on, and it was close to Teo's school. He could just swing by and pick him up so Nova wouldn't have to worry about rushing home from work.

He had put down roots. Without consciously trying he had made a good life here. He had been thinking about it lately, especially since he couldn't see his days without Nova and Teo. His life was better, fuller with them. He was happy; for the first time in his miserable life he was happy. But there was one thing that seemed to be left unfinished. His biological father.

He didn't want a relationship with the man. Tanner was fully formed. His life was complete enough and he didn't want to force his way into a family that would rather forget he existed, but he still wanted to meet the man who gave him half of his DNA. Tanner wanted to hear his voice. He wanted to know if he carried himself the way his biological father did. He just wanted to stand face to face with him and look him in the eye.

He deserved that. Without giving it another thought, he pulled up the public e-mail address that was listed for his birth father and wrote him a short note. Tanner had no idea if the man would ever see it, or if he would respond, but he sent it. He had taken a step. It was all he could do.

He got up from his desk and walked out into the

common space. Wylie sat there with one of their crew members. They were just opening their lunches.

"Join us," Wylie said. "I would have invited you sooner, but you were so quiet in your office that I thought you weren't there."

"I was taking care of something," he said vaguely as he walked toward the refrigerator and pulled out the lunch that Nova made for him this morning. It was a large bag and he was expecting leftovers or something simple, but when he pulled it out, he saw that she had done much more than thrown something together. She had made his sandwich in the shape of a bear's head, created with some kind of dark bread for color. He smiled immediately when he saw it and in the next box, there was some sort of cold noodle salad in the shape of a bird's nest, complete with two baby birds made out of cheese. There was a large homemade fruit salad and a snack cake for dessert but the best part about it was the note she included inside.

Tall, Dark, and Dummy,
    It took me a week's worth of groceries to make you this lunch. You eat like a pig. But you're a cute pig and you've been better to me than I ever deserved or expected. I appreciate you. You should know that, but don't expect me to say that to you ever again because I won't.
                See you tonight,
                Nova

"Where did you get that food from?" Ray, their cabinet guy asked him. "It looks like something you would give a first-grader."

"Nova," he answered. He thought back to that conversation they had in his kitchen, that he wished that he had someone who loved him that much when he was a kid. This was it. This was Nova telling him that she loved him.

"My sister made that for you?" Wylie couldn't hide his disbelief. "I didn't think she had that in her."

"Yeah. She does." Tanner stood up. "I've got to go."

"Where?" Wylie asked him.

"I'm going to go tell your sister that I'm in love with her."

Nova had gone through her day, trying to put the letter out of her head. But it stayed with her all day. So much so that she was tempted to go to Teo's school and pick him up. But that was foolish. Elijah was locked up over a thousand miles away. He couldn't get to them.

But he found her address. He knew where she lived. And that made her uneasy as hell.

"All done," she told her client as she spun her around to face the mirror. She had tried to be present, to chat, to ask the woman about her family, but she couldn't muster it. She just focused on the hair.

"It's gorgeous. I'll never get it to look like this tomorrow."

"That's a stylist's dirty secret. We do great blowouts so you'll have to come back to us over and over. But I cut it in a way that you can just wash and go. Just put the antifrizz serum on it and let it air dry."

"You're a genius. I know we aren't going to have you here much longer."

Nova attempted a smile, but didn't say anything. She had heard that comment so many times in the past few weeks. Her inbox was flooded with offers. Great life-changing offers. A famed stylist from New York stopped in the shop yesterday just to see her. He wanted her to come work for him.

He charged twelve hundred dollars for a haircut. He did hair and makeup for photo shoots. He worked with stars on awards nights. His looks were seen everywhere and he wanted her to join him. Not as one of his underlings, but as the lead travel stylist at his West Coast location. She could be doing hair and makeup for photo shoots, be with celebrities on awards night, too. He promised to keep her schedule flexible so she could be there to pick up and drop Teo off at school. He even had a house for her to live in and a car for her to drive. He would pay moving expenses. He was handing her more than a dream job. He was giving her an opportunity to really change her life. And she hadn't said a word about it to Tanner. She hadn't told him about any of the offers she had received. She had been biding her time. Waiting for the right moment. But there never seemed to be a right moment, because he was spending time with her son, or making her laugh, or making love to her. He was making her happy and that was making her not want to move on with her life. She wanted to stay in her little warm bubble for as long as she possibly could.

She walked her client over to the register and cashed her out, and as soon as the woman walked out the door, Tanner came in. He must have read her mind. He must have known that she was thinking about him. He came in with such a serious look on his face and immediately she knew something was up.

She rushed out from behind the counter. "What's the matter? Did Wylie get hurt?"

"He's fine. You're the one who's in trouble." He swept her off her feet and into his arms before giving her a long deep kiss. It was in the middle of the day, in the middle of the salon right for the world to see, but she didn't care because her damn heart heaved painfully. "She won't be back until tomorrow," he said to her boss after breaking the kiss.

She didn't object. For once there was no fight in her as he carried her out of the salon and to his SUV. They drove to her apartment and went inside, right to her bedroom without saying a thing.

He immediately began to strip her. There was no slow seduction. Her dress got pulled off over her head, her shoes flung across the room. Her bra and underwear were disposed of quickly, soon forgotten as she watched him stare at her body. They must have had sex a hundred times since they had gotten together. He didn't seem tired of looking at her. He drank in her naked body with his gaze, making her feel like the most beautiful woman ever created.

"Why?" she asked in a whisper.

"You didn't think you were going to get away with making me a lunch like that and me doing nothing about it." He removed his shirt, revealing his long war-scarred torso to her. Just seeing him aroused her. He didn't even have to touch her. But he did.

He took a step forward and slid his hands up her neck, till his hands were cupping her face. "I love you, Nova Reed."

He didn't give her a chance to respond before he kissed her. She was glad he didn't because as over-joyed as she was to hear him say those words, she was devastated, too.

She couldn't stay in this town. She couldn't be the partner he needed and live the life she had wanted for herself.

She reached and undid his jeans, her hands shaking, the need for him overwhelming. She shoved his pants down to his ankles and pulled him down on the bed, his large hot body landing on top of her. She wrapped her legs around him, and guided him inside of her, not allowing him to pause and fully undress. She couldn't wait that long.

"Goddamn it, Nova."

She moved beneath him, wanting their lovemaking to start as soon as possible and last as long it could. He gritted his teeth and stared into her eyes. He loved her. He was looking at her like he was in love with her. But more importantly he treated her like he was in love with her. This beautiful, good man. It was overwhelming and she suddenly didn't feel worthy of it. Her eyes filled with tears. She tried to blink them away, tried to focus on Tanner, on the way he felt inside of her, but it was too much. The tears streamed down her face.

Tanner stopped moving and placed his hand on her cheek. "What's the matter, baby?"

"Please don't stop."

"You're sad," he said, the surprise clear in his voice. He rolled off of her.

"No!" She reached for him. "I don't want you to go."

He sat up and quickly removed the rest of his clothing and then put them both beneath her oversized comforter.

"I make it a policy not to make love to a crying woman." He kissed the side of her face. "I need to know what's wrong with the woman I love."

"Stop telling me that you love me."

"Why? I do love you. I've loved you for so long."

"You're making this harder for me." She shut her eyes. She couldn't stand to look at him any longer.

"What am I making harder?"

"I've been getting job offers from all over the country the past month. Yesterday I was offered one that was too good to give up."

His body grew a little tighter, but his expression didn't change. "Where is the job?"

"Los Angeles. He's starting me out at two hundred thousand dollars a year. He has a house for me to live in and a car to drive until I find my own. He's letting me keep my schedule flexible. I wouldn't have to travel outside of L.A. unless I wanted to. I can be home with Teo and I'll get to do hair and makeup for celebrities and photo shoots. It's a dream job."

"But is it *your* dream job?"

"You knew I was planning to move off island when we started this up. You went with me into that salon in Boston. You're the one who encouraged me to take the job in Nantucket. You knew I always wanted a better life."

"And a life with me isn't good enough?"

"I never said that. Don't put words in my mouth."

"You can have whatever you want with me. I could give you a life you never even dreamed about. I can take care of you. You would never want for another thing."

He was saying the same thing Elijah had said to her all those years ago. It was the way her ex-husband had seduced her into giving up her dreams for him. She couldn't go through that again.

"I don't want you to take care of me. Everything I've done these past four years was to get to this point. I need to take this job to show all those people who thought I was nothing but trash, that I made myself into something. I have to take this job for Mansi who paid my way through school, and for my mother who had big dreams for me. I've got to take this job for Teo—"

"That's where you're wrong. You don't have to take this job for Teo. He would be happy here on this island, surrounded by the family that loves him. With the man who wants to raise him as his son. I love him Nova. I would be a good father to him."

There was nothing she could say to deny that. Teo loved Tanner. Teo was happier now that Tanner was a big part of his life. Teo would be terribly sad without him. And it would be all Nova's fault. "Don't do this to me, Tanner. Don't force me to choose between you and my dreams."

"I'll come out to L.A. with you. I'll find work out there eventually. I can take care of Teo until I do."

"You just went into business with Wylie. You can't leave him high and dry and you wouldn't be happy there. We both know that."

"You won't be happy there, either. I know you well enough to know that, but I love you enough to make the move. I love you enough to do anything you ask."

"Stop telling me you love me."

"No. It's true. I love you as much as you love me. Don't try to deny that you're in love with me. I know you are. I can feel it in everything that you do."

She wouldn't deny it. It was too hard to, but she wasn't going to admit it either. There was something big inside her blocking her from saying those words. "You don't really know who I am. You don't know the kind of person I am. You don't know what I'm capable of."

"What did you do? Steal to keep you and Teo fed? It doesn't matter. All of that is in the past."

"It's not in the past for me. It's there underneath the surface and it could all come back to get me."

He narrowed his eyes; some of the anger she had seen there was gone, now replaced by concern. "What are you talking about?"

"The reason I ran away." She had never told anyone about that. Not even Mansi. She had been far too scared, too ashamed to admit that she had left a man on the floor to die, but more than that, she had left her mother. Already dying from the alcohol that had poisoned her liver. She had left that night and had never spoken to her again.

"What happened?"

"When I was seventeen, I came home from work

to find my mother passed out on the couch and a naked man in our bathroom. He was the complex's maintenance man and someone my mother slept with from time to time when rent was due or she needed more booze. He—he tried to force me to have sex with him. My mother always had these men around. Ever since I was a little kid they would leer at me, or grope me. They would always say disgusting things to me when my mother wasn't around. And for a long time I avoided it. I never allowed myself to be alone with them, but that night my mother had been so drunk. And the guy just wouldn't stop and when he reached for my zipper, I grabbed a knife off the kitchen counter and plunged it into his chest and then I ran like hell. I left a man to die on the floor. I left my alcoholic mother with no one to take care of her. I left and I married an abusive asshole just because he promised me that I would have a home to always come back to. You see? There is no reason for you to love me. I can't even love myself."

He shook his head, but she didn't see condemnation in his eyes, just profound sadness. "He tried to rape you, Nova. What you did was self-defense. You wouldn't have been in trouble."

"For years I've waited for the police to come after me, but they never have. It's been nine years and I've never been able to piece together what happened. Did Mama see what I did and cover it up? That was a big thing she had done for me and I just left her there. She died alone, you know. If I had stayed I could have gotten her to a doctor sooner. She wouldn't have had to die alone."

"Damn it, Nova. It wasn't your job to take care of an alcoholic woman. You were a kid. Your mother was supposed to take care of you. You were neglected and abused your entire life. I know you loved her, but you didn't owe her anything more than what you already gave her. Don't feel guilty about it, and your mother was dying then. I doubt she was strong enough or clearheaded enough to carry out any cover-up. You probably didn't kill that man."

"There was so much blood. You should have heard the scream that came out of him. I still hear it. Sometimes it wakes me up at night."

"What was his name?"

"Archie La Forge."

"None of what you said makes me love you any less. In fact, I think it makes me love you even more."

A sharp pain surged in Nova's chest. "But I didn't want this. I told you that in the beginning. I was always planning to leave here. It took me so long to get here, and I refuse to miss my chance again."

"I'll go with you."

"No. You came to this island for a reason. You belong here. You'll meet someone else. Someone who is sweet and doesn't like to argue and who knows how to be loved. You'll be so much happier with her than you will with me."

"She doesn't exist!" He sat up and roughly rubbed his face. "There is no one else for me but you."

"I told him I wouldn't start the job until September. We can still have the summer. We can still go on vacation like we planned. We can still have these next few weeks."

"What's the point?" he asked, getting out of the

bed. "It won't be any easier to lose you then. I love you, Nova, and if you can't love me back then I don't think there is anything left for us to talk about."

He got dressed and walked out of the room without looking back at her. As soon as she heard the front door close, the reality of what had just taken place hit her. She had just lost the best thing that ever happened to her and it was entirely her doing.

"You look like shit," Wylie said to Tanner as he walked into Tanner's office.

"Well, I feel like shit, too. So there's that."

The corner of Wylie's mouth curved into a slight smile. "You still haven't spoken to Nova?"

"No. There's nothing left to say. We want two different things." It had been a week since he walked out on her. "Teo misses you. He was crying, he was so upset."

"Don't tell me that." He rubbed his aching forehead. "It makes this thing so much damn harder." There were a hundred times that he wanted to storm over there and force her to change her mind, but he knew that nothing would change her mind. She would just dig her heels in more. He loved her stubbornness, her determination, but it was also the thing about her that made him want to shake her.

"There's no handbook for a breakup like this. It's not like you can sue my sister for visitation. But Teo is miserable without you."

"His birthday is coming up. I was going to take him to a baseball game and then out to dinner."

"You can still do that. Nova will let you see him."

"You think so?"

"Yeah, because when he started to cry, she started to cry, too. I've never seen her so upset. She always hides her feelings, but she can't this time. She's a wreck."

"You think she's having second thoughts about us?"

"Fourth and fifth thoughts, but I doubt she is going to change her mind. She's already started packing. They are going to go out to California early. Nova asked Mansi to stay with them until they get settled. Cass and Sunny and I are going to go with them, too. We're going to Disneyland and do a bunch of touristy stuff for about ten days, to make the transition easier on Teo."

It was a good plan. Nova was taking her son from his entire family. The separation would be brutal. He was glad it wasn't going to be so abrupt. But he couldn't help but feel a little sorry for himself. Nova was going to California and taking everyone he cared about with her. "How do you feel about it? You moved here to be with your family and now half of them are moving to the other side of the country."

"I'm upset, but what the hell can I do? Nova worked hard for this. She's good at her job and people all over the country want her. She would be crazy to not take these opportunities. I'll miss them, but I can't be selfish. I just have to be supportive and make sure she knows that I'll be here if she ever needs me."

"What do you suggest I do?" He couldn't ask her to stay. She had said from the beginning that she didn't want anything serious. She had told him that there was to be no falling in love, but by that point it already had been too late.

"I don't know. I never know the right thing to do when it comes to my sister. It seems to me you have two options. You can let her go and move on or you can follow her to California and convince her that you will be happy making a life there."

"Convince her? You sound as if you don't think I'll be happy there either."

"You're a veteran. You work with your hands. You hated the wealthy people you grew up with. How are you going to fit in in L.A. where you'll be surrounded by people who are the exact opposite of everything you worked so hard to become?"

Wylie was right. He didn't want to leave Martha's Vineyard, or the quiet life he had carved out for himself, but he didn't want to let Nova go, either. It didn't feel like it right now, but maybe there was someone else out there for him. Someone who would like this life. Someone who would easily accept his love. Someone who wanted to make a family with him, because in the end that's all he ever really wanted. His own family.

"I got an e-mail from my biological father's office."

Wylie's eyes widened. "What does it say?"

"I don't know. I didn't open it yet."

"What are you waiting for?"

"I don't know. I have enough shit going on this week. I'm not sure if I want to deal with this now."

"If you ask me, one way to forget something is to get involved with something that's a bigger pain in the ass."

Tanner opened the e-mail that had landed in his box an hour ago. It was short, just two lines and some contact information. "It says that he would like to meet me. Next Friday. He'll meet me at my house."

"He knows where it is?"

"He probably does. I wouldn't be surprised if my mother and he snuck away and met at my grandparents' house here."

"It's your house now," Wylie reminded him. "I'm assuming you're going to want to change some things."

"I was going to let Nova do whatever she wanted to the house, but now . . ."

"I'm here for you, man. Just let me know what you need."

Tanner nodded. He didn't know what he needed right now, but he appreciated that he finally had a friend in his life that he could count on.

Chapter 18

Elijah had been arrested. It was the last thing she heard before she boarded the bus for Massachusetts. Her father-in-law had delivered the news to her. His face was grim, his jaw tight. She had gone to the police after Elijah had beat her. If it were just her, she wouldn't have bothered, but she had looked at the small baby in her arms and she knew she couldn't let it go. What kind of message would she be sending to her son if she had?

The police officer who sat at the desk when she walked into the station cursed upon seeing her. She hadn't known how bad she looked at the time. She was more concerned about her baby who had been flung across the room like he was nothing at all. She was in too much pain to make it to the hospital, but she had gone to the police first in hopes that they would get her boy checked out. They took them right to the hospital. A warrant was issued for Elijah's arrest and it was that night she learned that it hadn't been the only one.

He was wanted for questioning in a murder case in Mississippi. A wealthy family in Biloxi had had their home invaded. Their children tied up. The mother beaten. The *father shot. It had been the same time she had been in the hospital giving birth. They couldn't prove that Elijah pulled the trigger or even that he was there but they knew he was involved, that he was the ringleader for a crew that had been hitting rich families up and down the coast in three states.*

That was the kind of man she had married. Had had a baby with. She had turned a blind eye to his activities for so long. She knew he was up to something, but it hadn't been clear to her until last week when he brought home an antique diamond bracelet for her. It wasn't the usual stuff he brought for her. This one was far too exquisite to be slipped off some woman's arm as she walked down the street.

She had confronted him about it and he called her ungrateful. He had said his stealing was all to take care of her and the baby she had saddled him with. She knew he had been high at the time. He was far too twitchy and agitated, but she couldn't let his comment go. She raged back at him and he hit her. She hit him back, not wanting to back down, but he had gone ballistic. He had beaten her until she stopped moving.

She still couldn't see out of her left eye. Her in-laws had taken her in that night. She hadn't wanted to call them but there was no place left for her to go and she didn't want Teo to spend the night in a shelter. They gave her the bus money to go up north. Her father-in-law even promised to fly her back down for the trial. He said there would be one, that this time Elijah needed to be punished. At the time, he had no idea how heavily involved his son was involved in crime, but he would learn soon enough.

Mansi was going to be waiting for her at the bus station closest to Martha's Vineyard. She told her how happy she was that she was coming home. How much she had missed her all these years, but Nova was ashamed to go back to her grandmother like this. Totally defeated. Unable to take care of herself and her child. She was supposed to be better than her own mother. But she found herself in the same pattern. Alone with a small child to raise. With no education. With no skills and no way out. As she got closer to the bus station her stomach grew tighter, the anxiety in her chest making it hard to breathe.

Teo was fussy from being on a bus for two whole days. She couldn't seem to soothe him. Nothing she ever did with him seemed right and she wondered if she had made the right choice to keep him. If she would have left Elijah when she found out she was pregnant, she could have given him away to the nice couple who wanted to love a child so much, it was painful to see. But Nova wanted to keep her son, and because she had chosen to do that, her baby could have been killed. He could have hit the wall or bounced off the couch and broken his neck on the coffee table. It would have been her fault. She was the one who confronted Elijah. She was the one who decided to keep the baby. She was the one who married a man she knew in her gut was all trouble, and the more she thought about her mistakes, the harder it was for her to breathe. And just when she thought her lungs were going to collapse, the bus stopped.

They were at the station and her grandmother was standing there, her white hair loose around her shoulders, looking as anxious as Nova felt.

Tears pricked the back of her eyes, but she told herself that she wouldn't cry. She needed to be stronger than she was. But the moment she stepped off the bus in front of her grandmother and removed the hood that shielded her

*head and the sunglasses that covered half her face, she
knew that she wasn't going to make it.*

*Mansi was made of strong stuff, but the gasp that es-
caped her was one that Nova would never forget. Mansi's
eyes filled with so much sadness, so much pity, that Nova
wanted to hide from her again.*

*"I'll kill him. That son of a bitch. I'll kill him for doing
this to you." She took Teo from her arms, having never met
him before, and soothed the baby as if it were the most natural thing in the world. "It's okay, little one." She kissed
his hair. "You are home now." Mansi wrapped her free arm
around Nova and hugged her tightly as she began to weep.
"It's okay, sweet girl. You are home, too. You'll never have
to leave again."*

A few nights later, a knock on Nova's door shook
her from her thoughts. She hopped up from her
spot on her couch, knowing exactly who would be
on the other side of it. Teo followed by Wylie came
through the door when she opened it. She was glad
Teo was back. The apartment had been far too
quiet with just her and the kitten there. Last year at
this time she had been home alone a lot. Teo would
be off at Mansi's or with Wylie. Nova would be at the
apartment studying, trying to improve herself so
she could get them out of here. And now that time
had come.

There were boxes everywhere. The life she had
created here the past five years being packed away.
She thought she would be more excited about this
new turn in her life, but she was miserable. Her
anxiety was nearly choking her at night, and more

than that, she felt alone. There was no Tanner to turn to. His warm heavy body wasn't in her bed at night. All she had was the kitten he gave her. And even though she loved his sweet little face and loved stroking his soft fur, he made her even sadder. She would never be able to look at the cat and not think of the man who gave it to her.

"Hello, handsome." She picked up Teo and kissed the side of his face. "I missed you."

"Did you?" He scrunched his forehead. "I wasn't gone very long."

"It felt like forever to me." She looked over to Wylie. "Can you stay for a few minutes?"

He nodded, but Nova knew she couldn't keep him here long because he didn't like to be away from his wife and baby.

"How was your man's-only birthday dinner? I can't believe I have a six-year-old now. I still remember when you were a tiny little baby like Sunny." She sat down on the couch with him cuddled in her arms.

"We had a good time, Mommy. We went to Oak Bluffs. Mr. Tanner said I could get whatever I wanted so I got two shrimp cocktails and chicken wings."

"Sounds amazing. Did you have dessert?"

"Yes." He nodded. "We went for ice cream. Uncle Wylie, give Mommy the bag."

"I almost forgot. This is for you." Wylie handed her a small bakery bag, and without opening it, Nova knew exactly what was inside.

"Mr. Tanner bought these for you. He says they are your favorite."

"They are the best cookies on the entire island,"

she said, trying to keep her tears at bay. "You'll have to tell him thank you for me when you go with him to the baseball game this weekend."

"You could come with us, Mommy. Mr. Tanner would let you. He still likes you."

"I still like him too, baby. But the baseball game is just for you and him. He wants to spend lots of time with you before we go, and now that school is over you're going to get to do that."

"Okay," he said resigned. Nova had been preparing Teo for the move for the past two weeks. She showed him pictures of the house they were going to live in. It had a huge pool complete with a slide. There was a park nearby that he could play in. She promised to take him to dozens of places before school started and told him that he could pick out whatever he wanted in his room. He seemed to be okay with it all, especially since Mansi was going to be out there with them for at least six weeks, but he didn't understand why Tanner wasn't going to come with them. He didn't understand why he had stopped coming around just because they were moving.

"Go get ready for bed. Make sure you wash your face really good tonight. I'll be in soon to tuck you in."

He nodded and got off the couch and headed straight to Wylie. "Good night, Uncle Wylie. Thank you for driving me home."

Wylie picked him up and squeezed him. "You're welcome. I'll see you tomorrow."

A few seconds later Teo went into his bedroom, leaving them alone. "I'm going to miss the hell out of him, Nova. It's taking everything inside of me to keep it together."

"Please, Wylie, don't make me feel guiltier than I already do."

"I'm not trying to make you feel guilty. You need to take this shot. You worked hard for it, but I'm going to miss having my family close. Hell, you're even taking Mansi."

"She's *my* grandmother," she pointed out. "Plus she's only staying with us for a little while. She'll be back around Halloween."

"She'll stay with you as long as you need her to. She might not want to come back."

"I'm not sure she'll be happy there in the long run."

"I'm not sure you'll be happy there in the long run, either."

"I owe it to myself to see, don't I?"

"Of course you do. But why won't you let Tanner come with you and make that decision for himself?"

"Because, again, I'll feel too damn guilty. He's finally found a place he loves, where he's comfortable. I can't ask him to give up his home and his career to follow me across the country. We haven't even been together that long. I know what it feels like to give up things you've always wanted to make someone else happy. I can't ask him to do the same for me."

"He's miserable. I've never seen a man so low in my life. Why don't you just go see him?"

"I didn't want for this to end right now. I wanted the summer with him. He ended it. He walked away from me. It was supposed to be easier. I would just get on the plane and we would go our separate ways. Now I have to worry about seeing him every time I leave the house. Now I have to make plans for Teo to see him so I don't have to face my heartbroken kid."

"You can't plan a breakup to go the way you want. Love doesn't work like that."

"Apparently not." She wrapped her arms around herself, wishing that this wasn't so damn hard.

"Tanner's biological father is meeting him here on the island next Friday."

"He is? That's huge for him."

"You've been with him through this entire journey of finding out who he really is."

"Yes." From the moment he realized that the man who raised him wasn't his father, to the showdown with his mother, who was the orchestrator of this huge family secret. It seemed wrong not to be there in the end. "Teo needs new sneakers. Do you think you could take him next Friday?"

Wylie nodded slowly, his eyes widening with understanding. "Cass needs some stuff, too. We might have to go off island. Is it okay if we keep him overnight?"

"Yes. I think that would be for the best." She stood up and hugged her brother tightly. "Thank you, Wylie."

"Why are you thanking me? I love to spend time with him."

"Thank you for being my big brother."

Tanner didn't know what kind of food to put out for his lunch meeting. He had gone to the store and bought a roasted chicken, fancy cheese, crackers, olives, and three kinds of salad. He bought beer and wine, a cake and a pie. He just kept buying food. Enough for a party of at least ten. There were no rules to this kind of event. No etiquette to follow when you are meeting your biological father for the first time.

What the hell would he say to the man? There were so many questions he could ask, but as the hour drew near, they all went out of his head. Other thoughts clouded it.

Would he recognize himself in the man? Would he feel a connection with him? Feel like the man was his father? Feel that feeling he had been searching for his entire childhood? Or would he dislike the man? Would this entire meeting be a huge waste of his time?

The doorbell sounded and Tanner glanced at his watch, seeing that his guest was a few minutes early. He opened the door, trying to calm the pounding in his chest, but he didn't see a man who looked like him standing on the other side. His heart pounded harder. Nova was there, wearing a pretty pink sundress on her curvy body. She looked so uncertain.

He hadn't seen or spoken to her since he walked out of her apartment that day. He had seen Teo. Wylie had been their go-between arranging it so they never had to see or speak to each other. It had been beyond painful to do it that way. He was happy to be with Teo, but being with him and being without Nova felt wrong. It felt like half his family was missing.

"I'll go if you want me to. I heard that your father

was coming today and I . . . I don't know why I'm here." She paused for a long moment. "I thought you might need me today."

"Today and every day," he said. He wanted to touch her. To kiss her. To smooth his hands all over the body that he thought about so much. But he wanted to talk to her, too. To ask her how she had been. To know what she was thinking. How she was feeling.

He didn't do any of that. His biological father's car pulled up and he grabbed Nova's hand, pulling her inside to stand beside him as he got out of the car.

Richard Powell was just as tall as Tanner. His skin darker. His clothing well-fitting. His stride confident.

The instant rush of emotions Tanner thought he would feel didn't come. It was simply odd seeing the man who helped give him life. It was almost like watching a video instead of seeing the real thing.

"Tanner." He extended his hand; his shake was firm. "I'm glad you reached out."

"It's good to meet you, sir."

"Sir? I know you have spent most of your adult life in the military, but you don't need to call me sir."

"Father seems too much and Richard seems too informal for the man who gave me life."

Richard nodded. "I see your point. I was surprised the words *deadbeat* and *asshole* didn't come flying at me as soon as you saw me." The corner of his mouth curved. The man had a sense of humor. Tanner knew he wasn't going to be able to hate him.

"I wouldn't ask you to come all the way over here

just to curse you out. I would wait until the holiday, like all families do."

He laughed that time. It was a deep, warm sound. He had some charm. Tanner knew immediately why her mother threw away her marriage for him. He was the exact opposite of the man she had married. "Is this beautiful woman your wife?" he asked, looking at Nova.

"No," Tanner said, and it actually pained him. Technically she was nothing to him anymore. He couldn't bring himself to say "ex." Because everything thing he felt about her was just as strong and present as always. "This is the woman I'm in love with. Nova, meet Richard Powell, my biological father."

"It's nice to meet you, Nova."

"You, as well. Please come in."

Nova took over the hosting duties as soon as they got inside. She sat them outside on the deck overlooking the ocean, pulled the food out of the cartons it all was still packed in, and placed it on platters. Tanner had been too nervous to even think to put it on the fancy china his grandparents seemed to have an abundance of.

"I had forgotten how beautiful the Vineyard is," Richard said to him as he stared out at the ocean.

"You've been here before? To the house? You didn't ask for directions."

"If you want to know if your mother and I used your grandparents' home as a love nest, the answer is no. I respected your grandfather far too much. This was the campaign headquarters for his second reelection. We used to gather around the formal dining room table and strategize."

"How did it start between you two?"

Richard looked at him for a long moment. "You don't really want to know the answer to that one."

"I guess I don't. Give me the abbreviated version."

"I feel like you want a black and white response, where one of us is all good and the other is all evil. We had an affair. It's something I am ashamed of. Even more now because I have a wife. If she'd had a child with another man I would have been angry and devastated. I wish I could say I was a big enough man that I would forgive and not hate, but I can't say that. There is no excuse for what we did."

"But if you didn't do it, then I wouldn't be here."

"I didn't say I regretted it."

"Did you love her?"

"I did, but even in a perfect world with all the societal problems gone, it wouldn't have worked out between us. Your mother wanted a great romance and in the end I want what I have. A dedicated wife. A family. A quiet life."

It struck Tanner the similarities between them. That's all he wanted too, but Nova wanted more. She wanted off this island. She wanted out of island living, and this quiet life was the thing he had craved the most.

She walked out on the deck with a tray of food in her hands. He stood to help her, struck again by how stunning she was.

"Sit. Sit. I've got this." She put everything down.

"I need to go get the drinks ànd silverware. Keep talking."

She left them alone again.

Richard watched Nova as she left. "I'm starting to remember that your mother did tell me about Nova."

"You spoke to her?" He didn't know why he was surprised by this. His mother had admitted that she called Richard when Tanner went into the army, but he was surprised that this married man was still communicating with the woman he'd an affair with so many years ago. "You still speak to her."

"We don't really speak all that often. And when we do it only concerns you. She told me about the troubles you were having as a teenager, and when you went into the military. She told me every time you were being honored. She called me when you finally got out. And she called me after you two spoke about me in D.C. She was very upset that night."

"She doesn't even speak to me that often."

"No?" He seemed surprised. "She speaks of you as if you were the most important part of her life."

Tanner laughed but there was nothing funny about it. "She's the most important thing in her life. What did she tell you about Nova?"

"She said something like you were shacked up with a single mother divorcée who wore too much makeup. The picture your mother painted of her is in vast contrast to the woman I see here today. She seems lovely."

"She is." He nodded. "When exactly did you find out about me?"

"I think you were six. It was time for your grandfather's third reelection campaign to start again and she called me to see if I would be willing to run it. By that time, your grandfather was so well established and so popular, he didn't need my services. But your mother was insistent and she seemed hurt that I didn't want to come back to Boston. She wanted to pick things up where we left off. I had moved on by then. I was seeing someone seriously. My focus had changed. I told her that, and then she dropped the bomb on me. I had a son and he had no idea that the man he called Dad wasn't his father. We went back and forth for a while trying to figure out the best thing to do, but in the end we decided it was for the best not to rock your world then."

"I wish you had. I felt like an outsider in my family. I knew I didn't belong with them, but I didn't know why."

"We didn't know what to do. There's no handbook for that situation. I thought it would be best for you to continue to grow up with the man you thought was your father. When you were a teenager, I regretted that decision and your mother and I had a big argument when I told her I was coming to get you and knock some sense into you."

"You, a stranger to me, were planning to come take me from the only parents I have ever known and raise me?"

"I realized how stupid of a plan that was. Luckily your grandfather made you join the army after you were arrested."

"Why didn't you ever try to contact me after I had

straightened out? I was old enough to decide what was best for me."

"I wasn't sure if you would want to have anything to do with me. I'm still not sure if you want to have anything to do with me."

"What were you hoping would come out of this?"

"I'm not asking to be your father. I lost out on that, but I would like to hear from you from time to time. Know that you are well. It's a hell of a thing for a man to have a little piece of him walking around on this earth. There's a natural need for me to want the best for you."

It was nice hearing that. For so long he just wanted to know that there was someone in his life who cared and now, as he took stock of all the people in it, he realized that he did have a lot of love in his life. It just took going through hell to realize it.

Nova walked out again with the things that she had gone in to get. It took longer than it should, but he knew that she was giving him the time he needed to speak to his father in private. She hadn't been able to say it yet but he knew that she loved him, too. He wouldn't have been able to get through this journey without her.

Was she put in his path just to get him through this point in his life, or was the rest of his life meant to be spent with her?

Chapter 19

Nova stood at the kitchen sink washing dishes as Tanner and his biological father said their final good-byes. They had had a pleasant lunch with Richard, and Nova had to stop herself from staring at the man. The resemblance was strong between father and son, even the way they held themselves. They sat tall, their backs straight. Their smiles were the same. The shapes of their heads. They had similar senses of humor and that made Nova wonder how the hell Tanner's family could keep such a huge thing from him.

He must have felt like an alien among them and it made her sad for the boy he once was who never knew his place. When she first saw him today she had been so happy, so filled up that she wanted to throw all her common sense out of the window and tell Tanner to come along with her to California, but she would be doing that for her comfort, for her security. It wouldn't be for him at all, because after so long not knowing his place in the world, he had found it here on Martha's Vineyard.

She was going to have to stay strong. She was still going to follow her dreams. And she was going to make it easier for Tanner to make new dreams of his own. Ones that didn't include her.

She heard the front door close and Tanner's heavy footsteps as he walked back into the kitchen. "You don't have to hand wash dishes. The dishwasher works."

"I know," she said softly. "I want to."

"You were giving me time with my father. I appreciate that."

"Things seemed to have gone well."

"They did."

"You didn't need me after all." She felt shy around him now that they were alone. It was the last feeling she expected. He was the person who knew her the best. He knew all of her dark secrets, her insecurities. He could read her emotions before she could even process them. It was scary to have someone be that inside of her head and heart, because he could truly hurt her if he wanted to. He had the power to devastate her. "Let me finish cleaning up and I'll get out of your hair."

"No." He shook his head. "I can't ask you not to go to California, to stay and make a life here with me, because that would be selfish, but I will ask you to stay with me tonight. I crave you and I miss you and being with you makes my days a whole hell of a lot better."

She reached for him, wrapping her arms around him as tightly as possible. His sweet words only made her feel more terrible. "I miss you, Tanner. I miss you so damn much."

"You don't have to miss me. You can just marry me and have my babies and we can forget all this happened."

"Oh, shut up, Tanner."

"I do want to marry you," he whispered in her ear. "I'm not asking you, but I want you to know that. I want you to know that I love you enough to spend the rest of my life with you."

"I wish you didn't."

He sighed. "Why can't you let yourself be loved?"

"I'm too messed up."

He looked at her for a long time, as if he were weighing his words carefully. "I found out what happened to that man who assaulted you."

"Archie?" She pulled away from him, her heart racing so hard it was painful. She clenched her fist, bracing herself for news she desperately wanted to hear and never wanted to learn at the same time. "What happened to him?"

"He's dead."

She stumbled backward and grabbed onto the kitchen counter to keep her upright. Tanner stepped forward and lifted her into his arms.

"You didn't kill him, though. He died in prison. He was a predator. The other inmates took care of it."

"Why the hell didn't you lead with that part?"

"You felt bad. That man tried to hurt you and you felt bad for defending yourself. Don't you see you can stop running now?"

She shut her eyes and nodded, feeling close to tears. She wasn't sure what emotion was flowing through her, but it was intense and it made her breathless. "Take me to your bedroom."

He was heading in that direction even before she got the words out of her mouth.

Her heart hurt as she saw his room again. She had spent so many nights here loving him. She missed the room and the slight smell of the ocean air that wafted through the windows. He set her gently on his bed and removed her shoes.

She looked down at him, so handsome in his cotton blue button-down shirt and camel colored pants. She began to undo his buttons. He didn't say a word, just stared at her as he undid the buttons she couldn't reach. He went for his pants while she removed her dress and soon they were both completely naked. She wanted him. She throbbed for him, but she didn't want this time to be that fast mind-numbing sex that they were capable of. This was probably going to be their last time together. She wanted to savor every moment. She wanted to remember all of it. Every touch. Every moan. Every look he gave her.

She climbed beneath the covers and he joined her there, gathering her close, smoothing his hand down her nude back.

This felt like coming home. There was nothing on earth that felt as good as being this close to him.

"How are you feeling about the visit from your biological father?"

"I like him. He's easy to like."

"Do you think you'll see him again?"

"Probably. He won't be my father, though. He'll be a friend. I had a very difficult relationship with my father growing up, but I kept wondering if he would be bothered by this meeting. If it would hurt his feelings if he knew I liked Richard so much."

"Why?"

"I was the most awful teenager on the planet and he could have washed his hands of me. He could have completely disowned me at any time, but he was there. Cleaning up my messes. Bailing me out. Lecturing me on why it was important to be a good man. Looking back on it now, he was my father. When it was probably really hard to be. I'm not going to give up on him now."

He was loyal and sweet and kind. He would be such a good father, a good husband to some woman. Nova hated that woman already and she hated herself for falling so far into love so fast. "Make love to me, Brennan. Don't stop until tomorrow comes."

Nova left Tanner's house that next morning and picked Teo up at Wylie's before returning to her apartment, which was nearly all packed. She had given her notice to her landlord. Much of her furniture was gone, given to one of her friends who was moving to a bigger place. It was all set. The flights were booked. Her position at the salon, resigned. There was no stopping it. Her new life was about to begin.

She wished that she could muster up some excitement over it. She should be excited. She was moving to a gorgeous place. She was going to be doing what she loved. This was her dream coming true. This was why she'd worked so hard for all these years. But the closer she got to moving day, the more depressed she became. Instead of anticipation, she was feeling dread. It was going to be hard starting over again. She had done it before. Twice now. And each time she had changed.

Who would she be after this move?

Would she even like herself?

Seeing Tanner last night made it worse. Having made love to him all night made it worse. Hearing him say he loved her over and over made it almost impossible for her to walk out the door.

He didn't once ask her to stay. He didn't once tell her that he wanted to go with her. He asked to see pictures of the house she was going to be staying in. He wanted to know all about her new boss. He was being supportive and it nearly killed her. She had wanted him to ask her not to go. She had wanted him to be a forceful jackass and demand that she be with him. It would have made things so much easier.

But the last thing he said to her was that he loved her and Teo too, and in the process he made her feel like a monster. She was hurting him. She who had been hurt so many times was hurting someone else, and it wasn't a good feeling. But he would move on. He would find someone to love. Someone who loved him deeply in return.

"It feels empty here, Mommy." Teo wandered around the living room. Only the couch remained and some boxes.

"It does."

"It makes me feel sad."

Me too, she wanted to admit. "I know, baby." She picked him up and walked over to the couch with him, pulling her phone out of the pocket of her dress. "But just think about how much fun we're going to have in California. We'll have the entire summer to do great stuff. We're going to spend a few days at Disneyland and there's three other big amusement parks I want to take you to." She pulled up the Web sites of the places on her phone and for a few minutes they checked out the pictures. "And since Mansi is coming with us, she said we have to go to the redwood forest. Do you know about redwoods?" She pulled up pictures of the state park in Northern California for him. "They are the biggest trees in the world. We can rent an RV and go camping."

Teo looked up at her skeptically. "You said you'd rather get your fingernails pulled out than sleep outside."

"It won't be outside. It will be in a camper. Or maybe we can see about renting a cabin. We never stayed in a cabin before."

"Do you have enough money for vacations?" he asked her in a very adult way. "We never been on one before."

"No, but I've been saving a lot of money. I worked so much so I could do these nice things for you eventually. You know Mommy is getting a new job and I'll be able to do more things with you."

"You don't have to take me on vacation."

"Uncle Wylie and Aunt Cass are going to come. I thought you were excited."

He shook his head. "Mr. Tanner is staying here."

"He can't come, baby," she said softly. "He needs to stay here and work with Uncle Wylie."

He sighed and went back to looking at her phone. They had had this conversation before, but Teo still had a hard time understanding why they weren't going to be together anymore. His heartbreak was Nova's fault. She should have never let them get so close. She should have kept her guard up. Tried harder to push Tanner away.

A knock at the door distracted Nova from her train of sad thoughts. She shifted Teo from her lap and stood up to answer it. She had been so distracted, she had forgotten to ask who was at her door before she opened it. It was something she should have done this time because her ex-husband was standing before her. A ghost from her past that she had trouble believing was real.

He still had that impossibly long black hair. But he had filled out since she had last seen him. Beefed up. His arms were covered in tattoos. His face was hardened. There was not an ounce of softness in his eyes.

He was supposed to be in prison. She had gone down to Mississippi where he had been extradited just for the trial. He had only received five years and those five years weren't up.

"What are you doing here? You're not supposed to be out."

"You know why I'm here. I told you I wasn't going to let you get away with this."

"Teo, run to your room and lock the door!" She stood in her doorway, blocking Elijah as best as she could.

"But, Mommy—"

"Now!"

He did what she said and moved faster than she had ever seen him move.

"You bitch." Elijah shoved her aside. "You're going to make him afraid of me. I'm his father!"

"You're the man who nearly beat me unconscious and then flung a six-month-old across the room when he wouldn't stop crying. You aren't a father. You aren't even his father anymore. You're an abusive addict who should still be in prison for murder."

"They can't prove I had anything to do with that killing."

"You didn't say you were innocent. You just said they couldn't prove it. Do you think I want that kind of man around my child?"

"He's not just your child," he raged.

"Your rights were terminated. I have a restraining order against you. You're not supposed to be here. You're not even supposed to be out of prison. This isn't going to end well for you."

"Did I forget to mention I was granted parole? I'm a free man."

"Get out, Elijah!" She refused to be afraid of him. She had worked too hard to get where she was; she wasn't going to cower.

"You're moving." He walked farther into the place. "My mother said you were doing hair. That you had gotten yourself in with the rich crowd. I can see it in your face. You think you're better than me."

"It's not hard to feel superior to a violent thief."

"You can feel superior all you want. I know where you came from. What are all the fancy politicians going to think when they find out that your mother was a drunk with a record?"

"That was her. It has nothing to do with me."

"It has everything to do with you! Those are your roots. Your bad blood. You're going to end up just like her. A nobody who dies alone. You were a waitress, living in a shitty motel filled with hookers when I met you. I got you out of there. Where do you think you would be if I hadn't? You would be one of them. Selling your body for a few dollars in order to feed yourself."

Her hand cracked across his face. She hadn't meant to hit him. He had beat her. She knew better, but he cut her deeply. It was the same shit he used to say when they were together. He knew how to get to her, because he knew what terrified her the most.

"You've still got fire," he said with a grin as he advanced on her. "You're still the sexiest woman I have ever seen." He grabbed her arm and pulled her close to him. She recoiled from his touch. His fingers dug into her skin. He was always rough with her. He never knew how to touch her. "I hate you, Nova. But I thought about you when I was on the inside. Your hot little ass. The way your tits looked. The way it felt when I was in you."

"Get off of me." She tried to yank herself away from him but his grip was too tight.

"We can try it again." He wrapped his arm around her. "You can take me with you. We can be a family. It's hard for a convicted felon to get a job. You can take care of me like I took care of you. You need me. If it weren't for me you would have nothing. You would be nothing."

For so long she had carried that hurt around with her. It had taken her years to lose that feeling. It had taken being with someone who truly loved her to make her realize that she was good enough and strong enough to achieve anything on her own.

"What do you say, baby?" He dropped his voice to the pitch he always thought was seductive. "You and me again." He grabbed her behind and squeezed, as his mouth came crashing down toward her. A flash of panic went through her before calmness came over her. She relaxed and let herself be kissed, and when Elijah pushed his tongue into her mouth, she bit down on it, causing him to howl in pain. He backhanded her. Her face throbbed, but she wasn't going to let him beat her again. She stomped on his foot, remembering the moves from the self-defense class she had taken when she had first arrived on the island. Her knee came up and connected with his groin, just before the palm of her hand slammed into his nose.

Elijah went down with a loud thud and just after he did, she heard sirens and heavy footsteps rushing up her stairs. Tanner and Wylie appeared in her doorway, both of them looking ready to murder.

"I'm fine, boys."

"Your face." Tanner glanced at Elijah writhing on the ground, lifted him up, and slammed him so hard into the wall that plaster fell from the ceiling. "You like to hit women? You're really going to like having the life stomped out of you by a man."

"Tanner, let him go." Two police officers were in the doorway. Nova recognized one of them as the father of one of Teo's friends. "We'll take it from here."

"How did you get here?" she asked all of them.

"Teo called me," Tanner answered after he surrendered Elijah to the officers. "I was headed to the job site with Wylie."

"He also called the police, Nova," the officer said. "He said a man was trying to hurt you, and judging from your face, he did."

"Your lip is bleeding. His handprint is on your face." Tanner came over to her and wrapped his arms around her.

How different his arms felt around her than Elijah's. So much better. So right. Tanner always knew how to touch her.

"We're going to need your statement, ma'am," the second officer said to her.

She nodded. "I'll be right down." She didn't look at Elijah as they took him away. "Wylie, can you go check on Teo? Tell him I'm okay. I don't want him to see me hurt."

"I will." He kissed Nova's forehead before he went to the back to see Teo.

Tanner slid his hand over her uninjured cheek and looked into her eyes. "We came over here prepared to save you and here you were saving yourself."

"It's nice to know that I have someone willing to save me."

He kissed her nose. "Let's go give your statement. I need that asshole out of here as soon as possible."

Her statement was given, Tanner was by her side, his arm protectively wrapped around her. A phone call revealed that Elijah had been released from prison, but a condition of his parole was that he was not supposed to contact her, which he had broken before he ever was released. Nova realized she should have said something when she first got the letter nearly a month ago, but she thought he was still in prison and no threat. If she had said something, her son would have never had to lock himself in the room and be terrified that some man was going to hurt his mother. But it hadn't been just any man, had it? Elijah was Teo's father and she was going to have to address the issue now. No more pretending that he was dead.

She walked back upstairs and found Teo cuddled in Wylie's lap. The look on his face nearly broke her heart. It was pure worry and then relief when he saw that she was fine. "Come here, little one." She held out her arms to him and scooped him up. "You're my hero." She planted a dozen kisses on his face. "You're so smart. You did the right thing calling. I love you so much."

It was then he started to cry. He must have been holding it together since Elijah appeared at the door and now he was sobbing.

"I'm so sorry, Teo," she said, feeling helpless. "We're safe. Nothing is going to happen to us now. I promise."

"Why was that man so mad at you? I heard him yelling."

She left the room with Teo and sat them down on the couch and took a deep breath. Tanner stood there, his expression neutral. He had told her that she should tell Teo about Elijah. That he had the right to know. That every person had the right to know where they came from if it were possible.

"Teo, that man is your . . ." She hesitated. The word *father* didn't seem right. Elijah had never loved him. Even before he got locked up, he was never there. He was the other half of Teo's DNA, but he wasn't a father. "I lied to you about something, Teo. I told you your father was dead, but he isn't. That man was your father. He did some bad things and was in jail and I didn't want you to know that. He wasn't allowed to see us anymore. I'm sorry for not telling you."

Teo was quiet for a long moment as he processed what she said. She didn't know if he understood. If he would hold this against her for the rest of his life.

"I don't want that man to be my daddy." He looked up at Tanner. "I want you to be my daddy. Why can't you?"

Hurt flashed in Tanner's eyes and he looked at Nova briefly. "I love you, Teo. I love your mother, too. I—Damn it, Nova! I can't do this anymore. I refuse to hurt him. You're going to have to be the one to tell him. This is killing me."

He turned to leave and the panic that Nova felt just a little while ago returned, only it was much stronger this time. It choked her.

You won't be happy without him.

"I love you!" The words came tumbling out.

He turned around, looking stunned. She had never said it to him before. She had thought it a hundred thousand times, but she had never said it. "What?"

She placed Teo on the couch and stood up to face him. "I love you. I'm in love with you."

His expression softened. "I already knew that."

"I'll marry you."

The corner of his lip curled. "I didn't ask you to marry me."

"Then I'm asking you to marry me."

He tilted his head and studied her. "Why do you want to marry me, Nova?"

"Because you're a good man and you love my son as if he were yours. You make my heart beat faster when I see you. I want to be with you all the time. I want to marry you because I'm in love with you and I can't go through the rest of my life without you."

"What makes you think I want to be married to you?" he asked, his smile growing bigger.

"Tanner!"

He took a step forward and cupped her face, kissing her fiercely. "Did you think I was going to let you go? My plane ticket to California was bought the moment you left me this morning. I can't be without you. My life was no good until I met you. You and Teo are my family."

"So that's a yes?"

"I've been hiding a diamond ring in the house for a month. Of course I want to marry you." He stepped away from her and lifted Teo into his arms. "I want to be your daddy. Nothing would make me happier."

"It's about time!" Wylie said, having been quiet for the past few minutes. "I'm going home to tell Cass and kiss my kid. We're throwing you a party. I don't want to hear a damn word about it. You're getting a big engagement party. Cass is going to plan it. She's been talking about it for two months. You'll show up and you'll like it."

"Okay, Wylie," Nova agreed.

"No arguments?" He smiled and then kissed her cheek. "Congratulations. I'm happy for you." He slapped Tanner's back. "You too, man. Good-bye, Teo. I'll see you tomorrow."

"Good-bye, Uncle Wylie. Mommy, can I call Mansi and tell her?"

"Of course you can."

Tanner let him down and he scampered off to his room.

"We've got to start looking for our own place," Tanner said to her.

"Why?"

"I'm sure your boss would be okay with us staying there for a little while, but we're going to need to find our own house in California."

"We're not moving to California."

He frowned in confusion. "But what about your job? You worked so hard. It was your dream."

"Dreams change. This island is where I found myself and fell in love. This place is my home. I don't want to leave it. I can figure out how to have the career I've always wanted and the family I need. I want to have your babies, Brennan. I want Christmases here. I want memories here."

"That sounds like a damn good life to me."

He kissed her again and for the first time in her life she felt like everything was finally going to go her way.

Epilogue

Eighteen months later

"You're driving me insane, Reed! I'm this close to losing it."

"Shut up. I'm not sure who you think you are ordering me around."

"I'm your husband. That's who I am! And if you would listen to reason, I wouldn't have to order you around."

"No one asked for your opinion. I'm not sure why I married you in the first place. You are a bossy pain in my ass."

"You married me because you're in love with me and I'm good for you and deep down you know that I'm always right."

Nova glared at him and rubbed her lower back. "I am in love with you, you long-legged jerk. It's the only reason I put up with you."

He walked over to her and placed his hand on her large belly. His heart swelled every time he did so. She was entering her eighth month of pregnancy. They had just passed their one-year anniversary. A lot had happened in that year. They'd had a big wedding. Tanner's grandparents were so happy that he was settling down that they pulled out all the stops, but it wasn't a snobby event. Nova's whole tribe was there and nearly every resident of Aquinnah came out to wish them well. Both of Tanner's fathers were there, but any awkwardness they felt was well hidden. Tanner's mother, however, didn't come. She was in Europe with her new love. It was one relationship he had learned to let go, but he had gained so many more, that he had barely felt the loss.

He had adopted Teo. He officially had a son who called him Daddy and followed him everywhere he went. And now he had a new child on the way. A little girl that he couldn't wait to meet.

After they got engaged, Nova had taken some time off from working to decide what she wanted to do next. They did go to California after all. But for a month on vacation. They took Teo to Disneyland. They camped in the redwood forest. They drove up to Oregon and rode in a hot-air balloon, and when they returned to Martha's Vineyard, Nova decided she wanted to open her own salon.

Nova had been surprisingly relaxed about their wedding plans, but when it came to the salon everything had to be perfect. They had looked at every vacant building on the island at least twice. He was about to suggest they go off island until a space became available in Oak Bluffs. They bought it and completely gutted it. Nova meticulously planned out every detail all while still traveling a couple days a week to do hair and makeup for her growing list of clientele. She was the number one bridal stylist in the country, but this salon was going to be her home base.

And that's where they were today. Only she wasn't supposed to be there. Her doctor had ordered her to slow down. She had been all over the country in the last couple of months. She was supposed to be at home resting, but he found her there painting one of the walls. And she was doing it in four-inch heels.

"Please come home and rest. You're not supposed to be on your feet, much less painting walls."

"I don't want to go home and rest."

"Then I'm going to be forced to pick you up and take you out of here."

She glared up at him, but she knew he would do it. "I want to go eat. I want corn chowder and corn dogs and buffalo wings. And I don't want to hear any crap about eating healthy. I let you make me those green smoothie things every morning and tonight I want what I want."

"Okay. We'll go get Teo and then we'll feed you. I'll even buy you dessert."

"I want a brownie sundae with nuts and extra hot fudge, too."

"Of course. What's a brownie sundae without extra hot fudge?" He wrapped his arm around her and began to lead her out of the nearly finished salon.

"I want a milkshake, too. A strawberry one."

"Okay, but I'm going to sleep in the guest room

tonight because I can't imagine your stomach is going to be happy tonight."

"Okay. No milkshake."

"You're admitting that I'm right?"

"Of course not. I'm admitting that I can't sleep without you beside me." The annoyed look on her face melted away and she looked up at him. "I'm really happy, Tanner," she said softly. "I know I'm a miserable pregnant person and that I must be terrible to be married to, but I've never been so happy, or felt so safe or loved in my entire life. I love you." Her eyes filled with tears. "I'll never stop loving you."

Sometimes she got sensitive. Her hormones were making her rage, laugh, and cry all within a few minutes, but mostly she was sweet and, even after a year of being married to her, he found every day exciting. "Ew, don't be nice to me. It creeps me out."

"You're supposed to tell me you feel the same way!"

He shrugged. "You're all right, I guess. I really only married you because you have a nice ass."

"Tanner!"

She looked completely outraged and he threw his head back and laughed.

He cupped her increasingly round cheeks in his hands and kissed her gently. There was something about seeing his wife pregnant that made him want her even more. "You know I'm crazy about you, Reed."

"That's Mrs. Brennan to you." She kissed him back, a little longer, a little deeper this time, and it sparked that same fire in him that had been sparking since the first time his lips touched hers.

"Mmm." He slid his hands down her back and pulled her even closer. "Teo can stay at your brother's house a little longer. Why don't we go home and spend a little time alone?"

"Are you crazy? I'm pregnant and I'm hungry and if you don't feed me right now I'm going to bite your hand off." She walked away from him, mumbling, "I can't believe he just said that to me."

He laughed again. All of his days had been filled with laughter since he married, filled with joy. Tanner had never believed in perfect, but if such a thing did exist, his life with her would be it.

Connect with